P9-EEI-032

DROWNED TOWN

DROWNED TOWN

JAYNE MOORE WALDROP

**FIRESIDE
INDUSTRIES**

Published by Fireside Industries
An imprint of the University Press of Kentucky

Editorial and Sales Offices: The University Press of Kentucky
663 South Limestone Street, Lexington, Kentucky 40508-4008
www.kentuckypress.com

Library of Congress Cataloging-in-Publication Data

Names: Waldrop, Jayne Moore, author.
Title: Drowned town / Jayne Moore Waldrop.
Description: Lexington, Kentucky : Fireside Industries, [2021]
Identifiers: LCCN 2021019300 | ISBN 9781950564156 (hardcover) |
    ISBN 9781950564163 (pdf) | ISBN 9781950564170 (epub)
Subjects: LCSH: Land Between the Lakes Region (Ky. and Tenn.)—Fiction. |
    Relocation (Housing)—Fiction. | LCGFT: Short stories.
Classification: LCC PS3623.A35835 D76 2021 | DDC 813/.6—dc23

For my family and the many lost places.

Every man, every woman, carries in heart and mind the image of the ideal place, the right place, the one true home, known or unknown, actual or visionary.

Edward Abbey, *Desert Solitaire*

CONTENTS

DRY GROUND

Cam wandered through this uninhabited place, remembering each house and family and tree that had been here before the water came. She stumbled, nearly turning an ankle as she crossed a disintegrating asphalt slab, a remnant of the street where she had lived in a town that once existed. She glanced in both directions, more from childhood habit than necessity, since there were no cars left. There was nothing left, only a few shards of brick and stone, a faint curvature of sky and earth that felt vaguely familiar.

Her mother's unsealed wedding dress had made her feel nostalgic and drawn back to the old town. The ecru lace gown, preserved with care for future generations in a heavy cardboard box designed to keep out moisture and fabric-eating pests, had been brought out and altered to fit Cam. The wedding—her second, Owen's first—was in three days. She and Owen had been friends since childhood, when they both lived in this old town. Cam had been slow to see him as anything other than a buddy and hesitant about marrying again, but this time made sense, she thought. Now in their forties, surely they knew what they were getting into.

That morning she had met with the seamstress for a final fitting. The waistline had been let out a bit, the shoulders taken in, torn lace repaired in a few spots. In the small, cluttered tailor shop, she slipped the dress on and looked at herself in a three-way mirror.

"How does it feel?" the seamstress asked as she zipped up the back and tugged at the neckline.

"Like I've stepped back in time," Cam said, thinking about the framed wedding picture that had been on her parents' bedside table for as long as she could remember. Her mother wore the same dress in the photograph, her satin slingback pumps shining beneath the tea-length hem. The black-and-white photo had been snapped in 1955 as the smiling young bride and groom descended the steep concrete steps of the Eddyville First Methodist Church. And now, nearly fifty years later, Cam looked in the mirror and thought the dress made her look younger, too.

She was smiling as she left the shop, pleased with how the gown had turned out but drawn to the place in the photograph. For the last few months she had focused on the future—whether to get married, what kind of wedding suited them—but today the past pulled at her. She ignored the list of errands in her pocket and decided to drive to the old town. She still remembered the way.

The two-lane highway dead-ended at a lonesome knoll overlooking Lake Barkley. Cam parked in a grassy area beside the road and walked toward what used to be Water Street, the hilly one that had ended at the ferry landing. The broad lake sparkled in the midday sun. The sky was bright and cloudless. She watched as a large cabin cruiser, better suited for the ocean than an inland waterway, powered its way through the narrow, twisting channel marked by red and green navigation buoys. The markers served as both reminder and warning that the Cumberland River's deep channel still provided the safest passage on a lake that appeared vast but could be deceptively shallow in places. The cruiser spread an oversized wake that rocked nearby fishing boats and caused the captain

2

of a slow, scruffy pontoon boat to swerve at a defensive angle to keep from getting swamped.

A lone bronze marker revealed the spot's history as the former site of Eddyville, a thriving town settled near a series of bends in the Cumberland River, which snakes a course through the middle of the country from mountains to barrens to rolling hills. The plaque told the town's role in American history as an outpost on the western frontier, as an important junction during the Civil War, as a commercial center and county seat. The tarnished words also described midcentury government projects for flood control, hydroelectric power, and tourism when the flowing river was dammed. The sign memorialized U.S. presidents, vice presidents, and governors from Kentucky and Tennessee, but failed to mention the people who had lived in the town and given up their homes as the giant lake rose. They had been told their sacrifice was for the public good. They were never told how much they would miss it, or for how long.

Cam wondered if the adults had realized what they were losing when everyone was moved out. At the time she had been a child, not privy to their conversations about the relocation. Maybe some folks jumped at the chance to leave this place and its floodwaters, where the river crawled out of its bed and slipped into town at least once a year, usually in late winter or spring. They had tired of shoveling mud-caked streets and sidewalks, pumping out perennially musty, wet basements, and moving furniture to the attic. The chance to live on higher ground lured them away, enticed by the gift of free land for those who committed to build in a town that sprouted in a cornfield two miles away. Others had fought the taking of their land, but without success. In the end everyone was forced out.

"They're calling the new town Sycamore for that big old tree they left standing near the new courthouse," Cam's father announced when he got home. "And our lot's on Dogwood Lane." She looked up and saw him holding a piece of paper in the air.

"Here's our new deed, signed and recorded at the clerk's office as soon as they gave us the piece of ground," he said. "They're ready to start Monday, but we'll have to decide which model we want." His eyes were bright, as they always were when he was speaking to her mother.

"Those are pretty names," her mother said. She leafed through a stack of magazines on the sideboard and then saw Cam on the floor studying the catalog she needed. "Baby, bring me that house plan book," she called. "We need to pick out our new home."

Cam was only six and a half, but she loved looking at her parents' books and magazines. She had found the house plan book on the coffee table after school let out. She analyzed the cover photo, which showed a family of four, dressed up like they had been to church or a funeral, except they looked too happy to have come from a graveyard. The glossy parents smiled as they looked at each other. The mother wore a small sky-blue hat and pearl necklace; the dad was in suit and tie. Their children—a girl and a boy—looked like they would never fight or call each other names the way Cam and Becky did. The full-color family walked toward a fine example of a ranch-style home, the kind everyone wanted in the 1960s. Cam knew that her own family didn't look like those people or dress like them, even on Easter Sunday. Their clothes weren't as fancy and their car was old, but they too were getting a new house.

Cam flipped to the inside of the book and counted ten drawings of different kinds of houses. Some were long and straight. A few seemed to have upstairs rooms like their own house. In the illustrations she counted windows, doors, rows of bricks, and little shrubs planted along the front walls. She said the word *split-level* out loud. Each page had another drawing, a series of lines that formed boxes of different sizes labeled LR, DR, KIT, BR, BA. Cam didn't understand what the lines meant. She went to find her mother.

"Who drew these pictures?" Cam said as she slid the open plan book across the kitchen table.

"I heard it was some fancy architect from Fort Worth, Texas. He designed all the houses for the new town," Mama said. "What do you think?"

"These lines don't look like houses to me."

"Those are floor plans. They show how the house will look on the inside."

"But they're flat."

"Pretend you're looking into the house, like you're a bird looking down from a tree and the house doesn't have a roof. Each line is a wall, and the walls make rooms."

Mama pushed her fingernail along the drawing like she was giving a tour of the house.

"These are the outside brick walls, and this is the front door. You walk into the living room and here's a big picture window. This is the kitchen. Our table would go here. And then you walk down this hall. Here's Becky's bedroom, and our room, and this would be your room." She pointed to a small box.

"I get my own room?" Cam asked. She and Becky had always shared one.

"You sure do. Your room has a window so you can see the front yard and the street."

"What color is my room?"

"Whatever color you want, baby."

A new house in a new town sounded like a nice place to live, Cam decided.

Five months later, her family packed up at the old house and headed to their new town, a location flat and dusty with nothing to commend it but the fact it was beyond the reach of the river. Syca-more was a town of the future, not of the past.

As more houses were built, Cam monitored the construction and tried to remember which floor plan was being used. She watched as many of their former neighbors moved in. Although Cam knew almost everyone, she thought they all looked different here, living in brand-new houses and walking on uncracked side-walks. They looked familiar yet almost unrecognizable. Some acted busy and excited. Others looked worried or confused, like they didn't know where they belonged. All of them had changed their routines and now lived with altered boundaries. They weren't the same people. They couldn't see or smell the river each day. They no longer needed to worry if the water was high or low.

After the move, Cam turned seven and was ready for second grade. Becky was going into fourth. Sycamore's state-of-the-art ele-mentary school was mostly finished by September, and the towns-people marveled at the design patterned after the solar system with a large central hub that contained the gymnasium and principal's office surrounded by smaller round grade-specific satellites orbiting in chronological sequence.

"I think it looks cheerful. You're going to love it," Rose Weth-erford declared as she walked the girls to school on the first day. Word had spread that the newspaper was sending a photographer to document the stream of schoolchildren arriving for the first day of classes in the relocated community. The event was a big deal in Sycamore. Rose had gotten up early to style her own hair, to put on makeup and a nice dress, before she awakened the children.

Cam and Becky wore nearly identical plaid dresses with white collars and black Mary Janes that pinched their feet, which had grown unaccustomed to closed-in shoes over the summer. Their long, sun-bleached hair was tightly braided and tied with ribbons that matched their dresses. Their mother bought the dresses and shoes at Tot-2-Teen, a shop previously located in Eddyville's business district, across Water Street from the Lyon County courthouse. Like most established businesses in the old town, the owners of the children's shop had taken their buyout money and rebuilt in Sycamore. The fresh new store with its yellow-and-white-striped awning had opened its doors as back-to-school shopping began.

Inside the elementary classrooms, the floors were shiny, the desktops uncarved, and the seat bottoms not yet blemished by gum wads. The building smelled like fresh paint and plastic. The spines of the full-color textbooks crackled when Cam opened hers for the first time. Outside, the sun felt hot when the students played kick-ball at recess. There were no trees, and the newly sown grass wore down under the treads of sneakers. Their old school, with its rows of swing sets on a playground shaded by giant oaks, was scheduled to be torn down before the lake waters rose. So were their old homes.

In the second week of school, Neville Burgess approached Cam on the playground during recess. She had known Neville most of her life. In the old town he and her boy cousins had been best friends and played together all the time, but her cousins had moved to Princeton when their house got bought out. She hadn't seen them in a long time. She wondered if Neville had. Cam noticed a bead of sweat rolling down the boy's cheek from the little sideburns his barber had created.

"Your house is next," he said.

"What's that mean?" she said.

"The bulldozers parked next to your old house yesterday."

"How do you know?"

"I saw it. I ride my bike over to the old town every day."

"You're not supposed to. You'll get in trouble."

"Those old bastards don't need to know everything," he said, defiantly. Neville liked to cuss. Cam guessed he picked it up from

7

his dad. The Burgesses had lived three houses from the Wetherfords in Eddyville, and they used to hear his dad hollering during warm weather when everybody's windows were open. That man sure could cuss, her mother had often said. After the buyout and before the move, he shouted and cussed even more, and most of the bad words were aimed at the government and the U.S. Army Corps of Engineers. Mr. Burgess had held out for as long as he could. They were one of the last families to sell.

"They might be tearing it down right this instant," Neville said. He seemed proud that he knew something she didn't. "They're moving down the street and there's not much left. It'll all be gone by the end of the week."

"How far away is the old town?" Cam asked. She didn't have her bearings yet. It might have been a million miles away.

"Not far, really. We'll go the back way so nobody sees us. The government owns it all now and they've put up fences, but I know how to get in," Neville said, looking less defiant.

"I'll think about it," she said.

"If you want to see it before it's gone, meet me at the end of your street right after school," he said. "Better change clothes, though. I'm not towing you on my bike if you're wearing a dress."

For the last hour of school, Cam thought about where she used to live. She wanted to see the old house, but she had heard her parents talk about people being arrested for going back to see their land one last time before it was flooded. Trespassing, her dad had called it. She had heard the word in church and knew it was something bad, something she wasn't supposed to do, but she couldn't recall her parents specifically telling her to not go. She walked home from school, changed clothes, and told her mother she was going to play baseball with her friends. Neville was waiting for her, like he said he would.

"Get on," he said. They took off down a dirt path through tall grasses in uncut fields and blackberry thickets, staying away from the main road and eventually heading into hilly woods.

"You sure you know the way, Neville?"

"Don't worry. I can find it," he said. "I've been going every afternoon since school started."

Neville was standing up to pedal, so Cam had most of the seat to herself. She suspected Neville didn't want her to hang on to him. He never was one to hold hands or sit beside girls at lunch. And she knew there were certain rules to be observed as a passenger, like not to drag her feet or lean over too far in any direction. And not to hug up too close. She tried not to touch his blue plaid shirt any more than necessary, but she couldn't keep from grabbing hold when they bounced hard along the path. He pumped the pedals with all his might on the last steep hill, but her extra weight made the climb impossible. They got off and walked the bike the rest of the way to the top.

"Do you know where you're at?" he asked.

She looked around. "Not really. Everything looks so different," she said.

"We're up on Pea Ridge," he said.

She remembered Pea Ridge but still didn't recognize this place. Pea Ridge was a limestone bluff high above town that overlooked the river and the entire valley. A few old farmhouses on the ridge remained unchanged. They weren't part of the buyout because the lake level would never get this high. The cemetery didn't have to be moved either.

"But where is everything?" she said. She saw bare, rusty red dirt and uprooted trees, churned and splintered, as if an angry giant, awakened by the ruckus, had stepped down from the ridge to smash it all.

"This is all that's left, Cam," he said, pointing. "Looks like they took the roof off your house today."

"Where? I don't see it." She squinted to follow his finger but couldn't find the house. "Can we get closer?"

"We're not supposed to, but sometimes I walk around down there if nobody's working."

They listened for sounds of workers or machinery and heard none. Birds, singing like normal, were the only sign of life. They hid the bike behind a boulder and started walking down the road that led to town. The asphalt was undamaged, still striped in yellow down the middle. Just past the KEEP OUT warning barricade, Neville pointed to a hill of red bricks that caused the chain-link fence to bulge.

"That's the shirt factory where my mama used to work. The front door used to be there," he said, pointing again. Cam remembered the large building and the whistle that used to blow at noon to signal the workers' lunch break. It blew at the end of the day, too, a sound that was heard all through town, alerting kids that their parents were heading home from work.

"Where'd they build the new shirt factory?" she said. In her mind, everything from the old town resurrected somewhere in Sycamore.

"There's not going to be a new one. Those sonsabitches closed it for good," he said. When Neville scowled, he looked just like his dad. Sounded like him, too. "My mama's still looking for work."

They walked farther into town. Cam saw a sign that said Water Street.

"Now I know where we are," she said. She looked to the left and spotted her old house.

"Come on, Neville," she shouted as she ran toward it. When she got closer, she saw that its windows and doors were missing, and the walls were jagged where its roof had been torn off. As the children approached, bricks from the chimney fell into what had been the kitchen.

10

"We better not go in," Neville said. "It might come down while we're inside."

Cam wanted to go upstairs to the bedroom she had shared with Becky, but she was too scared. Without its roof, the structure seemed less like home and more like a drawing from the house plan book. She glanced across the street.

"Miss LaClede's house looks fine. Let's go over there," she said, turning toward a white frame house with a wraparound front porch.

Miss LaClede, Cam's piano teacher, had lived alone in the big house built years ago by some distant ancestor. She was an old woman, with eyes so clouded with cataracts she could hardly read the music books. That didn't matter because she could play the songs by heart. After the lesson, Miss LaClede always served lemonade and oatmeal cookies to Cam on the porch, where they sat in oversized wicker rockers. Sometimes as Miss LaClede told stories, Cam picked at the dark green enameled wicker with her fingernail, revealing a previous coat of dull white paint underneath. The old woman told Cam that she had never lived anywhere but that house. She was the last of the LaClede family. The others were all dead. Now she was, too. Cam's dad said Miss LaClede didn't want to leave her house, so she just died right before they made her move.

Cam and Neville climbed the concrete steps that led to Miss LaClede's generous front porch. From here, the river looked wider than Cam had ever seen it.

"Is the water coming up?" she asked.

Neville nodded. "That's why they're in a hurry to tear it all down."

From the outside, Miss LaClede's house looked sturdy, untouched, while its neighbors lay in ruins. A few smoldered from bonfires set to reduce the amount of demolition debris. Massive piles of brick and stone surrounded the house like the walls of a fort.

But inside, the process had begun. Pieces of the house were missing, like the stained-glass window on the staircase landing that once glistened lavender and pink in the afternoon sun when Cam arrived for her music lessons. Now, standing in the front hall and looking up, she stared through a hole in the ceiling all the way to blue sky. A carved fireplace mantel sat propped against the front wall. Bronze chandeliers were stacked nearby, and the fancy wood banister had been ripped off the staircase. Miss LaClede was gone, and the last remaining evidence that she ever existed—her house—was being picked apart as if by a wake of vultures.

A small object on the staircase caught Cam's eye. She climbed five or six steps, hugging the wall because the handrail was missing, and she saw an old photograph lodged against one of the risers. She picked it up and eased back down to the front hall to study it. The image of a boy, his eyes closed, lying in a casket surrounded by flowers. The wallpaper and mantel in the picture looked familiar. Cam looked around Miss LaClede's front room and saw the same wallpaper pattern. The dead boy had been here, in the very spot where she stood.

Cam turned the photograph over and saw pencil writing so faint and curly she couldn't read it.

"Neville, where are you?"

"Chasing birds out of the kitchen," he hollered. "They must roost in here."

"Come here. Look what I found," she yelled back.

He came into the hall carrying a broom. She showed him the photograph.

"Creepy," he said. "Who's that?"

"I don't know, but it looks like he's dead. There's writing on the back," she said.

He took the picture and studied the old-fashioned cursive for a long time.

"Can you read it?" she asked.

"I think it says 'Francis, Brother, April 17, 1938.'"

"Is that Miss LaClede's brother?"

Neville shrugged. "How would I know?" He stared at the photograph of the dead boy, then handed it back to Cam as if he wanted rid of it.

"Let's get out of here. I need to get home for supper," Neville said. He headed toward the front door.

For a second Cam considered putting the picture back on the stairs where she had found it, but she slipped it into her pocket. She would keep the photograph and never show it to anyone, not even Becky. Sometimes she would take it from its hiding place in her closet and look at it, thinking of Miss LaClede. The picture of the dead boy was Cam's only connection to her, the surviving proof that Miss LaClede and her people had ever existed.

A few months after their trip to the old town, the reservoir reached its expected high level. The town and its history drowned.

The old place often came to her at night. In her dreams she walked intact sidewalks, recalling each house and family and tree. She dreamed of Francis LaClede, the swings on the playground, and tiny pearl buttons, scattered in the dirt where the shirt factory once stood. But this time she had returned in daylight. A melancholy hung in the muggy air. Memories flooded her thoughts and bore down on her like the hot June sun. Cam stared at the lake's surface, her gray eyes filling with tears, knowing that somewhere out there— below the water—the shape of the land remained. She thought of her parents descending the steps of the Methodist church, dressed in their wedding clothes and carrying that familiar buoyant expression in their eyes. She knew that look well. They still looked at each other that way, as if each step in their life together launched a fresh start. Cam wiped her cheeks and walked toward the car, feeling Water Street's incline strain her thighs. She pulled the short to-do list for the wedding from her back pocket and prepared to relaunch.

View from Within

Every morning before breakfast lineup, men on heavy equipment returned to their work of demolishing the old town within view of Lester Elliott's cell. With the new lake rising, lapping above the ancient riverbanks, they labored with a new fury, even working weekends to finish the job. The sounds of front-end loaders and excavators came through open windows in the prison's thick stone walls, windows shaped like narrow slots, designed for ventilation, not escape. The noise bothered some of the inmates, who complained they couldn't sleep for all the ruckus, but not Lester. He had always been an early riser, and he liked watching life outside.

From his cell on the third floor of the penitentiary, which itself rose high on a bluff above the town and river, Lester looked through his tiny slot window, the view unobstructed by mountains or trees. Across the river stood a big brick house, the only house opposite among the vast bottomland that stretched for miles. As a crow might fly across the broad and open sky, the house was directly across the Cumberland from his cell.

Years ago when Lester first arrived, a guard had told him that the distant setting was called Mint Springs, a small community situated on a narrow strip of land known as Between the Rivers, bordered by the Tennessee on the west and the Cumberland on the east. And year after year as he served his sentence, he watched the house as seasons unfolded, as members of the farm family or field hands worked the land. To Lester, the place was like a dream, a mirage he was unlikely to reach.

From the outside the prison in Eddyville looked like a castle perched high above the river that over time had cut a particularly serpentine stretch of channel through Lyon County's gray limestone. Since the prison's construction in the eighteen hundreds from rock quarried nearby, it had housed men considered the worst, most violent offenders in Kentucky. One of its cell blocks was death row, a small area reserved for those waiting to be executed in the electric chair installed just steps from where they slept each night.

Lester became a resident of Eddyville—the town and the prison—on July 1, 1945, a date imprinted in his mind like a pattern on tooled leather. Twenty years ago now. Twenty years, gone. He was sent here after his conviction on an armed robbery charge. At a grimy filling station in Shelby Gap, he and his buddy Sam had stopped for gas on their way to pick up a blue Chevy for Pal's Used Cars in Prestonsburg. Pal bought cars all over eastern Kentucky, and he paid Lester and Sam a ten-dollar bill each for every vehicle delivered to his lot. It was easy work.

They had gotten out to stretch their legs while a pimply-faced kid filled the tank.

"What's your name, boy?" Sam said.

"Jesse, sir," the redheaded teenager said, looking at Sam with enormous dark brown eyes. The eyes reminded Lester of a milk cow's, slowly blinking, showing little emotion. He still remembered those eyes.

"Don't forget to clean that windshield and check the oil," Sam said.

"Yes, sir." The boy methodically completed the tasks as requested.

"You working here by yourself, Jesse?"

"This morning I am. Daddy went to town for some parts."

Lester saw Sam studying the boy, but he didn't think much of it. Tired and hungover from a late-night card game at the Curve Bar, he wanted to head home and climb back in bed as soon as they delivered the car.

"Got any coffee in there?" Lester said to the boy. His voice sounded dry and weary.

"No, sir. Daddy didn't make any before he left, and I don't know how to. We got cold pop, though."

While the boy topped off the tank and replaced the gas cap on the dark green Plymouth, Lester reached through the driver's side window for his billfold.

"Don't worry about it, Lester. I got this," Sam said. The boy walked back toward the concrete block building to write up the $3.58 ticket. Sam followed.

As Lester unwrapped a fresh piece of gum, he heard a single gunshot. He thought it came from inside the building and ran toward it, hoping Sam was okay. When he approached the door, he saw Sam pulling out two cold drinks from the Nehi soda cooler. Lester turned toward the short counter where the cash register sat and saw the concrete block wall behind it splattered bright red. Lester's heart pounded and his stomach rolled. He peeked over the counter. Jesse lay sprawled on the floor, brown eyes open, head surrounded by a halo of blood.

"What the hell was that for?" Lester shouted.

"Something about that boy pissed me off," Sam said as he opened the pop with a shiny metal opener tied to the cooler with a piece of hay rope. He reached one to Lester, who shook his head and stared, unable to speak or piece together Sam's calm offer of the grape soda and the dead boy behind the counter.

Sam had always had a mean, crazy streak, Lester knew, but he hadn't expected this. He felt unable to move or to grasp what had just happened. As a kid, Lester had watched eleven-year-old Sam twist the necks of newborn kittens and throw them down a well. At the time he also had felt paralyzed, unable to stand up to Sam or make him stop. Today Lester had stood outside, a few feet away, unaware of Sam's intentions or that he had taken the pistol from the glove box.

At trial Lester told the jury that he didn't remember much after seeing the dead boy. He recalled getting back in the car but being unable to drive. Sam had shoved him over to the passenger seat and taken the wheel. As they drove off, Lester caught a glimpse of a woman with long red hair in a yellow housedress, running toward the filling station.

Driving like a wild man, Sam flew down a curving stretch of road along the creek toward Elkhorn City. The police caught up with them before they reached the Virginia state line. Surrounded by troopers and every law enforcement vehicle for several counties, Lester raised his hands to show his surrender. Sam reached for the pistol one last time.

Lester testified that he had no idea of Sam's plan to rob or kill, but it didn't matter. In a unanimous decision, the jury convicted Lester of being an accessory to murder. He was twenty-seven years old.

"I wish I could send you to the electric chair," the white-haired judge said as he sentenced Lester to life in prison. "I guess this is the best I can do." As he was led out of the courtroom, Lester saw hate-filled faces in the crowd that came to hear his fate. The redheaded woman—the terror on her face that day as she ran toward the store flashed before him—slumped and cried into the chest of a gaunt man.

The day after his sentencing, a deputy with a blond flattop and a red face woke him before sunrise.

"Get up," he said, shoving a shallow bowl of lumpy oatmeal beneath the door. "It's my pleasure to take your sorry ass to the pen this morning."

"Hell, do we have to leave in the middle of the night?" Lester said, weary from lack of sleep. All night he lay awake, thinking about his wife Marie, who hadn't shown up for his sentencing. They had been married six months before the shooting.

"Eddyville's clear at the other end of the state," the deputy said. "It's a hard day's drive. We won't be stopping to let you buy no souvenirs or postcards."

Lester sat up on the cot and eventually got to his feet. He ate a few bites of the cold oatmeal before they came to get him. In shackles and handcuffs, he was led to the back of a Pike County patrol car. The sheriff himself was driving Lester to the state penitentiary, accompanied by the same deputy who had brought breakfast to his cell.

Lester watched familiar countryside pass as they traveled Highway 80 along narrow hollers, fertile valleys, and sharp curves. In Prestonsburg they passed Pal's Used Cars, where prices were painted on each windshield, and he wondered if anybody ever picked up the blue Chevy.

As they drove west, the landscape changed and the sky widened. The mountains transformed into hills, then flattened to rolling pastures. This was new country for Lester.

"Are we still in Kentucky?" he asked.

"Yes, you dumb son of a bitch. It's a full day's drive both ways," the deputy said. He had been driving since he and the sheriff switched seats at the last gas stop. The sheriff didn't respond, and Lester guessed he was asleep, judging by the angle of his head against the window.

Lester watched the sun grow larger and brighter as the road seemed to head straight into it. The deputy pulled down the felt visor and shifted in his seat to try to block the blinding light. The sun sank into the horizon about an hour before they pulled up to the gates of the Kentucky State Penitentiary, where Lester was turned over to guards awaiting his arrival. He'd never been so far from home.

The guards soon realized Lester was not a troublemaker. They treated him better than a lot of the prisoners, even gave him his choice of jobs. Every inmate had to work, but some jobs were less desirable than others. He chose the leather workshop, where he learned to make wallets and purses and belts, tooled with flowers and curlicues, which he then stained with a variety of dyes. He signed every piece by tapping his initials into a hidden spot that wouldn't mar the design. At the little shop on Water Street where inmate crafts were sold to the public, customers searched for leather pieces with an *LE* inscription. Word got around that a fellow by the name of Lester turned out quality work.

In the workshop, he worked at a table next to Billy Morgan, a young thief from Lexington. Three large windows allowed light to flood in, with metal bars that didn't completely obstruct the view of the river and the town. The smell of cowhide and leather dye filled the hot, humid air.

"I heard they're going to flood this place and let us all drown," Billy said. A scowl pinched the space between his eyebrows.

"They can't do that," Lester said. He kept hammering. He was working on a belt with a fancy design of cactus against a desert sunset.

"I don't know," Billy said. "Seems like they can do anything they want, by the looks of that town."

"That's the damned truth," Lester said. He stopped working and walked over to the windows. Eddyville was nearly leveled. For the last three years, he'd watched as the town was deconstructed. The houses and businesses were gone. The people had moved away. He'd heard that the dam about ten miles downstream was finished. The water was rising. The river was becoming a lake according to plan.

He turned around and looked at Billy, who fidgeted with a piece of unworked leather, pulling it between his fingers, over and over. He figured Billy was nervous because he hadn't been in long enough to have witnessed how the river regularly came up out of its banks.

"The water never gets high enough to reach us, even in the big floods," Lester said. He'd watched the town nearly go under in 1950 and again in 1957. The river came up, went back down, a rhythm he had noticed through the years. He'd been told that the projected lake level would get no higher than the worst of the floods.

"I've seen them townspeople riding boats down Water Street, in the middle of winter, cold as hell, and the water lapping up along the Rexall Drugstore," he said. "Sometimes it makes me happy to be in here and not out there."

"It gets up that high?"

"Sure does. Be glad we're up on this hill."

"Did they make you sandbag?"

"In 1950 we had to. It got close to coming in the basement here."

"How long you been in here, old man?"

Lester wondered if Billy thought of forty-seven as old because he was a stupid boy or because of the toll twenty years in this place had taken on Lester's face. When he thought about what all he had missed in life, he imagined a slow draining of his soul from his body. There wasn't much left. Maybe Billy only saw an empty old husk.

"About as long as you've been alive, son," Lester said.

"You ever think about getting out?"

"Early on I thought about it, but I decided I didn't want to get shot. Anyway, I don't have much reason to be anywhere else. My old lady divorced me once I got here, and Mommy's dead. Besides, I hear the prison's gonna have the best lake view around." He smiled. "Wonder if they'll let us out for a swim?"

Billy shook his head and chuckled. "I can't swim. I never learned how."

"Boy, you better hope that water stops where they say it will."

In the past, when natural floodwaters overtook the town, Lester watched from his cell as row upon row of houses went under. When the river receded, the people returned to salvage what they could. They hauled furniture out to the yard to dry, scooped out the mud left behind, and replaced waterlogged floors, walls, and appliances. They'd clean up again the next time it flooded. Over and over. He didn't understand why anybody would go through it. He'd get the hell out of town.

"Don't know why, but people love that old town. I think I'd get tired of smelling mud and pulling dead fish out of my basement," he said.

Billy laughed and nodded.

Lester sat back down at his table and repositioned the long strip of leather he had been working. He picked up his mallet and selected a stamping tool to make a decorative border along its edges. The mallet hit the stamp solidly, making a clean impression of a rope pattern in the hide. Lester checked the quality of the imprint, then moved the tool a smidge so the pattern formed a continuous line. Again and again he tapped, until rows of rope design met at the point where the buckle would be attached. When he saw that his work was flawless, he tapped a nearly invisible *LE* close to a larger cactus design, then carried the belt over to a cart of finished pieces ready to be sold.

After Lester worked his mandatory hours, a guard escorted him back to his cell. He stood close to the open slot window and looked across the river. This was the time of day that he loved, and his favorite view in a foreign place that had become his world. For twenty years Lester had watched the house as the setting sun cast its warm light over the landscape. It was a fine old home, surrounded by pastures, fields of crops, and acres of forest beyond. He'd watched it through the seasons and imagined what life might be like over there.

When a westerly wind blew across the land, it collected the smells of grass and dirt and animals, then crossed the river toward the prison. The breeze blew through Lester's window with a freshness he attempted to capture by inhaling, deeply, holding it in for as long as he could. Its purity was quickly overpowered by the stale air trapped between men and stone.

From his high, small view, Lester caught sight of something different about the landscape. He leaned into the window and squinted, the skin around his eyes creasing into a fanlike pattern of wrinkles. The water inched closer to the house. Its back wing and its double porches were gone, and he spotted a pile of rubble dumped on what had been its gravel drive. Giant trees were uprooted and on the ground. The barns were down, too. The house, his oasis, was surrounded by bulldozers and tractors, its fate sealed. Lester stood at the window, looking, breathing, until his eyes and lungs were filled.

WEEKEND VISITOR

Margaret Starks sat at her lacquered desk, surrounded by two younger lawyers, a paralegal, and a personal assistant who stood in silence and awaited her final approval of a brief that had wearied them all. The filing deadline was in four hours, the work on behalf of Sunderman Inc., a valued client that kept the Louisville law firm of Marshall & Dodson busy.

The hovering at the edge of the desk didn't distract Margaret as she analyzed the brief line by line, word by word. She expected—no, she demanded—that her staff remain on standby ready to receive her next order, just as she had expected the associates to pull the all-nighter to finish the rewrite after yesterday's loud pronouncement that the previous draft was shit. When she arrived at her spacious corner office overlooking the Ohio River at 7 a.m. sharp, she had warned them, it had better be right. As morning became afternoon and the deadline approached, Margaret lived up to her in-house reputation for rants that bordered on emotional abuse of staff.

"When we finish here, I have hours of driving to get to a wedding rehearsal, but I'm not leaving until this brief is perfect. Better hope your collective missteps don't make me late," Margaret said as she gestured toward a stack of discarded drafts. She returned her attention to the document, then looked up and glared at one of the lawyers, a tall blonde with a depleted expression who shuffled from one navy blue pump to the other. The shuffling stopped.

Margaret didn't care if her style of legal practice exhausted the people around her. She had a history of dumping team members whose work product didn't measure up to the standard of care she reserved for her clients. She had no patience for the thin-skinned who couldn't take correction of their grammatical or stylistic weaknesses. Her undisputed status as the hardest-working partner in the firm gave Margaret some measure of satisfaction.

She handed the document to the tired blonde. "Text me when it's filed. I've got to get on the road," she said, the only indication that the brief met her expectations.

Without another word or a hint of appreciation, at half past two Margaret collected her black Chanel handbag and Prada briefcase, then headed to the nearest bank of elevators. At ground level she dashed toward the parking garage at Sixth and Market Streets, undeterred by her tailored pencil skirt and tall black heels. Her precision-cut dark hair grazed her shoulders with each stride. When she reached the silver BMW in its reserved space, she lowered its convertible top, stripped off her suit jacket, tucked her hair under a straw fedora, and sped away. With three hours of hard driving, she might make it to the rehearsal on time.

Tomorrow was Cam Wetherford's wedding. It would be Cam's second marriage, and Margaret's second stint as her bridesmaid. The first marriage, right after college, lasted barely a year. Margaret had told Cam not to marry the jerk, but she didn't listen. Margaret hoped this one would work out better. "This is my last tour of duty in a bridesmaid's dress, even for you," Margaret had told Cam, her dearest friend since they met in college.

Margaret admitted to herself that she'd been a lousy member of the wedding party this time around. She'd missed their engagement party, dropped the ball on hosting a bridal shower, and failed to plan a bachelorette weekend. She'd been working too much. She'd also decided the traditional feting rituals seemed silly for people in their forties. They'd done it all before. Besides, she had quit going to weddings since Robert died. Five years after her husband's death, she missed him every day, but weddings in particular magnified his absence.

"Are you sure you even want me in your wedding? I'm not much fun anymore," she said when Cam asked her. "You won't hurt my feelings if you'd rather have someone else."

"Stop it. I want you with me," Cam said.

"I'm too old to be a bridesmaid," Margaret said. "You know I don't wear ruffles and I don't do pink."

Cam laughed. "I know better than to ask you to wear pink ruffles. Seriously, pick out your own dress. Any color you want, because I don't care. There's no color scheme. No matchy-matchy anything," she said.

"That helps," Margaret said. She tried a few more excuses. Cam nixed them all. Ultimately Margaret said yes. She couldn't skip Cam's wedding. Somehow she'd get through it. She'd also get to be with Cam's family at the lake house in western Kentucky. She didn't dread that part of the weekend. Since Robert died, they were the only living people she really missed.

On Chestnut Street she steered around a large beer delivery truck double-parked with its hazard lights blinking, then punched the accelerator to make it through the intersection. She winced when she caught a whiff of the Butchertown stockyards as she wheeled onto the I-65 ramp and headed south out of town. In a few miles traffic slowed, then stopped, in all lanes. Through the fibers of the hat she felt the hot sun scorching her scalp. Sweat broke out across her body, making her white shirt stick to her back.

"This is unbearable," she said aloud, as if talking to the strangers in cars in front, behind, and alongside. Lately she often caught herself talking out loud. Usually no one was near. Margaret lived a solitary existence, except at the office where people were paid salaries to be around her. She knew those relationships were transactional. So was the loyalty. She suspected the associates had a long list of nicknames they called her behind her back, including the inelegant "Mags" she once heard whispered as she walked into a conference room. That one had an ugly ring to it, she thought, but she let it go, deciding Mags wasn't as insulting as bitch or ballbuster. Margaret pushed a button to return the roof over her head and cranked up the air conditioning, leaning into the vent to cool her face and stop the flow of perspiration. She might not have time to change clothes before the wedding rehearsal. She tossed the hat onto the backseat and fluffed her hair with her fingers.

Tomorrow Cam would marry Owen Moss, a nice guy she'd grown up with but too country and fleshy for Margaret's taste. Owen wasn't her type at all, not that she was looking for anyone. To further complicate the day, the wedding was out in the woods at a remote church called St. Stephen's in a nature preserve or national park or something that was better known for hunting and camping than for weddings. Why would anyone get married out in the woods? Why not Nashville, where they both lived? Nashville made a lot more sense as a wedding venue, especially for Margaret. Nashville was as close a drive and had better hotels, too. Instead, Cam and Owen picked a place in the exact middle of nowhere.

"You have to be on time for the rehearsal so you can ride with us. You'll never find St. Stephen's on your own," Cam had told her a week ago.

"Even with GPS? I can't believe there's a spot that hasn't been mapped," Margaret insisted.

"There's no street address. There's no phone signal. There are no signs, so you have to know exactly which little gravel road to take," Cam said.

"Are you kidding?"

"And bring bug spray. There are lots of ticks," Cam added.

"Ticks? That's an unusual warning for a wedding guest," Margaret said.

"And occasionally wasps. And don't wear heels. They'll sink into the ground, especially if it's raining."

The description sounded like the last place on earth Margaret would have chosen to get married, but St. Stephen's was the only one Cam and Owen had considered. For some reason they loved the spot.

Margaret and Cam had been close friends since their first semester at Commonwealth College, but they were as different as daylight and dark. Cam grew up in rural western Kentucky where rivers, lakes, and woods were part of everyday life, and her large extended family had lived in the area for generations. An architect, Cam spent a lot of time outdoors. She always kept a pair of muddy boots in the back of her Jeep.

Margaret was not a muddy-boot kind of woman. She preferred pumps with the highest heels she could walk in. She thought the shoes gave her an advantage, both in height and attitude. She was a city girl, born and raised in Louisville, accustomed to urban life and its amenities. Louisville had world-class restaurants, old Victorian neighborhoods, manicured parks, museums and performing arts centers. It was big enough to feel like a city, her parents always said, without the problems of a real city. Both of her parents had grown up on the East Coast.

After graduating from law school at the University of Virginia, Margaret toyed with the idea of a larger city. Her parents had encouraged her to look at the big firms in New York and Boston, which they considered to be real cities, but Margaret wanted to come home. She missed her hometown. She accepted a generous offer from a firm whose named partners were a former Kentucky governor and a senator. The offices were on the top floor of the city's tallest glass tower and brimmed with Chippendale sofas and oriental rugs. Autographed pictures of presidents and CEOs lined the walls. Marshall & Dodson had an air of importance that suited Margaret and her parents. By that time Margaret was in love with Robert. They were engaged and planned to marry right after the bar exam. Moving to Louisville was fine with him. He knew it meant a lot to Margaret. Robert took a job with the public defender's office, the type of work he always intended to do. The tired-looking office filled with mismatched furniture and located near the county jail was also fine with him. He fit in.

Margaret fit in at Marshall & Dodson, too. As the only child of two doctors, she was groomed for success and its trappings. Her parents, both Harvard-trained physicians, moved from the Northeast to Louisville as the city developed a reputation as a healthcare destination for heart transplants and intricate surgery on hands blown apart by fireworks and wars. Dr. Elaine Starks was a pediatric oncologist and Dr. Alfred Starks an orthopedic surgeon. Soon after their arrival in Kentucky they purchased a home, a fine example of neo-Georgian architecture nestled in a well-groomed enclave atop the bluffs along the Ohio River. A sought-after interior designer filled the house with English antiques and his signature color scheme of yellow and coral. They cultivated a circle of friends that included members of Louisville's old guard whose names firmly announced lineage and prominent roles in Kentucky history. Names like Taylor, Clay, and Crittenden.

During Margaret's school breaks, the family vacationed on the East Coast or traveled in Europe. "Nothing but the best" became their mantra, a type of family motto suitable for needlepointing. Margaret never doubted her parents wanted the best for her. And from her. Even as a child she believed that if she worked hard enough, she would be enough. She wanted to make them proud.

As a teenager she began to notice the barrage of dings and digs her parents slung at their colleagues, their friends and Margaret's, and sometimes Margaret herself if she didn't live up to their expectations.

He's not very bright. And, heavens, that accent makes him sound like he grew up in a trailer park.

They moved from the wrong side of Bardstown Road to the right side of Brownsboro Road. Good for them.

I think she's had some work done, don't you?

They're from old money. You can just tell.

Surely you're not wearing that dress, dear. That's not a good look for you.

In Margaret, her parents nurtured a need to rise to the top, whether the win was in academics, tennis, or the country club swim team. If she succeeded, they lavished praise and gifts to reward her. If she failed, together they would analyze her mistakes and set new goals. She felt their disdain for anything less than perfection. She carried their expectations with her like an overloaded backpack until she landed back in first place.

When the Doctors Starks heard talk at the club that Margaret's high school wasn't sufficiently rigorous for an Ivy League–bound student, they researched the possibility of boarding schools. Margaret cried and begged not to be sent away. Against their better judgment, they relented. She surprised them again when she chose Commonwealth College, a small liberal arts school less than two hours from Louisville. Margaret surprised herself by bucking her parents.

Before she made her final college decision, the family toured the campus, an old one founded back when Kentucky was still part of Virginia. Its landscape was dotted with columned brick build-ings and enormous heritage ginkgo trees said to have been planted by Henry Clay. Commonwealth had a strong reputation for both academics and partying. The town was small, with few options for entertainment. The school administrators generally turned a blind eye to underage drinking so long as students stayed on campus, didn't drive drunk, and didn't vandalize the historic structures.

"It's a nice little school, quaint even," Margaret's father said. "But you understand you're turning down Wellesley and Smith to stay in Kentucky?" He peered at her over tortoiseshell half-frame readers.

"I get it, Dad," she muttered. "My teachers say Common-wealth is an exceptionally good school. And it's my choice."

"Fine. Let's quit arguing about this," her mother said, casting a glare at her husband. "We just want the best for you. That's all."

Margaret and Cam met soon after they arrived for freshmen orientation, ending up in the same group led by a peppy senior girl who tried to instill camaraderie and school spirit through scaven-ger hunts and role-playing games. By the second day, as their lead-er droned on about football tickets and finals-week study snacks, Margaret glanced around the circle and made eye contact with the girl in cutoffs who slumped in her chair. Her printed name tag said *Camilla*, but the last four letters had been marked through. At the next break, Margaret ran into the girl at the vending machine.

"I'm dying. I can't believe we gave up a week of summer for this," Cam said. Her voice was unexpectedly twangy to Margaret's ear.

Margaret nodded and inserted coins for a Tab. "It's like being in middle school again," she said.

When they rejoined their group, they sat together, glancing at each other when someone said something stupid. With the country twang and hippie clothes, this girl wasn't like the ones Margaret had grown up with in Louisville's east end.

31

Cam lived in faded jeans and rarely wore makeup. She paid no attention to labels on clothes and handbags. Margaret's dorm closet brimmed with bright Lilly Pulitzer dresses and Marimekko print slacks. She wore enough makeup to look well groomed but not slutty or like she was from somewhere out Dixie Highway. Their study habits were different, too. On nice days, Cam spread her bedspread on the grass in the quad and studied outdoors. Margaret used the same cubicle each day in the windowless basement of the library. Margaret decided not to pledge a sorority, despite her mother's urgings. Cam never considered it. A few weeks into the semester, Cam moped about. "God, I miss my family," she said. "I wish I could go home this weekend." Cam's words surprised Margaret, who was happy to be away from hers.

Early on, Margaret had laughed at Cam's accent, but by midterm she stopped. Even though Cam sounded like a hick and her vowel sounds dragged on for days, she was way more interesting than Margaret's high school friends.

"You lived next to the Luxembourg Gardens?" Cam said as Margaret casually described her family's last vacation. At the time Cam thought she wanted to be a landscape architect.

"Yeah, we had an apartment that overlooked the park," Margaret said.

"Do you realize how lucky you are? I'd kill to be there. Those gardens were designed in the sixteen hundreds, and by a woman," Cam said.

Margaret nodded. She hadn't given it much thought.

Over Christmas break Cam visited Margaret in Louisville. After introductions in the marble front hall, Margaret watched as her mother gave Cam the once-over and then dismissed her. "Where did you find this girl?" her mother said after the visit. When summer came, Margaret traveled to western Kentucky for the first time, the first of many weekends spent at the Wetherfords' lake cottage.

She had never been "out in the state," as Louisvillians referred to the rest of Kentucky, a phrase conveying that everything beyond the city limits was provincial, inferior, backward. Margaret thought the landscape's flatness matched the sound of the local accents. Row upon row of crops—she had no idea what was growing—stretched as far as she could see. Ubiquitous smokiness hung in the air from the region's famous barbecue joints and tobacco barns. People waved from their car or truck or boat as they passed, even if they didn't recognize the driver.

From that first visit, Cam's parents had welcomed her. When she addressed them as Mr. and Mrs. Wetherford, they insisted that she call them by their given names, Lowell and Rose. She'd grown attached to all the Wetherfords, not just Cam. Robert had loved them, too. They were the closest thing to family that she had left. Even if she wasn't thrilled about the wedding itself or being a bridesmaid, she wanted to be part of their circle again.

At last the traffic began to move again along the interstate's six southbound lanes. To make up for lost time, Margaret darted in and out of the lanes, always looking to gain an advantage over her fellow drivers. She reached the Jefferson County line and set the cruise control to 78, fast enough to make good time but not so fast that she couldn't brake for a radar gun. She might make it on time.

The hot, humid June day reminded her of many others spent out on the lake with Cam's family. She had no idea how many times she had made the trip, the first leg down the busy interstate and the second on the nearly deserted West Kentucky Parkway. Cars were few, and for long stretches the landscape nondescript. Drivers sometimes found themselves drifting off from fatigue or monotony. A cable barrier had been installed in the median a few years back.

As she drove, Margaret thought back to another hot summer weekend when Cam's dad taught her to water-ski behind their speedboat. Margaret had watched Cam and her sister Becky ski like Cypress Gardens pros for what seemed like miles across the lake. They made it look easy. Margaret was eager to try, confident in her ability to be the best.

"Your turn, Margaret," Lowell said. He was a tall man who never appeared rushed, with thinning hair that he kept slicked back from his face. He wore plaid swim trunks and worn slip-on sneakers that he called boat shoes. He handed her a narrow white ski belt.

"I don't wear a lifejacket?" she said. The belt looked too flimsy to hold her above the surface.

"You don't want all that bulk. The belt's enough, but you might have to tread a little while you're in the water. The trick is to get on up out of the water on your skis, and you won't have to tread for long," he said.

Cam laughed. "Just trust him. He loves teaching newbies. The rest of us endure these lessons several times a summer," she said.

Margaret strapped the ski belt around her waist and then plunged into the deep bluish green water from the side of the boat. She resurfaced with a squeal. "It's colder than I expected," she yelled. Her skin, which had warmed under the sun for hours, rippled with goosebumps.

"Here, catch your skis," Cam shouted before tossing them overboard. The first one smacked the water then sailed straight toward Margaret. She caught it, then reached out for the second one, which took a slightly different trajectory. She had to kick and paddle to catch it. While she was still on the boat, they had given her basic instructions and she thought she understood, but out in the cold lake, shivering, treading water, everything felt awkward and difficult to accomplish. She wallowed to get the skis onto her feet, grab the rope, and manage to keep it untangled and between the tips of her skis. Her heart started to race.

"Ready?" Lowell called to her.

"Almost." She tried to concentrate, to remember what she'd been told. She saw another boat speed by, pulling three skiers.

"Ready?" he repeated. His voice sounded upbeat like he had more confidence in her ability than she did. His optimism surprised her. Her own dad never sounded like that.

"Ready!" she yelled.

When the boat took off, she tried to hold on to the rope, but her arms felt like they might be ripped from their sockets. She let go. The next attempt wasn't much better. She fell again and again, but he wouldn't let her quit. Somehow his good-natured push for her to ski didn't feel as stressful as her own parents' insistence on perfection. He smiled each time he brought the boat around to better position the rope in her favor.

"You've almost got it. Keep your knees soft, like shock absorbers," he called out as the boat circled around her. She reached for the handle and missed. He circled the boat again. She was cold and nervous; her teeth chattered. Her hands shook as she grabbed for the rope again. Neither of Cam's parents showed signs of irritation or impatience, but Cam and Becky seemed hot and bored.

"I could try again later," she offered, wishing the lesson would end.

"Let's do five more tries, or one good trip around the bay once you're up," he yelled back. As she attempted to keep the ski tips parallel and above the water with the rope between them, she felt sick at her stomach from the waves and the fear of falling again. She gritted her teeth and told herself she could do this. She would do this.

"Go," she yelled.

He gunned the boat. Her arms burned like fire, but she kept them straight, white-knuckling the red plastic handle. She followed her arms up out of the water, and her legs solidified under her. She was skiing. Cam and her sister stirred from their spectator stupor and cheered, giving her thumbs-up signs. Her skin was no longer chilled by water but warmed by air.

She stood on two skis long enough to qualify as a trip around the bay. When she attempted to cross the wake, she took an ugly spill, more like a cartwheel than a fall. She came up coughing, choking from a mouthful of water, and then aware that she was topless. Her orange bikini top must have slipped off in the impact from the fall.

"She's down!" she heard someone shout above the engine.

Margaret watched as they made a fast U-turn and headed back to get her. Her eyes darted around to see if her swimsuit was floating nearby. She groped herself until her hand felt extra fabric at her waist and, looking through the clear water, she saw something orange twisted around her ski belt. As the boat got closer, she worked to get the top free, struggling to pull it back up and rehook the straps. With shaky arms she stroked the water to collect the skis, which also had slipped off in the fall. She pointed one ski up toward the sky so other boaters could see her.

"Good job!" Cam's dad bellowed as they approached. He hooted and hollered, then threw up a victory sign. Margaret nodded her head in acknowledgment and tried to smile. She hated skiing.

"The rope is right behind you. Grab on as it passes and you won't have to swim too far," Rose said, showing the simple yet authentic grace she always exhibited in Margaret's presence. She never missed an opportunity to take good care of those around her. Lowell cut the engine. The lesson could officially end. Margaret Starks had gotten up.

Feeling drained, she hauled herself up the small aluminum ladder at the back of the boat, where she collapsed onto the beige outdoor carpet without grace or vanity. Her legs felt weak and shaky, her arms already sore. A bruise was forming where something—rope or ski—hit her shin in the last fall. Cam, whose face was sunburned and covered with more freckles than when the lesson began, threw a towel to her.

"What'd you think?"

"Please don't ever make me do that again," Margaret whispered.

Cam laughed. "You just became another notch on Dad's ski belt. He loves first lessons," she said.

"Sorry mine took so long," Margaret said.

"We're used to it. Complaining doesn't help," Cam said.

"If we whine, he makes the lesson longer," Becky said.

Lowell fished down into a metal cooler, plucked out a bottle of Grapette dripping with icy water, and handed it to Margaret.

"Girl, you did great!" he said. His smile was wide and toothy.

"Thanks for teaching me. It's harder than it looks," Margaret admitted.

"We'll take you out again tomorrow, and it will get a lot easier." He coiled the rope and stowed the skis. Margaret glimpsed at Cam and silently shook her head. She didn't want to ski again.

They spent the rest of the day on the boat touring the lake, with Cam's parents pointing out landmarks. Both had grown up nearby. A large structure of gray stone with turrets and a high wall came into view.

"What's that? It looks like a castle," Margaret said.

Cam and Becky giggled. "You don't want to live there, Cinderella," Cam said. "That's the state prison."

Margaret squinted and saw razor wire strung along the walls. Guards stood watch in the tower.

"That's where we used to live," Becky said.

"The prison?" Margaret said.

"No, that was our town. Our old house was just a few streets from the penitentiary," Becky said.

Margaret couldn't envision a town there. The prison was perched on a steep hillside with the lake at its base.

"There doesn't seem to be room on that cliff for an entire town," Margaret said.

"Nothing looked like this before the lake, honey," Rose said. "The river level was much lower. There was room for everything." She stood and turned to the east, steadying herself against the movement of waves and a gentle breeze. Her blue one-piece swimsuit had a thick nylon layer for coverage that was topped by a thinner, swirly-patterned blouson designed to flutter across her midriff. A teal-colored scarf tied back her light brown hair. She pointed toward the shore, indicating how the town had been laid out. "The business district lay over this way. The courthouse and the hotel were about here, and the churches and the movie theater over there. And most of the houses ran along a road that's now under the water." For a time Rose stared out at the lake's surface. "I have to admit it's getting harder for me to remember it," she added.

Margaret watched Rose's warm smile fade, her expression grow distant, perhaps sad. Margaret didn't know how to respond. The adults in her life rarely showed how they felt. She averted her eyes.

"It was a beautiful old place. Full of history," Lowell said.

Margaret listened, nodded as appropriate, and watched a man who walked along the prison wall.

"Margaret, look there. See that slab of concrete on the bank?" Rose said as she pointed toward the prison, then spun around to point in the opposite direction. "That was the ferry landing. When I growing up, we had to take the ferry to get home. That's Between the Rivers, where I'm from. Mint Springs. There." She seemed to be pointing to the middle of the lake.

"Under the water?" Margaret asked.

"Yes, under the water," Rose said. "My family's homeplace, where we Clarksons had lived since 1840, is somewhere down there."

Lowell whirled his captain's chair around so he could be heard over the engine. "Once they built Kentucky Dam, nothing was the same. Then came Lake Barkley. And then somebody in Washington decided we needed a recreation area, a wilderness, so they moved everybody out from Between the Rivers and renamed it Land Between the Lakes." He pointed toward the shore, a lush green strip of land without houses or boat docks or other traces of humans.

"We fought it, but we couldn't win," he said, then he swiveled to face forward and drive the boat.

"I'm starving," Becky said. Cam nodded in agreement.

"Let's head over to Mint Springs. We can anchor and eat our lunch there," Rose said.

"Sounds good," Lowell said. He slowed the boat's speed and steered to cross the lake, due west from the prison. As they ventured outside the channel buoys, he stood to look for obstructions in the water.

"By the time the government thought up the idea for Land Between the Lakes, they'd already torn down all the old river towns for the lakes. They had gotten real good at moving people off their land," Rose said. Her face, usually soft and pleasant, tightened. Lowell cut the engine and tied the anchor rope to a cleat on the bow, then slipped the anchor down to the muddy lake bottom.

"Only about seven feet of water here. We're just about over the site where her house used to stand," he said.

Rose nodded, surveying the small bay to get her bearings. "That's about right. I see the cemetery on the hill there, beneath that big tulip poplar," she said. She opened the cooler and began to set out sandwiches, cold drinks, and sliced watermelon on a small pop-up table at the back of the boat. Cam and Becky ate their pimento cheese sandwiches, hardly paying attention to the conversation. They'd heard it before, Margaret guessed.

"It was hard on people around here. Some never got over it," Lowell said. Margaret wondered if the Wetherfords had.

For years Margaret would listen to their stories, but she never understood the depth of their bitterness. She viewed the area with the eyes of a weekend visitor who arrived long after the dams were built, the towns were flooded, and the last resident moved out to make way for LBL, as they all now called Land Between the Lakes. As a tourist, she didn't have to see beyond the scenery. After the government had decided what was needed in western Kentucky and Tennessee, Margaret and others like her became beneficiaries of the actions. She swam in the lakes and biked the LBL trails without much reflection on who had been there before or what was sacrificed to provide this place for her, the weekend visitor. Privately she applauded the successive decisions designed to transform the area into a destination, but she never told the Wetherfords how she felt. She didn't want to insult the people who had hosted her, accepted her, treated her like a daughter. She loved them, so much so that her younger self wondered if she should take up their bitterness and carry it as a sign of her loyalty to them. She had tried, but she found she couldn't sustain any meaningful level of regret that the lakes had been created. In its current form, the area was interwoven with her dearest memories, including Robert. He had loved it, too.

Margaret glanced at the dashboard clock and eased the cruise control up to 82. She would take her chances. She'd talk her way out of a ticket if she got pulled over, or she'd hire a local lawyer and get it dismissed for defective equipment. She had a shot at making it on time, perhaps with a few minutes to change into something more appropriate for a wedding rehearsal than her serious dark suit. She had a room reserved at the state park lodge, not far from the Wetherfords' cabin. Once she got checked in, they could pick her up to go to the rehearsal.

She rolled past exits to destinations called Beaver Dam, Providence, and Princeton. She never thought about these little towns unless she was heading to see the Wetherfords. She never heard much about them, either. The land flattened and the sky seemed to grow broader as she headed west. She was making good time when the gas gauge warning light came on.

"Damn. I'll never make it now," she said. She relaxed a bit when she saw that the next exit—Sycamore Kuttawa—was the one she needed. Sycamore was the nearest town to the Wetherfords' place on the lake. The road south from the four-way stop was the way to the cottage. At the end of the ramp, she turned toward Sycamore and stopped at the first gas station, a midcentury marvel with a Jetsons-style roofline jutting into the sky. As she pumped gas, she glanced around and remembered that Cam had grown up here. Her family hadn't built their lake cottage until Cam was in high school.

Margaret had always seen Sycamore as a rather featureless place where 1960s ranch-style houses and randomly placed, low-slung shopping centers dominated the architecture. One large tree with dappled white bark appeared older and taller than anything in town, even the courthouse. She could never figure out where to find the center of town, if one existed. With no obvious grid layout in the small business district, the town looked as if it had been built all at once by a real estate developer on a tight budget. Decades later it still felt unfinished and unrooted.

Her phone chimed. She checked the screen and saw a text from Cam.

Where r u? We need to leave for church.

She typed hurriedly.

Almost to your house. Wait if you can. Leave directions if not. I don't have to change.

Inside the gas station, she headed to the restroom and glanced in the mirror. She smoothed her hair and reapplied lipstick, knowing there wasn't time to freshen up at the hotel. There was no hiding the fact that she was arriving late, looking disheveled and unprepared for her best friend's wedding. When she got back to the car, she double-checked the trunk to make sure she had brought her dress for the wedding. She hadn't meant to disengage from the celebration, but she knew she had. Cam had always been there for her, attentive, on time. When Robert was sick and then dying, Cam had been by her side. Cam deserved better from her.

She programmed the Wetherfords' address into the GPS to keep from missing a tricky turn, then headed south on KY 273. The road roughly paralleled the lake, with occasional hills blocking the water view. Impressive vacation homes had been constructed on the hillsides, giving them panoramic views of the lake through expanses of glass and decking. Rumors swirled last summer that a couple of country music stars from Nashville were building a vacation home, more mansion than lake cottage, with a garage wedged into a hillside to conceal their tour bus from fans and gawkers.

"Can you believe those are weekend houses? They look more like hotels," Lowell had said. He was the pleasantest man Margaret knew, but she heard a tinge of resentment in his voice as he gazed at the newcomers' mansions. She remembered that nearly all of Cam's family—the Wetherfords and the Clarksons—had been river people. They had a long, unbroken history on the Cumberland. Despite her strong bond with the Wetherfords, she too was still a newcomer. A weekend visitor.

Knowing the turnoff was close, she slowed and squinted to see. A small sign appeared with two white balloons floating above—*Wetherford-Moss Wedding*—and Margaret recognized Cam's familiar artsy lettering and stylized flower borders. The fleeting image of the sign, the merest suggestion of Cam, stirred a sense of relief in Margaret as she made the final turn. For years Cam had been a constant in Margaret's life, a true friend, a guiding force that led to this spot where Margaret had found welcome and comfort countless times before. Feeling a small surge of rekindled strength, Margaret knew she was at the right place.

FOR WHAT IT'S WORTH

Occasionally someone would stop Elmer Newby in a store and ask him why in the world he'd help the government run people off their land. Elmer always clenched his teeth and stiffened his shoulders. His cheeks turned red. "Hell, I didn't decide this. That was some fool in Washington," he told them. Elmer hated that folks had no choice about leaving, but he had to make a living. Every morning as he headed out to appraise property, he reminded himself that he had a family to support. A job to do.

Elmer started his real estate appraisal business after he returned from the war in Europe and attended college on the GI Bill. In the early years he struggled to keep the business afloat. He got his real estate license and sold a few houses when the bank account grew lean, but he preferred appraising land to showing homes. He was good with numbers. Coming up with the fair market value on a piece of property required figuring parcel size, square footage of structures, and finding the value of comparable tracts. Comparables were crucial to the calculation. The goal was to be as objective as possible because, in Elmer's mind and according to the standards of his profession, objectivity led to fairness for both the buyer and the seller.

During one long stretch without much work, Elmer decided he might need to close his business and take a job with a weekly paycheck. He knew Judy worried about the rent and whether they could afford things for the kids. He could get a route selling life insurance policies for Joe Flynn's agency or selling clothing for the men's suit factory. About the time he was ready to call it quits, he heard talk about another federal dam project, this time on the Cumberland River. The dam and the resulting massive reservoir required the government's acquisition of thousands of acres. Each parcel would be appraised to determine fair market value and a purchase price. Elmer felt like he'd struck gold.

His business took off. He appraised all sorts of property—houses, businesses, schools, tilled farmland—most of which would be under water or along the new higher shoreline when the lake filled. Through the government's power of eminent domain, entire towns were taken. People lost homes and farms that had been in their families for generations. Old-growth forests were leveled. The sight of a mountain-sized stack of downed trees had caused Elmer to grieve for days, but that was the way of progress, even if it hurt to look. When the dam was finished, Lake Barkley would fill and flood the land, forever altering the place. There would be no going back.

The Barkley Dam project changed Elmer, too. For the first time in his life, he had money. He hadn't inherited a copper from his people, but now he had money. He and Judy took the kids to Florida for a summer vacation. They built a modern ranch-style home with a brick façade, by far the best house he had ever lived in. Elmer wanted his children to have a better life than he had known growing up. His own father had a hard time holding a job—he was bad to drink—which meant the family moved often to find work. From one rental house to another, one school to the next, they kept moving, never calling any one place home. Elmer didn't want that for his kids. He wanted them to know where they belonged. When he and Judy built the house, he knew exactly how much it cost, each two-by-four and every window, even down to the price of a brick or a roof shingle, and he had earned every cent needed to build it.

But he grew anxious as the last few Barkley tracts were acquired. The appraisal work would dry up with the dam's completion. He thought his business was sufficiently established, but he hated the thought of losing everything he'd worked for.

"Did you see the paper?" Judy had said when the news broke a few years ago. She stood at the sink washing breakfast dishes, already dressed for work in a yellow sleeveless shift, her auburn hair combed, a hint of orange lipstick applied. Two days a week Judy worked in the children's section of the Mayfield Public Library. Their three boys had caught the school bus a few minutes earlier.

"Not yet," Elmer said as he poured himself a cup of coffee.

"There's big news," she teased.

He leaned toward her and gave her a peck on the cheek, glimpsing the freckles on the back of her bare arms. He wanted to lean down and kiss them too, but he didn't. He splashed milk into his coffee, then dropped in two saccharin tablets and stirred until they dissolved. He wore a white shirt with a narrow black tie, and after he had his coffee, he would slip on a jacket grown shiny from pressing and head to his small second-floor office over the Ben Franklin on the courthouse square.

He sat down at the table, picked up the *Sun-Messenger*, and read the headline: *Kennedy Administration Proposes New Recreation Area Between Lakes.* Elmer's heart raced as he read. The Tennessee Valley Authority proposed buying out every property owner on the narrow strip of land between the rivers—now lakes—to re-create a wilderness for hiking, boating, fishing, and other leisure activities.

Three hundred miles of shoreline stretching from Kentucky into Tennessee. As many as 170,000 acres, 1,500 dwellings and farms to be appraised. The story quoted governors and congressional delegations from both states, who were delighted with the news. So was Elmer Newby. The Land Between the Lakes project was a godsend, assuring steady income for years.

Judy's hands grazed the back of his neck. "So, what do you think?"

"That I'm the luckiest son of a gun that ever lived," Elmer said.

She laughed and squeezed his shoulders. "I'm glad you realize that," she said.

Elmer stood and, putting his arms around her, pulled her close. "I'm not taking anything for granted," he said, then left for the office. His mind shifted into high gear, making plans, deciding who to talk to at the local TVA office. Because of the Barkley work, he was on a first-name basis with several of the land acquisition superintendents. It might be years before actual appraisals began—federal projects were notoriously slow and cumbersome—but Elmer wanted to be the first guy in line.

His wait for the work to begin went on and on. A few months after the LBL announcement, President Kennedy was shot and killed in Dallas. Then the feds argued over whether the land should become a national park or a recreation area. They argued with the people over how many acres would be acquired and whether commercial development would be allowed. The people fought to keep their property, now destined to become a tourist attraction. Some residents wanted to develop their own resorts on the lakes. President Johnson stepped in, insisting that landowners deserved more time to protest and let their voices be heard. The people got their hopes up.

When the acquisitions finally commenced, the government took it all. The protests had changed nothing. TVA claimed every tract in the forty-mile peninsula that straddled the Kentucky-Tennessee line. Nobody wanted to leave their homes. Some claimed the government was stealing their land with lowball offers for now-lakefront property. All the people Elmer dealt with were mad as hell, regardless of their circumstances. Nice homes and rusty trailers, owners rich and poor, Black and white, young families and old widows. "Don't get out of that car" became a common greeting when Elmer arrived on assignments, and a few times, he believed he'd not survive the job.

A farmer named Warren was particularly convincing. Elmer had driven more than an hour to reach Crooked Creek, a remote area where every other homeowner had been bought out for Barkley. Only Warren remained. His house sat at the end of a long road—more dirt than gravel—that few traveled these days. As Elmer parked and climbed out of the car, he spotted a man with a headful of white hair waiting near the corner of a log corncrib. Warren was ready for him, perhaps alerted by the rooster tail of dust thrown up as Elmer's car approached.

"Stay where you are," Warren said. Elmer saw that the man held a shotgun. From his years in the war, Elmer recognized its shape. A Winchester Model 12. The Perfect Repeater. His heart thumped in his chest.

"Sir, my name is—" Elmer stopped as he saw Warren lift and shoulder the shotgun, preparing to draw a bead on him. Elmer raised his hands shoulder high. "I'm not armed, Mr. Warren, and I don't want any trouble," he said.

"Get off my land and we won't have any trouble," Warren said.

"I'm just trying to do my job, sir, but this can wait," Elmer said. "I'm getting back in the car now." He eased back into the driver's seat and turned the car around. When he checked the rearview mirror, Elmer saw that the old man had not moved or relaxed. He

48

remained in a fighting stance, ready to follow through. Elmer drove off. From that day forward, he kept a loaded snub-nose Smith & Wesson in the glove box. His children understood to never turn the latch when they rode in his car.

Though he was glad to grab as much work as he could, some jobs stayed with him. Some nights he lay awake, remembering Donnie and Evelyn Richards being forced to leave. Unlike most of these assignments, he knew Donnie and Evelyn. They were Judy's distant cousins. Evelyn's eyes were the kind of green that only rivers possessed, and she had looked deep into his own. "Where will we go, Elmer?" she said, refusing to blink. "We've never lived anywhere else. This is our home." The fact that she spoke so tenderly to him had struck him harder than if she had shouted or cursed.

The clock ticked beside his bed as he wondered who came up with an idea that exiled them all and why it had ever been approved, but when morning came Elmer went back to getting the work done, keeping his family of six fed and his business afloat.

One day he rose early to recalculate the Richards appraisal. He had kept it in a separate file and held back on submitting his final valuation, but he needed to turn it in. He needed to get paid for the job. On a fresh form, he reentered the same details—square footage, acreage, number of rooms—but he changed the home's condition from fair to excellent. When he got to the office, he'd find new comparables to justify the higher sale price.

At breakfast when they had their coffee, Judy had to say his name twice to get his attention. "What is it, honey?" she asked, sliding her hand over his.

"I can't stop thinking about Donnie and Evelyn," he told her. "It's pitiful," and then he found that he was choking on the rest of his words. She didn't press him further, tightening her grip on his hand. He finished his coffee and looked at her, noticing flecks of river-green in her eyes, too.

"Some of these folks will never get over this," he predicted.

The phone rang as Elmer unlocked the office door. He left the keys in the lock and scrambled to answer the call. It was Clyde Edmonds, who ran the land acquisition office over at Golden Pond. Clyde handed out appraisal assignments.

"I've got a holdout over in Pleasant Grove. Old colored man won't talk to anybody. Already run off two other appraisers. We can't have any bad publicity," he said.

Elmer remembered the newspaper stories about Ada Chilton and the public outrage over what had happened to the old woman during the Barkley buyouts. He said, "You've got a bunch of amateurs working for you. You need somebody who can get the job done."

"You want to try?"

"Have I ever let you down, Clydie?

"I'll up your fee by fifty dollars if you can get Nate McCracken's property appraised without any trouble."

"Sign me up," Elmer said. He could use a little extra money. School started in a few weeks, and his children looked like they had outgrown everything in the closets. Elmer liked a challenge. He also liked the job security of being Clydie's first choice whenever the agency needed an appraisal.

But Elmer worried. He remembered Ada Chilton, the old woman who had used her shotgun to blow out a windshield when an appraiser came to talk about buying her property. She too had been a holdout. The situation turned ugly when somebody lured Miss Chilton into town on the pretense of a meeting. While she was away from home, government-hired crews moved in with bulldozers, leveling her still-occupied residence and then torching it. As fire engulfed all of Miss Chilton's worldly possessions, smoke was seen for miles, like a signal of things gone wrong.

When Elmer heard what had been done to the old woman, he couldn't believe something like that could happen in America. He assured friends and family that he had nothing to do with Miss Chilton's file.

Before heading to Pleasant Grove, Elmer filled a couple of mason jars with ice water and packed two sandwiches and an apple to last him through the day. All the restaurants in the area known as Between the Rivers had closed. A few small general stores with rough wood floors were still open if he needed a cold bottle of pop late in the day.

Elmer drove toward Gilbertsville, where two lanes of US 62 crossed the top of Kentucky Dam. Built in the 1940s, the dam was the first of the big local federal projects designed for flood control and to generate hydroelectric power for rural western Kentucky. To the right of the narrow highway Elmer glimpsed Kentucky Lake beyond the low guardrail, its surface glistening in the morning sun. To the left, in between passing cars and power lines that carried electricity generated by the dam's turbines, he saw the swirling currents of the Tennessee River below the gates. The lake was wide and calm; the river narrow and wild. As he gazed, he heard the honk of a horn. He looked back to the road and corrected his unintentional drift toward oncoming traffic.

Two decades had passed since the first impoundment, but Elmer still viewed the lake with awe. Numbers churned in his head about the yards of concrete that went into the construction, the cost per yard, workers employed, gallons of water flowing per second. Even when he wasn't appraising, his mind automatically put a cost-benefit analysis to everything around him.

The lake itself was stunningly beautiful, the dam a technological wonder. Elmer never imagined a body of water so big right here in his own backyard, like an ocean had been plopped down in the middle of the country or a sixth Great Lake had formed. He never dreamed of something like this so close to home. Elmer was from an adjoining landlocked county, a place more of soil than water that hadn't lost an acre or a dollar in tax revenues from the building of two dams, the resulting reservoirs, or Land Between the Lakes. In fact, he and his neighbors benefited from the creation of thousands of jobs and cheap, plentiful electricity. It was progress, plain and simple.

Optimistic to his core, Elmer remained excited about what the lakes meant for western Kentucky, both for business and on a personal level. Nearly every dollar he had earned came from his own hard work, much of it connected to the federal projects. He was a self-made man. He liked progress and wanted to be part of it.

A couple of summers ago, he had borrowed a friend's long-stowed army surplus tent for a camping trip to the new Kentucky Dam Village State Park. Judy was six months pregnant with their fourth child.

"I'm not sleeping on the ground," she said.

"You don't have to. I borrowed a cot for you," Elmer said.

"It's so hot, honey. My feet might pop if they swell any bigger."

"I bought one of those inflatable rafts for you. You can float in the water to stay cool."

Judy's scowl lifted a bit. "We don't have sleeping bags, either," she said.

"Roscoe let me borrow a couple. The boys and I can make a pallet with blankets. It'll be fun," he said. He put his arms around her. "I promise I'll do the work."

In a red metal Coca-Cola cooler, he packed hot dogs tinted a deep pinkish color, milk, lunch meat, mustard, and ketchup. He filled the picnic basket with potato chips, corn flakes, Little Debbie oatmeal cakes, thin-sliced Bunny Bread, hot dog buns, a large stack of paper plates, and tin mugs to use for drinks and as cereal bowls. He stashed a watermelon and a carton of pop on the backseat floorboards. The melon rolled over the boys' feet when Elmer braked or took a curve too fast.

At the state park they found their campsite at the lake's edge and Elmer tried to pitch the tent. Eventually he got it to stand by roping it to nearby trees.

"I think Roscoe forgot some of the tent poles," he said. "It should hold for the night, though."

For almost twenty-four hours at the lake, they swam, watched ski boats zip by, and fished from the bank with a borrowed pole they all shared. One of the boys caught his first fish, a small bluegill with vibrant orange markings. Around the campfire, they roasted two packages of hot dogs on straightened coat hangers and drank cold pop, something the kids didn't get at home. The boys chased tiny toads until dark, when they switched to catching lightning bugs. When they could run no more, they collapsed onto a pallet made from damp-smelling sleeping bags and blankets that nearly filled the tent. As his family slept, Elmer sat alone by the fire, watching the embers and looking at the stars. Water stroked the shore at a level the old river people never dreamed possible.

"If my luck holds and the work keeps coming, I want to buy a lot or a cabin over here," he told Judy on the drive home the next day. "There's something about this place."

Pleasant Grove, a crossroads originally situated near a bend of the Cumberland River, had been settled in the eighteen hundreds around an iron furnace built by enslaved laborers. More recently the community had its own motel and restaurant, both listed in the Negro Travelers' Green Book. They'd already been torn down. A white frame Baptist church and a one-room school had been leveled and burned last month.

Elmer thought about the tract of land owned and occupied by the holdout, Nate McCracken. A title search at the Lyon County courthouse revealed that McCracken's family had owned the land for nearly a hundred years, the recorded deed dated shortly after the Civil War. Title had been passed from generation to generation of McCrackens. While Elmer was at the courthouse, he found several recent transfers of similar properties on which he could calculate his comparables.

As Elmer got farther from home, WNGO-AM faded to static. He spun the dial to find a closer station, WCBL in Benton, and heard the morning news, weather, and livestock reports. The forecast was a hot one with a chance of rain in the late afternoon.

His dusty white Ford Fairlane rolled past razed farmhouses, dogtrot barns, and churches. He recalled the earlier demolition work in preparation for the lakes where everything—buildings and trees—was cleared. This time was different. For LBL the forests, creeks, and ponds were to be left untouched; only signs of human settlement and industry were doomed. The plan was to return the area to wilderness as if no one had ever lived here.

Elmer turned down a lane bordered by honey locusts twisted and knobby with age. A KEEP OUT sign had been nailed to the tree closest to the road. Elmer's breathing quickened and his fingers tightened around the steering wheel. He took his foot off the gas. Since the incident with old man Warren, he had changed the way he approached a property. His car crept up to the house, this one a neatly kept but unpainted frame structure not far from a large barn, also unpainted.

Elmer relaxed a bit when he saw a man working in the pasture between the barn and house. At least he knew he wouldn't be looking down the barrel of a shotgun right off the bat. Elmer took a deep breath as he parked the car and turned off the engine. He reminded himself that his work was backed up by the law. He had it in writing, a court order that gave TVA and its agents the right to trespass to accomplish a buyout. He kept a worn copy in the glove box, next to the pistol. He hoped he didn't have to reach for either.

He got out of the car and slammed the door. "Mr. McCracken?" he said in a loud voice as he walked toward the pasture. The man's shovel slowed and he turned, standing beside the trench he was digging. He was a tall man, unstooped, and he wore work clothes, a faded checked shirt and bib overalls covered in dirt. His heavy boots were caked with dried mud. He didn't smile or wave or approach in welcome, but he leaned on his shovel as a big brindle dog of an unidentifiable breed came from under the porch, barking and loping toward Elmer. Its tail curled over its back.

"Can't you see I'm busy?" the man said with a directness that surprised Elmer. Most Black men of a certain age in this part of the country still followed the well-known rules of engagement when addressing a white man, although Elmer had never set much store by that way of thinking. He decided he preferred Mr. McCracken's rude tone to looking down a shotgun barrel, and besides, his immediate concern was the approaching dog, now closer and starting to growl. He braced himself.

"Can you call off your dog, sir?"

"Rufus! Get over here," McCracken hollered.

The dog stopped, then turned and walked toward his owner.

"Thank you, sir. I see you're busy, but I need to talk to you. My name's Elmer Newby and I—"

"And you're from the government," the man interrupted.

"Not really. I'm from over at Mayfield, and I'm a real estate appraiser. I need to see your land so the TVA can make you a fair offer for your place."

"Don't have time today. Got to dig this ditch before the rain comes," McCracken said. He went back to digging.

"Well, sir, we're running out of time to give you a fair price. You've got a nice piece of ground, and the government ought to pay you what it's worth. If I can't see your property, we might miscalculate," Elmer said.

"Not today," McCracken said. He kept digging.

Elmer thought about his next move.

"How far you going to take that ditch?" he said.

"Out to the road."

"That's going to take you the better part of a day."

"Reckon so. Don't have time to waste," McCracken said, pointing toward the sky.

Elmer thought hard. Why the man was digging a new ditch confounded him, knowing that the government would hold title soon. But the man said he needed the ditch dug before the rain began, and Elmer needed to finish the appraisal. Pulling out the court order wouldn't help accomplish either task.

"How about this? I'll help you dig your ditch, as long as it takes us to finish. And when we're done, you spend the same amount of time showing me around your place so I can finish my work," he said.

Elmer waited. Presently McCracken stopped digging. "There's another shovel in the barn," he said.

"All right, sir. Let me get my boots from my car." Elmer walked back to his sedan, took off his coat and tie, and rolled up his sleeves. He exchanged his shoes for work boots and headed to the barn for the shovel.

They worked side by side for two hours. Neither said much, only questions and answers about the ditch. In that time Elmer thought about the years McCracken had spent working this land, surely never imagining being forced off so late in life. He watched McCracken's efficient movements as he cut straight into the earth and sent wide arcs of dirt into the air. By midday they finished the job. Both were covered in sweat and dirt. McCracken extended his right hand, and Elmer shook it.

"Come get a drink and wash up," McCracken said. He led Elmer around back of the house to a well, where he drew up a bucket of fresh water. Elmer washed his hands and face, then ran his wet fingers through his hair to slick it from his brow. He cupped his clean hands for a drink of the shockingly cold water coming from deep in the ground.

"You want a bite to eat?"

"Thank you, but I've got a sack lunch in the car. I'll sit here in the shade and eat if you don't mind."

McCracken nodded and went inside. Rufus scooted under the porch.

Elmer got his food and sat on the edge of the steps, hoping for a breeze to help him cool off. He ate a bologna sandwich and listened to the kitchen sounds coming from inside. A rattle of dishes and maybe a skillet. Then the screen door opened and McCracken reappeared. He carried a plate mounded with scrambled eggs and two pieces of light bread. He scraped half of the eggs into a tin pie pan on the rough wood floor and called his dog. Rufus leapt onto the porch and gulped his share. McCracken sat down in a straight-back chair to eat his meal.

"How long have you lived here, Mr. McCracken?"

"Name's Nate. Been here all my life. Born here. My daddy before me, too. Never lived anyplace else," he said.

"Must be hard to give it up."

"Never thought I'd ever have to." Nate's aged brown eyes looked straight into Elmer's younger blue ones. "We worked hard so nobody could take it away from us. Now I'm supposed to just hand it over," he said, shaking his head. "My great-granddaddy was born into slavery over in Christian County. And my great-grandmama's people worked the iron furnaces between the rivers. Also slaves. They worked right alongside those Chinamen."

"Folks came all the way from China to work these furnaces?"

Nate nodded. "Paid 'em next to nothing and worked 'em to death. Worked 'em like slaves. They're buried right over by the old furnace. Never made it back home."

Elmer looked in the direction of the barn when he heard a riot of blue jays, squawking and diving at a calico cat that walked toward the house. He turned back to Nate.

"You've always farmed?"

"All I know is farming and tending this place."

"Ever think about selling it?"

"Never, but we about lost it a couple of times. It's hard to hang on after a bad flood like 'thirty-seven. We'd have a flood once or twice a year. Or we'd have a drought, like in 'fifty-two. Hard to pay the taxes when your crops don't make nothing," Nate said.

"How'd you manage?"

"We'd get work at another farm over in Hopkinsville or Paducah, getting in hay or setting tobacco. Sometimes my daddy got on with a road crew," he said. "We might not have much else, but we paid those taxes. As long as we owned this farm, we were free. And we wouldn't starve to death, either."

Elmer nodded. His throat tightened; he didn't say anything for a few minutes. His face grew hot as he thought about the damned fools who came up with this plan, who decided to take this tract and many others from the rightful owners. Those damned fools were the same ones who paid his fees. He sighed, feeling the weight of his own complicity in the plan, but there was no going back. He thought about Nate's parents and grandparents, how they'd worked for generations to provide this home, a rightfulness in their title that derived from the good-faith exchange of taking care of the land and then living off its bounty. Elmer had never experienced a long connection to one spot. He'd never known a homeplace, but he understood the desire to provide for a family. He carried it with him every day as he headed to work.

When he saw that Nate had finished his food, he stood up. "I need you to show me all the good parts of your property. Just the good. Don't show me anything bad or tell me about a leaky roof or a well about to go dry," he said.

Nate called for his dog, then offered some advice. "You watch your step. We've got plenty of rattlesnakes and water moccasins since the lake came up. Guess they're looking for high ground, too," he said. "Rufus here is good at finding snakes before they find me."

For the next two hours Elmer followed Nate across his cornfields, hayfields, and meadows blooming with cardinal flower and goldenrod, through woods thick with tulip poplars, oak, and beech. They walked along gravel creek beds, ponds, and former river bottomlands that had become lakeside property. Elmer paid close attention as Nate explained his farm and his practices, details spoken with a quiet confidence that stemmed from years of working the same land. They stood on the shore and looked across the lake, its waves lapping against his fifty-five acres.

"When they built Barkley Dam, did they pay you right for your river bottoms?"

"Not near enough. That was my best ground. It's been hard to make up for it," Nate said.

They stopped by a small, fenced cemetery with simple limestone markers. All the names began with M. "There's my mama and papa," he said, pointing where small bouquets of faded red plastic flowers were planted at the headstones. Grandparents and great-grandparents were nearby. Nate looked around the cemetery.

"It's just as well, I figure. I'm the end of the line. Got no children, nobody to heir it but some third or fourth cousins that never lived here anyway," he said.

Elmer's view of the property shifted, and he began to see the land through its owner's eyes, not as a collection of objective facts and figures. A few times he had shaved small corners by reconsidering one subjective assessment or another when a price didn't reflect true value. Evelyn Richards's river-green eyes and her soft, haunting voice had nudged him before. He looked at the McCracken house, its unpainted boards, wavy-glassed windows, each log in the old barn, and decided he had no measure of its worth. The generational labor that had built the place made his numbers feel thin, his own new house cheap by comparison.

It was late afternoon when Elmer walked toward his car to leave. The western sky had darkened.

"Looks like we got our work done just in time," he said, pointing to a line of clouds moving in. Nate eyed the storm and nodded. The men shook hands, and Elmer patted the dog's head. Before Elmer got in the car, he turned back.

"Where will you go, Nate?" he asked.

"Some of the neighbors plan to stay together. They've bought a piece of ground not far from that new town. Sycamore. I guess I'll go with them," he said.

As Elmer drove off, the rain began to fall. He turned on the windshield wipers and thought about Nate McCracken having to pack up and leave a homeplace that had withstood floods, droughts, births, deaths, joy, hard times. A true home. Elmer started working the numbers in his head, wondering how he'd calculate a fair price. There were no comparables.

Wedding Chapel

The house at the end of the long gravel driveway seemed unchanged except for the front door's fresh coat of red paint that popped against the wood siding. The place looked deserted, except for an old green pickup truck. They must have left her, Margaret thought.

As she walked toward the house, she saw a note taped to the door, flapping in the light breeze.

> *Dear Margaret,*
>
> *We couldn't wait any longer, but Neville offered to stay and bring you to the church. Hope you get here in time to know where to stand during the wedding :) Change your shoes (I know you're wearing heels) and come on!*
>
> *Love,*
>
> *Cam*

Margaret looked around but didn't see anyone waiting. She hoped Neville, a name she recalled but couldn't connect with a face, wasn't driving the rusted-out pickup. It was covered in dust and, with the windows rolled down, she suspected it didn't have air conditioning. The sun was still high, and so was the temperature.

She tried the door and found it was unlocked, so she stepped inside. Its familiar slight mustiness—a mix of old wood, fabrics, and humidity—offered more comfort than offense in this setting. Memories from a thirty-year connection to the Wetherfords welcomed her. She had known this place longer than she had lived in her own parents' house or the one she had shared with Robert. In some ways, the rustic lake cottage felt more like home than her own house in Louisville, which was of exquisite design but empty and quiet. This home felt like people actually lived here.

As she turned to go back for her suitcase, she noticed a man, asleep, on the quilt-covered sofa. She tiptoed back toward the porch.

"So, you must be Margaret," the man said in a sleepy voice. She turned around as he sat up.

"That's right. You must be Neville. Thanks for waiting for me," she said.

"Margaret, the one who's always late unless she's heading to work. That's what Cam says, anyway."

"Not always," she said. What a jerk, she thought. She took a breath. She needed his help to get to the church. "I'm sorry I'm late, but I had a hard time getting away from the office. And traffic getting out of Louisville was horrendous," she said.

He ran his hands through his curly dark blond hair. "Are you wearing that?"

She bit her tongue. "If we have time, I'd like to change. I was just getting my things," she said.

"We ought to get on the road as soon as we can. They left about fifteen minutes ago, and they don't need long to rehearse. I hear the wedding's pretty simple," he said.

"I'll be quick," she said, heading toward the car. She rolled the suitcase over the gravel and up the front steps. She didn't see Neville when she came back inside. She heard a toilet flush in the bathroom down the hall.

She climbed the stairs to Cam's old room, where she changed into crisp white jeans and platform shoes, her concession to Cam's warning not to wear heels. Cam and Owen were out of their minds to get married at a chapel in the middle of the woods, she thought. She brushed her teeth in the upstairs bath, applied lip gloss, and headed downstairs.

"Was that fast enough?" she said.

"Not bad, for the one who's always late," he said. "I'll drive."

Surprised by his ongoing brusque tone, she took a deep breath. Let it go, she decided. The guy was not worth the effort. As he headed out the door, she found herself gauging his height in comparison to the doorframe, the way a convenience store clerk would size up a robber. About six feet tall, she thought, a tad shorter than Robert had been. He looked lean and athletic in his faded jeans and red-and-white-striped shirt. Probably a construction worker, she thought.

She grabbed her handbag and followed him to the old truck. Her speculation had been correct. She opened the passenger door and saw a filthy, cluttered interior. The cab smelled of dog, or dogs, plural. She moved a stack of papers and dusted off the bench seat. Her white pants would be ruined, she thought, as she kicked aside a couple of empty Sundrop cans in the footwell. When Neville started the engine and took off down the driveway, she realized she had also been correct in assuming the vehicle had no air conditioning. The vents blew hot air. She leaned into the open window for relief.

She darted a quick glance at Neville as he turned onto the main road. His stubbly beard glistened a gingery silver color in daylight, and more traces of silver threaded his hair and sideburns. She hadn't given much thought lately to a man's facial hair or his shaving habits. She missed the smell of Robert's shaving cream and the sound of a razor blade pushing against stubble, a sound not heard unless standing awfully close. It had been five years since her bathroom sink showed the telltale signs of a man's recent shave.

"So, you've known Cam since college?" Neville asked. His question reined in her thoughts of Robert.

"Yeah, a long time. She was in my wedding, too," Margaret said.

"I've known her since we were little kids. We were neighbors back in the old town," Neville said.

"The old town?"

"Before the lake. Our town was flooded, so we all picked up and moved to a new one. Sycamore," he said.

"Oh, yes, I've heard that story," she said. She gazed down at her hands and noticed two chipped nails. She hoped she could get a manicure before tomorrow's wedding. She glanced up to find Neville watching her, his deep blue eyes a hard stare, until he finally looked back toward the road. She couldn't tell if he was angry or crazy, and she wondered if she had said something to offend him. She was trying to get along. She tried again.

"I can't believe we haven't met before. I mean, since Cam's my best friend," she said.

He looked at her again with an expression like disbelief. "I think we met, years ago, here at the lake," he said. "You don't remember?"

Margaret shook her head.

"I remember Cam brought a bunch of people to the lake while her parents were out of town. I saw a girl who looked a lot like you leaning over the edge of the dock, throwing up," he said.

"Hmmm, I don't recall that weekend," she said.

"I bet you don't," he said, chuckling.

What an ass, she thought to herself. This time she took several deep breaths, a trick she'd learned as a litigator to keep from saying things she'd later regret. She looked out the window. The empty road cut through rolling fields of tall grasses dotted with wildflowers with a backdrop of deep woods. She spotted a large bird perched in a dead treetop where meadow met forest.

"Look, there's an eagle," she said, pointing at the snag. "I haven't seen one in years."

Neville leaned over the steering wheel and squinted. "I believe you're right. You've got a good eye," Neville said.

The last time she had seen one was on a cold January day at Pisgah, a large bay on LBL's Kentucky Lake shore. In winter, Pisgah attracted a reliable eagle population. In summer, its high rock quarry wall drew thrill seekers who jumped from a narrow limestone ledge into the bay's deep waters. On what turned out to be their last trip to western Kentucky, she and Robert had sipped hot chocolate from a thermos while they waited for an eagle, binoculars in gloved hands. Now she worried that memories of Robert were resurfacing at an alarming rate. Maybe she shouldn't have come.

"Hey, I really appreciate the ride. Cam tells me the church doesn't show up on GPS," she said.

"It doesn't. No one knew it was still here until a few years ago," he said.

"But it's an old place, right?"

"It is, but every known building between the rivers was torn down when the government turned it back to wilderness and re-named it Land Between the Lakes. LBL. Somehow St. Stephen's survived only because TVA didn't know about it," he said.

The small Catholic church had sat abandoned on a hillside, he explained, defunct as a congregation when most of the old German immigrant community died out years before the lakes were created. When the waters rose, the lone access road to the church flooded, cutting off the only way to drive there. Most people forgot the remote church existed. During the LBL buyouts, no one remembered it. The parcel didn't show on county tax records.

"Its obscurity saved it," Neville said. Bulldozers razed every house, barn, business, and school on the peninsula that strad-dled the Kentucky-Tennessee line. Twenty years later backpackers hiking above the shoreline stumbled upon the old structure, still standing but just barely. Its paint was gone, the roof leaked, and it was nearly off its foundation.

"It was almost beyond repair. If we hadn't had some of the best carpenters around, like my buddy Tom from over at Kuttawa, I don't think we could have saved it," he said. He recounted how he, the Wetherfords, Tom Wallace, and other volunteers had lobbied the park administrators to let them restore the church for public use. The plan to save St. Stephen's was approved. A new road was cut through the woods to reach the site, and hundreds of volunteer hours went into its restoration.

"Most of us think it's sacred ground. Somehow it survived when so much was lost," Neville said.

"Like it was just waiting to be found," she said.

Neville nodded. "Especially when we thought everything was gone," he said. Margaret recognized the same melancholy she heard when Cam's parents spoke about the taking.

"That's an amazing story. No wonder Cam and Owen want to be married there, even with the ticks and wasps," she said.

Neville looked at her. She felt childish mentioning the bugs.

They drove in silence for the next mile or two, watching the sun sinking in the distance. Neville took a left onto another paved road, two turns onto gravel ones, and then onto a dusty lane cut through deep forest. Each turn brought a successive narrowing of roadway and a tightening of the tree canopy. Neville slowed the truck on the final stretch to keep down the dust and to navigate around holes so deep they still contained enough rainwater to splash. Branches encroached and arched over the lane so that they were driving in a green, leafy tunnel that shut out much of the slanted late-day light. Margaret noticed that the air had grown cooler, even inside the cab.

"Cam was right. I never could have found this on my own," she said. None of the roads had names, only numbers designated by TVA or its successor, the U.S. Forest Service. A few years back, the forest service had inherited LBL's management when TVA went back to its primary job of generating electricity.

Margaret felt gritty and windbeaten by the time they approached a clearing with patches of open sky. She saw several cars parked alongside the road.

"And here we are," Neville said.

Then the church came into view, its white clapboards and silver tin roof illuminated in the lingering near-solstitial sunlight. The front gable was topped by a simple black metal cross pointing toward deepening blue sky. The chapel looked magical as it sat surrounded by towering oak and sycamore trees, seemingly untouched by time or loss.

"Oh, my, this is astonishing," Margaret said. "I never dreamed the place would be so beautiful, so idyllic." She continued to stare after they parked and got out.

Neville opened a gate in the picket fence that surrounded the churchyard with its neatly clipped grass. Orange and yellow daylilies planted next to the fence mingled with bright pink sweet peas. A giant hydrangea bush growing near the foundation was loaded with large greenish white blossoms. Limestone slabs half buried in the soil formed an uneven walkway to the building. In the far left corner of the fenced area was a small ancient cemetery, each grave marked with a rock and a yellow plastic bouquet.

"Someone takes good care of the place. You'd never know it didn't always look like this," she said.

"We take turns. We all pitch in," Neville said.

Cam appeared at the arched door, then waved and started toward them. She wore a sleeveless floral dress that looked fresh despite the heat.

"Is it really you?" she called out. They hugged and looked at each other and grinned, then hugged again. The sight of Cam made Margaret feel like a different person, and Cam's touch made her remember how it felt to be loved. For as long as they'd been friends, Cam had made her feel loved, as if Cam saw something valuable and worthwhile in Margaret that other people never seemed to see. Robert had made her feel that way, too. Both loved her, one like a sister, the other as a husband, and through them Margaret found a happier, freer, better version of herself. The Margaret who was worth loving. She had lost Robert, but she still had Cam.

"You look more gorgeous than ever," Margaret said. "And I'm so sorry to be late."

Cam winked and turned toward Neville. "Thanks for getting her here," she said as they embraced. Cam took Margaret's hand and led her into the one-room church.

"I'm so glad you're here. I wouldn't want to do this without you," Cam said.

The Wetherford family gathered around Margaret when she entered, and each one held her close, especially Cam's parents. Margaret wanted to linger in their arms as if she belonged to them. Their touch felt different from the obligatory social hugs given and received at cocktail parties, or a business handshake at the office or a casual brush of shoulders in an elevator. She missed the touch of other people. Margaret wondered how she ever considered not coming.

She hugged Owen, who waited his turn to approach her, looking overheated in jeans and a long-sleeved blue gingham shirt. He introduced her to his family and then to the minister. She apologized for being late. Cam motioned for Margaret and pointed to her position at the altar. Margaret noticed that Neville stood next to the groom, and it dawned on her that he was the best man. He hadn't mentioned it, and neither had Cam. Realizing everyone had waited for them, she felt the urge to apologize again.

The rebuilt altar and pews were painted glossy white. Floors were wide-plank oak, and the walls were a light sky blue. Long windows of clear glass, not stained, allowed somewhat wavy views into the surrounding woods.

The rehearsal was short. Everyone headed back toward Sycamore where Owen's parents hosted the rehearsal dinner, a cookout in the backyard of their neat red brick, split-level home. One of the original houses built when the town was established, it sat a few blocks from the elementary school that Cam, Owen, and Neville had attended. Their families still called it the new school, even though it was more than forty years old.

Margaret stood on the concrete patio with a glass of white wine, nodding and laughing as they told her stories about their school in the old town, which had been demolished hurriedly as the lake rose. She thought she must be the only one who hadn't grown up there.

"The workers were in such a rush, they forgot to take down the old basketball goal in the parking lot behind the school," Cam said. The folks from the old town knew exactly where the metal backboard and pole still stood, just beneath the surface at winter pool. They fished the spot regularly but knew to avoid the area when the water was low. They cackled as they took turns telling about tourists in expensive new boats or rentals, unaware of the hazards of the drowned town below.

Margaret tossed in her double bed at Lake Land State Park Lodge, anxious about the wedding in a matter of hours, at a chapel in the woods with no electricity or air conditioning, on a remote road that tended to wash out in heavy rains. The wedding plans had too many what-ifs to suit Margaret, and her worries grew as the hours ticked away. Cam and Owen seemed unconcerned as usual, but on their behalf Margaret fretted about everything that could go wrong, fixating on a worse-case scenario. She rolled over and stared at the green glow of the digital clock on the bedside table. Ten minutes had passed from when she last checked the time.

For as long as they'd been friends, Margaret had wondered how Cam survived without planning or worrying about details. Things always fell into place for Cam. Maybe she was just lucky. Margaret, on the other hand, needed organization, order, and predictability. Their friendship had a certain yin-and-yang quality about it, a back-and-forth rhythm in which each woman's quirks balanced and complemented the other's.

"You know you're a real tight-ass sometimes, right?" Cam had declared numerous times over the years.

"Whatever. I happen to like things done right," Margaret said.

"You sound like somebody's mother. Or maybe someone's boss. Let go, just a wee bit. Nothing's perfect," Cam said.

Their annoyances with each other never lasted long. They found ways to restore balance.

Eventually Margaret fell asleep. When she awoke three hours later, her first thought was to check the weather. She threw back the faded earth-toned bedspread, tugged at the coordinating plaid drapes, and slid open the glass doors onto a balcony that overlooked Lake Barkley. The month of June could be hot and sticky here, even early in the day, but this morning the air felt cool, refreshing, no trace of mugginess or rain. The sky was clear. Margaret smiled. Cam lucked out again.

When she went back inside, she looked around. She had checked in late after the rehearsal dinner and hadn't noticed how tired and dreary the room looked. At one time Kentucky state parks had been considered nice, but the dated décor wouldn't suit most modern tastes, nor was it up to Margaret's standards. Used to staying at boutique hotels with impeccable white duvets and gleaming marble baths, she ranked Lake Land as downright shabby in daylight. The only redeeming quality was its proximity to the Wetherfords' cottage. No doubt it was the best option for the weekend, but she worried about bedbugs. Despite her exhaustion when she arrived last night, she had checked under the mattress pad for traces of infestation. She kept her luggage off the carpet.

Tired from the sleepless night and a hard week at work, she needed a leisurely morning. The wedding was at three. If she got to the Wetherfords' house after lunch, dressed and ready to head to the church, she had time for a workout at the gym, maybe a swim in the pool, and a fresh manicure. She had missed her weekly nail appointment at Posh Salon, something that she never skipped, but finishing the brief kept her at the office. She picked up the bedside phone and called the front desk.

"Good morning, Mrs. Starks," the clerk said. "How can I help you?"

"You can start by not calling me Mrs. It's Ms.," she said, drawing out the word until it sounded like a hiss. "I need to schedule a nail appointment in your salon."

"I'm sorry, Miz Starks, but we don't have a beauty parlor here," he said.

"Are you kidding? I thought this was a resort," she said.

"We are a resort, Miz Starks, but our primary focus is on the lake. Most people are more interested in whether the fish are biting than getting their fingernails painted," he said.

Margaret's jaw tightened. "I have to be in a wedding this afternoon, so I need my nails done."

"I can give you the list of beauty parlors in Cedar Bluff and you could give them a call."

"How far is that?"

"About twenty minutes by car."

"I'm not sure I'll have time, but can you send someone to my room with the list?"

"I'd be happy to, but I'm the only person on duty right now and I can't leave the front desk. I'll have it here for you," he said.

"That's not really helpful. Forget it," Margaret said and slammed down the phone. She sighed as she checked out her nails and saw even more chipping, as if her hands were taunting her for such bad planning. She guessed she would have to do them herself, something she hadn't done in years. She doubted she had nail polish or remover in her toiletry bag.

Margaret began to pace. Her stomach churned. She knew she had overreacted with the desk clerk, but she couldn't stop herself. Lately little things, seemingly inconsequential ones, ramped up her anxiety. What she once attributed to stress or grief now felt like episodes of panic. She thought about the bottle of Xanax she still carried in her briefcase. The pills had helped after Robert's death. She rarely took them anymore, but she didn't leave home without them. If she took one now, she wouldn't be able to drink at the wedding reception. She needed the social crutch of a drink in her hand to make it through the day.

She wondered if there was another pill for loneliness. Maybe one for unbearable emptiness. She could use some of those. She no longer felt the daily sadness from losing Robert but, God, she missed him. She also missed the person she had been with him, a much better version than her present iteration. When his prostate cancer metastasized to his bones and he died, maybe the old Margaret had died, too. She watched Robert and the life they had built together—everything she wanted—slip away. The world they had made for themselves was lost, and Margaret's personal landscape demolished. She didn't know where she belonged.

Just being alone wasn't the whole story. She'd known solitude as a kid, an only child growing up in a big empty house with a succession of nannies. That was her childhood normal. This felt different, a combination of loneliness, isolation, and incompetence all rolled into an achiness she couldn't get rid of. Nothing she had done from the time of his diagnosis—from nonstop research on treatments to finding the most skilled doctors—had made much difference. He suffered. He died. Her inability to control the outcome had staggered her. It still did.

Margaret's dread of the wedding crept back. She wanted to be with Cam on her wedding day, but she feared what was coming. She'd watch from the sidelines as other people celebrated love, joy, and hope, the parts of her life she had lost. For each wedding invitation she had received in the past few years, she made excuses and *regretfully* declined. She wished she could have gotten out of this one, too.

In the tight brown bathroom with no windows, Margaret riffled through her monogrammed cosmetic bag hanging from the hook on the back of the door, looking for nail polish or remover, cotton balls or a file. She found nothing. She marched back to the bedside phone.

"Good morning, Miz Starks," the same desk clerk said. "What can I help you with?" She decided his solicitous tone irked her. It had to be fake, an act, because so far he had not helped her at all.

"By chance, would this resort have a gift shop with toiletries?"

"Yes, we have a well-stocked gift shop where we sell a few toiletries, as well as T-shirts and other souvenirs. It's on the ground level, near the restaurant if you're having our breakfast buffet this morning."

"I don't eat breakfast. I just need some nail polish and remover," she said.

"The gift shop opens at eleven," he said.

"I don't think you understand. I need them now," she said.

The clerk was slow to respond. There was a long pause, long enough that Margaret wondered if he had hung up on her.

"Miz Starks, I'm sorry I've not been able to meet your expectations," he said.

"What would it take to get someone to open the gift shop early and let me get the things I need?" Her voice grew louder.

"Let me talk to my manager and I'll call you right back."

She put the receiver back into its cradle. She hadn't intended to start the day off with a fight. *Let it go.* She didn't want to spend the day pissed off, but she wasn't used to being treated like this. Ordinarily the amount of money she was willing to spend made things happen for her, but not here. The world operated differently here.

"Screw the nails," she said aloud. She dug through her suitcase to find black running tights and a hot pink tee. She'd feel better if she got in a workout. She dressed and laced her running shoes, then grabbed the room key and her phone. She headed to the hotel's cramped exercise room. The only treadmill was occupied by a matronly woman wearing baggy jeans and unscuffed white athletic shoes, walking like a cardiac patient on the first day of rehab. She won't even break a sweat at that pace, Margaret thought. With earphones in and her regular workout music playing, Margaret looked at her watch and circled the room, occasionally glancing at the woman. As soon as the woman stepped off the machine, Margaret jumped on and cranked up the speed and incline. She was warming up when a text from Cam came through.

Are you coming for brunch? Bring your dress and change here. We'll all go together.

"Oh, hell," Margaret said. The pre-wedding meal at the Wetherfords' house had slipped her mind. Cam mentioned it for the first time late last night before Margaret left for the hotel.

"We just put it together," Cam said. "You know me. Not much of a planner."

By the time she got a shower and dressed, she'd be late. She guessed that Neville would note her arrival time and not let anyone forget that she was late again.

Sure. I'll be there. What time?

She stopped the treadmill, ran back to her room, and turned on the shower. As the water heated up, she stripped off her exercise clothes and left them scattered on the tile floor. It didn't matter if she made a mess. No one ever saw.

Forty-five minutes later, Margaret drove up the car-filled driveway. She wasn't that late, she told herself, but she braced for the comments, especially from Neville. He had annoyed her from the start. She dismissed him as another angry white man, a redneck stuck here without a shot of escaping. She knew Cam and Owen were different. They had left and made lives for themselves in Nashville. They had escaped.

She parked in the grass along the driveway and grabbed the hanging bag that contained her dress for the wedding. It was simple and summery, made of silk in a shade between aquamarine and cyan, something between sea and sky. Cam hadn't planned a color scheme, so Margaret picked her favorite. She had a pair of earrings in the same shade, a gift from Robert. He had bought them for her on their honeymoon. On their last morning on Capri she had found an elegant mother-of-pearl box tucked beside her coffee cup.

"What's this?" she said, looking at him across the table.

"A little something to remember this place," he said.

She beamed at him and opened the box. A pair of earrings hung against velvet, each with three small aquamarine stones strung together, delicately, with tiny links of gold. The faceted stones danced in the light.

"They're lovely. They're the same color as the water when the sun hits it," she said.

"I figured you had noticed," he said.

Whenever she wore the earrings she thought of Robert and that halcyon time on Capri. She had always worn them on their anniversary and other special occasions. When he was sick, getting weaker as the cancer spread, she wore them nearly every day, a reminder to him that they would return to that dreamlike place when he got better, a reminder to herself that their life together had not always been so hard. She wore the earrings to his memorial service, then she put them back in the mother-of-pearl box. The earrings had remained there, unworn, until today.

As Margaret walked toward the house, she heard the laughter and voices of the wedding party. She touched her right earlobe and felt the earring. She reminded herself that Robert had loved her. She needed to remember.

The main room of the Wetherfords' house had a high sloped ceiling and a wall of windows facing the lake. About thirty people sat around the house, some at tables and others on sofas where they balanced paper plates filled with egg casserole, hash browns, and country ham biscuits. Margaret saw Rose and went to give her a hug. Rose wore pink cropped pants and white Keds that looked brand new. In daylight Rose's hair was whiter and her face more deeply lined than Margaret expected. She pictured how Rose used to look when they first met nearly three decades ago: wearing a swimsuit on the boat, cheering on a new skier, or putting out a spread for a picnic lunch. Margaret could have sworn Rose used to be taller, too.

Rose pointed to an empty seat at the picnic table on the screened porch. "Fix yourself a plate of food," she said. "Make sure you get enough to hold you. It will be late afternoon before we get to the reception."

Margaret wasn't hungry, but she put a few spoonfuls of egg casserole and fresh fruit on her plate. She headed toward Cam on the screened porch.

"Hey, there you are. We were laying bets on when you'd arrive," Cam said. Everyone laughed. Margaret smiled, determined not to let their jokes get to her.

"Neville said you'd arrive so late you'd miss lunch and be calling for a ride to the church," Owen said.

Margaret nodded at Neville, who sat on the long bench on the opposite side of the table.

"Here I am. Sorry to make you lose your wager," she said, as she slid into the seat next to Cam.

"No problem. I never bet more than I can afford to lose as the cost of entertainment," Neville said. He was wearing a white dress shirt with a frayed collar and a different pair of old jeans. She wondered if he owned a suit.

"Guys, ease up on Margaret. We've gotten a head start and she deserves a chance to catch up," Cam said. "Hey, Dad, can you bring Margaret a drink?"

Lowell came by with a pitcher of mimosas. "Good morning, sweetheart." He bent down to kiss the top of her head. Margaret smiled up at him, thinking he set the standard for dads, hands down. "What shall it be, a mimosa or a Bloody Mary?"

"Bloody Mary, please. Just in the nick of time," she said. "I need something to put up with these jokesters." She pointed toward Owen and Neville.

"Don't pay any attention to them," Lowell said. "They're good boys, just ornery. Always have been."

Two Bloody Marys and a plate of food improved Margaret's attitude. She relaxed. She and Cam told stories and laughed as much for the parts they didn't disclose as the parts they told. Even at their age, they didn't need to tell everything they knew on each other.

Lowell came back to the table, leading a man and woman she didn't recognize.

"Margaret, here are some folks you ought to meet. This is David and Kate. They're from Louisville too, and they own a cabin down the road," he said. Margaret stood and shook hands. David was tall and dark haired; Kate, a strawberry blonde, was somewhat familiar looking, but Margaret couldn't place her.

"We've known David since he was a boy. His parents bought the cabin right after the lake was built," Lowell said. "I sure miss them. They were good people."

"What do you do in Louisville?" Margaret said.

"We both teach," David said. "High school biology for me, English for Kate. How about you?"

"I'm a lawyer. Marshall & Dodson," she said.

David nodded as if he recognized the name.

"My brothers are lawyers," Kate said. "They have a firm in Louisville. O'Brien & O'Brien."

"Plaintiff's lawyers, right? I may have had a case or two against them. I don't know them, but they certainly advertise a lot," Margaret said. Kate nodded but said nothing.

"Do you get down to the lake often?" David asked.

"Not very. Cam and I have been friends since college. She's my connection to western Kentucky," she said.

"It's too far for weekends, isn't it?" Kate said. "We don't come to the cabin as much anymore, either."

A young girl came up and took her hand. "Mom, are we ready to go yet?" she said.

"In a minute. Please don't interrupt," Kate said. "Margaret, this is our daughter, Lily."

Margaret offered her hand, but Lily wasn't looking in her direction. She was staring at the Wetherford grandchildren, about Lily's own age, sitting on the sofa and wearing headphones, oblivious to their surroundings.

Rose stepped out onto the screened porch.

"Sorry to break up the fun, but we need to dress for the wedding," she said. "It's too hot to make the guests wait for us."

Everyone pitched in to put the food away and clear the kitchen. Cam grabbed Margaret's hand and pulled her up the stairs.

"Are you doing okay?" Cam said.

"I'm fine," Margaret said.

"Sure? You looked anxious when you got here."

"I'm feeling better. Anyway, today isn't about me. It's all about you," Margaret said.

"I know it's hard, but I'm really happy you're here," Cam said. As they reached the second-floor landing, she gave Margaret a long hug.

Margaret pulled away and looked at Cam, her eyes already brimming with tears. "You know how much I loved Robert. I see that you and Owen have that, too, so that makes me feel better," she said.

They reached the second door on the left, Cam's bedroom, and went inside. Little had changed about the room since their days in college, though the white-and-gold French provincial twin beds were now pushed together to accommodate Owen's arrival.

"You can dress while I go brush my teeth and put on some makeup. I'll be right back," Cam said.

Margaret slipped into her dress, then touched up her lipstick and fluffed her hair.

"Oh, that luscious color," Cam said when she walked in. "It reminds me of the lake on a sunny day."

"Me too. Are you sure I can't wear heels?" Margaret said.

"The flats look fine. You'll thank me when you don't ruin your nice stilettos out in the woods," Cam said. "And did you use bug spray like I told you?"

"Can't you smell it? I feel like I'm in a toxic cloud," Margaret said.

"And you'll thank me again when you don't get tick fever," Cam said. She reached for the tea-length wedding gown hanging on the closet door. "Will you help me get dressed? I need your opinion on a few things."

"Oh, I love the dress. Where did you find it?" Margaret said.

"It was Mom's. Seems right this time around," Cam said. She had a short and unhappy marriage right out of college. Margaret had been her maid of honor then, too.

Cam slipped on the 1950s-style ecru lace dress and turned for Margaret to help with the zipper and a row of satin-covered buttons along the back. Margaret noticed Cam's fair, freckled skin through a small gap between the last button and the zipper further down the bodice.

"You look amazing," Margaret said. "Do you have 'something borrowed, something blue'?"

"Blue hydrangeas in the bouquet. I guess my dress is borrowed. It's definitely old," Cam said.

"Do you want to borrow something of mine?"

Cam thought for a moment. "What if we trade earrings? You wear my pearls, and I'll wear the blue ones that match your dress. We'll look like we planned a color scheme."

Margaret paused, not knowing what to say. She wore the earrings to feel close to Robert during the wedding, to steady her as she walked to the altar, as she listened to vows like the ones they had made to each other. Still, she couldn't refuse Cam's request.

"Of course. Wear them. But I need them back. Robert gave them to me," Margaret said.

"No, no, no. I can't wear them," Cam said.

"I want you to. Robert would, too. He loved you very much," Margaret said as she unlatched an earring back. She pulled the stem through her pierced ear and handed it to Cam. Margaret watched as Cam adjusted the earrings in the mirror, and she saw her own blue dress reflected beside the bride. Cam turned around for Margaret to see.

"What do you think?" she said. Her pale gray eyes sparkled and her cheeks were flushed.

"Perfect, like we planned it all along," Margaret said.

They hugged again and headed downstairs. Owen was waiting for Cam at the foot of the stairs. Rose and Lowell carried coolers filled with bouquets of hydrangeas and wildflowers toward the car. Neville, who had changed into a gray seersucker suit and pale yellow silk tie, stopped Cam on her way out the door. He took her hands and looked at her. She smiled broadly.

"You've never looked lovelier, Camilla Wetherford," he said. "I love you like my own sister." The look they shared brought tears to Margaret's eyes.

The family caravanned to St. Stephen's, crossing the narrow bridge over the Cumberland River and a second one across the canal that led to Land Between the Lakes. When they arrived at the church, Margaret saw cars already lining the narrow lane. Nicely dressed guests milled about the churchyard in flat-soled shoes. The younger ones wore sundresses and flip-flops.

Inside, sunlight flooded the church. Wildflowers in large vases decorated the altar. Crowded into a front corner of the tiny sanctuary was a quartet made up of fiddle, banjo, guitar, and recorder. Margaret hadn't seen a recorder since Mrs. Bell's music class in grade school. With no piano and no electricity for an organ, she guessed it was the best they could do.

The gathering bore slight resemblance to her own wedding, an evening candlelight ceremony at Christ Church Cathedral, a black-tie social event in Louisville with music by an acclaimed church organist and vocalists who blasted the crowd of three hundred guests. Margaret had worn a crystal-encrusted designer gown with a full-length train, with Cam as her honor attendant and seven bridesmaids in identical peach silk dresses. Flowers marked the aisles and banked the altar, their fragrance nearly overpowering. A reception at the Brown Hotel's Crystal Ballroom followed, with a band, a sit-down dinner, and an open bar. The opulent affair meant a lot to Margaret's parents. She was their only child, they reminded her. A big bash was expected from a family of their standing. The wedding planner worked for more than a year securing the venues, the right caterer, a spectacular band. Nothing but the best. With a great deal of handwringing, no detail was overlooked. To Margaret, that wedding seemed so long ago. A lifetime ago.

They took their spots facing the altar, Margaret and Cam on one side of the minister, Owen and Neville on the other. The minister wore a suit, not robes or even a clerical collar. Nothing distinguished him from the rest of the male guests except that he carried a Bible from which he read in a quiet voice befitting the scale of the church. The quartet played music that Margaret didn't recognize, tunes that sounded ancient and unadorned.

The lower windows had been raised for ventilation, causing a light breeze to flutter the altar flowers. Margaret looked out the upper panels of clear glass, wavy with age, and saw azure skies above the crowns of tall oaks, tulip poplars, and white-barked sycamores in the woods surrounding the church. In the distance she glimpsed a sliver of the lake, its water reflecting the clear blue of the sky. She thought of Robert in this mix of sky and water, the way she saw him the day he gave her the earrings. She felt as if he could be standing beside her here.

As the couple prepared to exchange vows, Cam turned to Margaret, smiling as she handed over her bouquet. For an instant, sunlight danced through the aquamarine earrings. Margaret hadn't seen anything so beautiful in a long time.

DRIFT

From the screened porch, David watched his daughter, perched at the end of the dock, elbows bent and hands on her hips, looking down into the water, frozen in a graceful stance like a bird fishing for its next meal. If not a heron or egret, only a nine-year-old kid could hold that position so long, especially in the noonday summer sun.

He'd come inside for a drink and a short break from mowing knee-high grass that covered the steep slope to the water. The weekend's work, part of the ritual of opening the cabin for the season, combined scrubbing, yardwork, and celebration of the return of summer. Yesterday, the last day of school, he had packed the car, ready to leave for the lake after the final bell. The trunk was crammed with cleaning supplies, a mop, mouse traps, hornet spray, jugs of water, and enough food for the weekend in the large red cooler. Lily tossed in her pink backpack and a fleece pillow for the three-hour drive. Kate hesitated, then announced she wasn't going.

"I'll drive over tomorrow," she said as she hugged Lily and handed her a packed picnic basket. "I've got some work I need to finish here."

"Mom, it's summer. School's over," Lily said.

"I know, sweetheart, but I'm behind. I've got a few more papers to grade and enter before the deadline," Kate said. "I promise I'll be at the lake by the middle of the afternoon."

Lily scowled.

"It's just you and me, kid," David said. "We'll get the work done and be ready to play by the time Mom arrives." He smiled at Kate and bent down to kiss her. She offered her cheek and a light embrace.

The winter had been particularly long and dreary, taking a toll on them. It felt as if they—and their fifteen-year marriage—were in an extended period of hibernation. As the days lengthened and light returned, David began to feel normal again. Kate was slow to reawaken, still sluggish as spring shifted into summer. Together, their world remained tilted toward winter.

Like ants streaming in straight lines, cars and RVs headed south on the interstate out of Louisville, a type of recreational migration, straining to carry many times their weight with boats, ATVs, bicycles, and camping gear. The belt of knobby hills that ringed the city was solid green, a lush, dark backdrop for giant billboards planted by the road that advertised upcoming fast-food restaurants and adult bookstores. Swaths of weeds with bright yellow flowers sprouted by the roadside.

"Hungry?"

Lily looked up from her book. "A little. Do we have anything?"

"Look in the picnic basket. I'm sure Mom sent something."

She turned toward the back, stretching her seatbelt to reach the woven basket. She grabbed its handles and fell back into her seat. He glanced as she dug through the contents.

"Woohoo!" she said. "Cookies!"

"What kind?"

"Red, white, and blue. With sprinkles. Want one?"

"I don't think she's made those before," he said. He'd expected oatmeal. Maybe peanut butter.

"She didn't make them, silly. They're the fancy ones from the grocery, the kind I always beg for and she always says no," Lily said. She grinned at him, her lips stained purplish from the first bite of frosting.

Store-bought cookies were no big deal. They'd all been busy as the school year ended. But Kate, his Kate, would never have sent these. She was a stickler for real food, a regular at the food co-op and farmers' market. Either homemade cookies or no cookies. She had made all of Lily's baby food, fresh, in a small food processor. He didn't care about the cookies, but some days he hardly recognized Kate. Her expression had a flatness that confused him and left him feeling helpless. Paralyzed. He felt incapable of making headway against her slow, continuous drift away from him.

They'd been through rough patches before, but somehow they'd managed to circle back to each other. Sometimes the hard, sad places were predictable and sharp due to circumstances, like when his parents died. The stillbirth. The miscarriages. Times of identifiable grief. Sometimes it crept up on them, quietly, for reasons more difficult to figure out. Like they were sinking from some unknown weight, slowly and gradually, waiting to touch bottom in order to push back up, hoping to have enough breath to last until one or both resurfaced. For David, the promises they'd made to each other when they married had evolved over time to become a commitment to help each other, an obligation to search and rescue. The first one to surface, to breathe again, would find the other, perhaps still struggling, and together they'd reach shore. They owed it to each other.

"I need to go to the bathroom," Lily said. She had chugged two or three juice boxes in the first ten minutes of the drive. David was surprised she'd lasted this long.

"We'll stop in Elizabethtown for gas. Can you wait?" David said.

"I don't know. How far is that?"

"Fifteen minutes or so."

"I guess," Lily said, looking out the window. He pushed the cruise control a bit faster. In a few minutes she asked again. "Are we close?"

"Almost. Hang in there," David said. He took the next exit and pulled into a gas station. Lily ran to the bathroom inside.

David pumped gas, cleaned the bugs off the windshield, and waited for her to return. He checked his texts—the remote cabin had limited phone signal, much less internet—hoping that Kate had sent a message. Saying that she missed him. That she regretted not coming with them. There was nothing. He considered sending one to her, but she might think he was nagging. Maybe she needed space. Whatever it took, he wanted her to feel better, to return to herself, to return to him. He'd suggested counseling, for both this time. She had refused.

"I'll be okay. I'm just blue," she'd said.

"I think it's more than that," he said. "This has been going on for a while."

"I know I'm a drag."

"I didn't say that."

"You didn't have to."

"Give me a chance to understand, Kate. I don't know what's going on, and I hate it. I hate feeling like this. I don't know where we'll end up."

After a silence, she spoke quietly.

"I thought there would be more by now," she said.

"More what?"

"I'm not sure. I love you and Lily. I love teaching. But this emptiness," she said, trailing off. "Like I'm waiting on something to come along, a piece that's missing."

"What the hell's missing? I don't get it."

"It's hard to explain. Maybe I don't understand. Life doesn't look the way I thought it would," she said.

David felt a shadowy presence elbowing into their lives, and he wondered if there was someone else. Perhaps she didn't want or need to be rescued. He had left the room that day, wondering how far to push.

He didn't notice when Lily opened the door and slid into the seat next to him.

"Dad," she said. "Hey, Dad," she repeated, waving both arms to get his attention. He put down the phone. "All good?" he said. She nodded and he started the car. Lake Barkley was another two hours west.

From the steep gravel driveway lined with old ribbon-barked cedar trees, David saw the cabin, waiting for him to return each spring since his boyhood. He also caught a glimpse of the lake in the late-day sun. His mood tempered, even about Kate.

They had a couple of hours of daylight to check out the cabin and turn on the necessities—lights, water main, water heater. By opening the windows and flipping a few switches, the house would come back to life after its winter rest.

"Let's haul everything in and get to it," he said. He could almost hear his own dad's voice issuing the same instructions. For forty-one seasons—all his life—David had returned to the place. He knew every square foot of the cabin and the land. He wanted Lily to feel the same connection, one of the few remaining links to his side of the family.

The small cabin had a covered front porch with a few rocking chairs. Plastic hummingbird feeders hung empty and light, blowing in a slight breeze. He remembered asking Kate to bring them in as they closed up last fall. She must have forgotten or been distracted if Lily needed something. He noticed several fresh dirt-dauber nests built above the window frames. The wasps, disturbed by their arrival, hovered around their mud homes. He'd deal with them later. The yard needed mowing, but otherwise everything looked good.

David's parents had bought the cabin not long after the dam was built and the lake level began to rise, but he didn't know who had owned the land before the lake. His family wasn't from the area. His dad had heard about the recreational possibilities for land around the lake and bought the property for next to nothing.

Back then, the cabin was primitive, more like camping than living in a house, with an outdoor toilet and no running water. Eventually his folks had added plumbing, a bathroom, and a couple of extra bedrooms. Over the years his family had made friends around the lake with other folks who liked being on the water, friendships that felt different, less hurried, than their city connections. His parents had thought the world of Rose and Lowell Wetherford, whose house was down the road, and David had his own tender memories of them. Lowell had taught him to water ski when he was a little boy, and each summer he reconnected with the Wetherfords here at the lake. He'd see them next month at their daughter Cam's wedding. David was a few years younger than Cam, so they were never close friends, but he enjoyed spending time with the Wetherfords. They reminded him of his own parents.

Real estate agents would still call the cabin rustic, if they had a chance to list it, but David had no plans to sell. It would be like selling off a part of his family, which was already small. Other than some distant relatives he had met as a child, Kate and Lily were it.

He hadn't thought much about the size of his family until he saw Lily's drawing of her family tree, an assignment for school. Her tree was lopsided yet accurate. His side was nearly vertical, more like a utility pole than a tree. There were few branches, owing to several generations of only children. Not many aunts, uncles, or cousins. In contrast, his wife's side of the family tree was lush, covered with many names and branches, vigorous and abundant at each level.

Opening the house often meant a surprise or two. One year they'd found a snake in the attic; another time birds had come in through the chimney. In their panic to get out, they pecked and pooped all over the house, finally breaking a window. After the cleanup and a trip to the nearest hardware store for glass repair, David had climbed along the roof to screen the top of the stone chimney. He remembered the worried look on Kate's face as he ascended the ladder.

"Can't we get someone else to fix this?" she had said.

"It won't take long," he said. His heart pumped as he clung to the rim of the chimney, trying not to look down, telling himself that he couldn't fall, not in front of Lily. When he finished the job and climbed down, Lily ran to him, hugging him around the waist. "Please don't do that ever again," she said, sounding more like parent than child. He was surprised that she realized, at her age, what might have happened. She seemed to notice everything.

David opened the screen door, unlocked the rough wooden one, and stepped into familiar space.

"Let's get the windows open and air it out," he said.

Lily knew the drill. She headed down the narrow hall to her tiny bedroom and he soon heard shutters opening and sticky windows being coaxed upward. David opened the back door, instantly creating a breeze through the musty interior, and stepped out onto a large screened porch that overlooked the wide lake and doubled the cabin's footprint.

David looked toward the lake, and the panorama almost took his breath. The sky always looked bigger here, he thought, its blueness fading into deep green hills that touched the glassy lake, creating layers of sky, land, and water. These horizontal slivers defined the landscape, parallel lines that ran one on top of another, occasionally dipping into or overlapping the adjacent layer. The late afternoon light created reflections and shadows that further blurred the lines.

In a short time, the water was on, beds were made, the most obvious cobwebs swept away, and the toilet bowl sprayed with bleach. David rolled the cooler from the car, and Lily unloaded the food into the refrigerator.

"Mom packed sandwiches for us," she said.

"Let's take them down to the dock and watch the sun go down," David said.

They walked through tall grass, past the fishing boat covered with a tarp, to the dock at water's edge. A few feet above the water, a thin line of driftwood, still damp and laced with several plastic soda bottles and pieces of Styrofoam, showed that the lake level had been higher recently. As they approached, frogs leapt from the bank into the water.

They sat on the dock's rough boards and ate turkey sandwiches. David watched as Lily rolled up the bread crusts into tiny dough balls, dropping them into the water through the cracks between the planks. She threw some toward a pair of Canada geese swimming close to shore. As they ate, the smooth water turned pink and orange with the setting sun. A lone boat engine strained in the distance, somewhere on the lake, making its way home.

"Red sky at night, sailor's delight," he said.

"Mom always says that," Lily said.

"It means tomorrow's going to be a good day. Calm. No storms. Sailors used to use the sky to predict the weather, back when they didn't have radar and weather reports on their computers."

"When's she coming?"

"Tomorrow."

"I miss her."

He nodded. He missed her, too. He'd never felt so disconnected from her. There had been no fighting or arguing, just distance. Silence. He guessed Lily didn't realize.

A mosquito buzzed around his ear. "We better head in. Check yourself for ticks and don't tell your mother we forgot to use the bug spray," he said.

Later, after Lily went to bed, David sat on the screened porch for a long time, watching the moon's reflection shine across the water and listening to the night sounds in the woods. Spring peepers and cicadas reminded him of nights spent there as a child, sleeping in seersucker pajamas and hearing his dad's snore through the open windows. Here, more than anywhere, he remained connected to his parents. The only part missing was Kate. He needed to hear her voice, to make sure she was okay. He decided to call her. To get a phone signal, he'd have to walk out to the road. The moonlight made a flashlight unnecessary; even in the darkest section through the cedars the driveway gravel glistened. But when he got to the road, he couldn't get a signal. He couldn't talk to her tonight. Maybe, he thought as he walked back to the cabin, things will be all right.

After David and Lily left for the lake, Kate wiped off the kitchen table to have a clean workplace to grade her students' final research papers. She fixed a cup of Earl Grey tea, turned on some music, and got to work. She had several still to read, but she figured she could finish before dinner. Not wanting to eat alone, she called her sister.

"I'd love to," Charlotte said. "Paul's exhausted from work, and I've shipped my kids out for the night. They all had sleepovers to celebrate the end of school."

"How about that new restaurant on Frankfort Avenue that just opened? The one where Allo used to be."

"That sounds good. They still have the patio, and the weather's great," Charlotte said. "Wait. I thought you all were going to the lake this afternoon."

"David and Lily went on. I'll go tomorrow. I'm still grading papers."

"Okay. Then I'll make a reservation for us. Two sisters, out on the town, not a worry in the world."

Kate laughed. "Not sure I'd go that far." Being around Charlotte would be good for her, she thought. Her older sister often made her get up and do stuff. They remained close as adults, but they hadn't had a night out together for a while.

The restaurant's flagstone patio was covered with a wooden arbor intertwined with lavender wisteria and twinkling white lights. Each tabletop had a white cloth, a candle, and a sprig of lily-of-the-valley in a clear vase. Kate had arrived first, claimed the table, and ordered a drink before she saw Charlotte strolling through the door. In looks there was no question they were sisters: fair-skinned strawberry blondes with the same straight noses and square jaws they also shared with their brothers, a strong resemblance that cropped up generation after generation in family photos. But Charlotte was like a stronger, tougher version of Kate, as if she had demanded and gotten all the milk in the house when they were kids. She was taller and carried herself with the stride and confidence of an athlete. Charlotte had played volleyball from Catholic grade school through college where she became team captain. A natural leader, she had been told since childhood. She still coached her daughter's team as a volunteer. Kate had always been known as the bookish sister, the quiet one who tended to be overlooked or maybe overshadowed. While she admired Charlotte's strength, that ability to dig deeper when called upon, Kate sometimes had to step back to keep from being overwhelmed by the big personality. At times Charlotte's leadership felt downright bossy, and Kate wanted a sister, not a coach.

When Charlotte arrived at the table, Kate stood up and they embraced. "I'm already ahead of you," Kate said, pointing to her glass of white wine.

"We may have to call a cab tonight," Charlotte said. "Moms gone wild, or something like that." The server came for Charlotte's drink order. She picked a craft beer with a crazy name from the list. Kate had never heard of it.

"How have you been? Seems like forever since we've had any sister time," Charlotte said.

"I've been okay. Well, if we're being honest, not great," Kate said.

"What's up? You feeling all right?"

"Just all right. Physically I'm fine. But it's taken a long time to come back."

"Come back? Where have you been?" Charlotte laughed. The server delivered the beer.

"I'm not sure," Kate said. "Haven't had a lot of energy, other than covering the necessities at work. At home. I'm glad it's summer." The conversation was slow and labored. Although Charlotte was her closest sibling, Kate had difficulty telling some things to her sister, or anyone else for that matter.

"Would you ladies like to hear our specials tonight?" the waiter said, standing beside the table with a notepad. His age suggested he had made a career in the restaurant business and, after straightening his black glasses, he read with tedious precision a list of nightly specials containing countless ingredients for each dish. Kate had difficulty keeping it all straight. She guessed she was feeling a buzz from her first glass of wine. She hadn't eaten much all day.

"Those sound delicious," Charlotte said. "I'll have the lamb." The waiter looked toward Kate.

"Did you say you had some kind of ravioli? I've already forgotten," she said.

"Housemade butternut squash ravioli, stuffed with pecorino and pine nuts, and finished with a light fresh sage and white wine sauce," the waiter repeated.

The description didn't sound good—the scent of fresh sage reminded her of body odor—but Kate didn't want to ask again. "That's fine. And another glass of pinot grigio." The server left the table and headed toward the kitchen to place the order.

"So, you've been down?" Charlotte continued.

"Yeah, very down."

"The miscarriage?"

Kate nodded.

"I didn't know you were still having problems from it," Charlotte said.

Kate tried to smile, wishing she could end the conversation, but Charlotte charged forward.

"Is everything okay with David?"

"David's fine. He thinks everything's fine."

"What does that mean?"

"Nothing. Really, he's fine."

"Lily?"

"Lily's fine, too. She's had a good school year. Yeah, she's fine."

"Sounds like everything is fine. You've used that word over and over. What is it, then?"

Kate hesitated. She had changed her mind about wanting to talk about things with her sister. "Seriously, I'm okay. Let's talk about you."

"Kate, come on. You can't lead me down this path and then leave me hanging. What's going on?"

Kate wanted to run from the table. Her words would sound silly and childlike to her older sister, who never whined about anything. "I guess I've been sad, really sad since we lost the baby. Then the other miscarriages. Life just isn't turning out the way I expected."

Charlotte looked at her and touched her hand. "Honey, how many years has it been since you lost the baby?"

"Six. He would be six."

"That's a long time. Have you talked to anybody about this?"

"Yeah, right after it happened. And this most recent one . . . it all seems pretty hopeless."

"I'm so sorry."

"I'll never be able to have the kind of family I wanted," Kate said. She saw Charlotte's expression change.

"What are you talking about, the kind of family you wanted? Really? You have a beautiful family. A husband who loves you and a little girl who is smart and sweet and lovely in every way. What other kind of family are you dreaming about?"

"A bigger one. The kids that we wanted. I've always wanted more. You know that."

"That's true, but it's not what you've got," Charlotte said.

Kate glared at her sister. She should've known that Charlotte wouldn't offer much sympathy. Charlotte was always the tough one, the strong one who never buckled.

"Let's change the subject. I don't think you understand."

Again, Charlotte took her hand. "I think I do. This isn't how you thought your life would look, but hear me out. It's the way it is. Quit moping about what might've been and neglecting the people who love you now."

"I know, I know."

"I'm not sure you do. Lily sometimes looks at you like she's afraid you're going to break. She knows something's wrong. You don't want to put that load of shit on your kid."

Kate thought of Lily's sweet face and tears flooded her eyes. "You think she's worried?"

Charlotte nodded. "How's David?" she asked again.

"He's an adult. He'll be okay. We'll be okay."

"I wouldn't take it for granted. Have you and David talked?"

"I'm tired of talking. Tired of everything, really."

"When was the last time you had sex?" Charlotte asked. The question shocked Kate. The sisters never talked to each other about their sex lives.

"Charlotte, stop. It's none of your business."

"The last week?"

Kate shook her head.

"Last two weeks?"

"No."

"Last month?"

"I don't remember. It's been a while."

"Is there someone else? Tell me."

"No, I'm not messing around with anyone else. If I wanted sex, I'd have sex with David. Truth is, I never think about sex."

Charlotte shook her head. "Don't get mad, just listen to me. Quit wallowing in this and get some help. You've got to move on."

Kate nodded. Hearing the comments about Lily shook her to her core and shamed her for not seeing it until now. How could she be so blind?

"Talk to David. Let Lily spend a night or two with us so you can have some time together."

The waiter brought their food. Kate looked at the ravioli and caught a whiff of sage. The smell repulsed her, but she needed to eat something. She took a bite and found that it tasted better than it smelled. She ordered another glass of wine, thinking the next one might make her feel happy again.

"Let me drive you home in your car," Charlotte said. "Paul can pick me up at your house and we'll come back for mine."

She didn't argue. She knew her sister was right.

Kate woke with a splitting headache and a strong taste of garlic in her mouth. Her head pounded when she got up to go to the bathroom, where she popped three ibuprofen gels and drank two glasses of water. She climbed back in bed. She didn't intend to go back to sleep, only to give her head a chance to calm down. She recalled the conversation with Charlotte and thought about Lily.

While she figured that she and David would work things out—they always had—she worried about Lily. She admitted to herself that she'd detached from them, but it hurt deeply that Lily had noticed. She started to cry. She never intended to shift her burden to her little girl. She rolled out of bed, took a quick shower, and packed a few things. She needed to get to the lake.

When Lily woke to the sound of the lawn mower, she got up, changed out of her nightgown into shorts and a top, then pulled her long brown hair back into a ponytail. She was ready for the day. She fixed a bowl of cereal and went out on the screened porch, where she sat in the swing and took slow bites in rhythm with the light kick of her bare feet that sustained the back-and-forth motion. She watched her dad pushing the mower along the hill. It stalled every few feet.

"Damn it," he shouted, and Lily looked up to see what was wrong. His face was red and sweaty. He ripped off his dark T-shirt and wiped his eyes before slinging it toward the cabin. He turned the mower on its side and reached around the blade, scraping away handfuls of grass clippings. He repeated the routine a couple of times. When it stopped again, he kicked the back wheel and headed toward the car. He returned with the weed trimmer grinding on high speed, knocking down the tallest grass and anything else in its path.

Lily thought about her mom and wondered what time she'd arrive. After breakfast she planned to make the cabin clean and pretty for her mother, who had looked tired yesterday, as she often did. Lily knew her mother would be happy to see it clean with no bugs or mouse droppings or snakes or wasps. And Lily would find some flowers to surprise her. Mom used to keep flowers on the table at home, but not lately.

Lily started by dusting and sweeping up piles of Asian lady bugs that had lived—and died—in the cabin over the winter. A few groggy survivors were released outdoors. She found the outside cushions in a closet and distributed them to the porch swing and chairs. She sprayed cleaning foam and wiped the sink and counter-top. When she finished the inside work, she went out and picked wildflowers before Dad reached them with the trimmer. She put the yellow and white blossoms in a glass of water and set the bou-quet on the table.

"She'll like this," Lily said to herself as she looked around.

For a while Mom had seemed different. Mad or sad, Lily couldn't tell. She thought it had something to do with those babies. Even though her parents had never mentioned them, Lily knew about the ones who had died. She'd overheard Nana and Aunt Charlotte talking about them. The only thing Dad had said to her was that Mom wasn't feeling well. Each time one of those babies died, Lily stayed at Nana's house until Mom got better.

"Your mom needs to rest, honey. That means I'm the lucky one who gets you for a few days," Nana had said, wrapping her arms around Lily. Lily liked staying a night or two with Nana, but some-times the stays were much longer. When she was younger, she and Nana had tea parties with the dolls and played Candy Land or Go Fish. The last time she stayed with Nana when her mother didn't feel well, they made cookies and played Monopoly. The house was full of people—her mother had three brothers and two sisters who lived nearby—so there was always a crowd around Nana's table.

When Lily came home, their house seemed quiet. Her mother held her and wouldn't let go. They said that Mom was doing better, but Lily knew that wasn't true. She'd seen her crying at the kitchen sink when no one else was looking. She spent so much time in bed that Lily wondered if she might die. Nana had told Lily to be a good girl and help her mom, so Lily tried to do just that. Since kindergarten Lily had been known as a helper at school, too.

With her work done, Lily headed down to the dock where the rest of the morning floated past her. Her eyes followed a sailboat as it crisscrossed the lake, its jumble of ropes and cloth fluttering in the wind. She had never been on a sailboat, and she tried to understand the wild movements of the people on board as they tacked back and forth. She sat down and let her bare feet dangle, getting wet with each wave. Speedboats roared by, towing skiers and kids on tubes riding the waves. Sounds of splashing and laughter bubbled to her ears.

Behind her, the roar of the mower and the trimmer had stopped. She looked toward the house and saw her mom's gray SUV. Dad carried Mom's duffel bag and another picnic basket toward the house.

"Mom!" Lily yelled as she ran toward her mother. "I've been waiting for you." When she reached the top of the hill, her mother's arms were open wide to catch her. Lily felt her deep hug and smelled her mother's familiar scent. When they released, Lily looked at her mother's face, searching for clues.

"I picked flowers for you," Lily said. "And the house is all clean."

"Oh, sweet girl, I can't wait to see it," Kate said as they walked to the cabin.

"I'm glad you're here, Mom."

"Me too. Are you hungry? I brought lunch."

"I'm starving," Lily said.

"Let's take a break now that your mother's here," her father said.

Lily studied his sweaty face, too.

With most of the cleaning done, the afternoon was free. David and Lily swam near the end of the wooden dock. She needed to be a strong swimmer, he thought, able to reach the shore on her own. They made a game of it, swimming out further each time and racing back to the dock. And they horsed around a lot. They played until she was tired and ready to go in. He never quit first. He remembered what it was like, a kid at the cabin with only grown-ups around, expecting him to entertain himself.

Kate read and dozed in the hammock. Lily made lemonade and served it to her mother as soon as she awoke. They spent the rest of the afternoon brushing and braiding each other's hair. David heard them laughing, too. He stopped by and asked Kate how she was doing.

"I'm good. I got the grading done. Had dinner with Charlotte last night."

"How was that?"

"She let me cry and feel sorry for myself, and then she kicked my ass like she always does."

"Feel better?"

"A little."

"Want to talk about it?"

"Not now. Lily and I are hanging out," she said.

He bent down and kissed her cheek. "We missed you. It's not the same without you."

He went back outside to unwrap the fishing boat and hose out the bugs that lived in it. He dragged it to the water by himself and tried to start the engine, which turned over after a few pulls. The lake had grown quieter and calmer as the sun sank toward the hills. Waves were gentle, shadows long, and the water smooth as polished glass. The crowds had headed home.

"They don't know they're missing the best part of the day," David said as he stepped onto the porch. "Let's go out on the water."

"Are you sure? I don't want to get stranded again," Kate said.

"I'm sure," he said. Her fearful look reminded him of last summer's near disaster when the boat engine stalled and left them adrift without working navigation lights as darkness approached. Before a passing boat finally spotted them and stopped to offer help, Lily had cried and Kate yelled. He was angry at himself for putting his family at risk, embarrassed about looking helpless. They were towed back to the dock and the engine later repaired at the nearest marina. Ever since, he made a point to get home before dark.

After supper, he asked again. Lily nodded and looked at her mother.

"Please, Mom? Can we take the boat over to the little beach?"

Kate shot him a warning look, then turned back to Lily.

"If you want to go, let's go. I'm sure your dad means it when he says the boat is fine."

They headed down the hill to the dock. David got in the boat and then steadied it as Kate and Lily took their seats. They were already wearing life jackets. He cranked the engine and it hit. Its puttering sound turned into a purr as they pulled away from the dock; then it sputtered and died.

"That doesn't sound good," Kate said.

"It's a little fussy," David said. "I took it out earlier today and it did fine." He pulled the start cord over and over until it hit again.

Black smoke roiled from the motor. Please let it run this time, he thought.

"Dad, are you sure?" Lily said. She fingered the straps on her life jacket.

"We'll be fine. Promise."

He guided the boat toward a small gravel beach on the opposite side of the lake, a national recreation area called Land Between the Lakes where there were no houses or hotels and few humans at the end of the day unless they had a permit to camp. The boat chugged along, hiccupping occasionally, rising and falling as its flat bottom rolled over a few slight waves. As they approached land, David cut the engine to glide ashore, silently. Rocks crunched beneath the boat as they came to a stop on the bank.

"An eagle's nest," David whispered, pointing toward a tall tree across the bay. Near the top of the tree the nest looked like a huge bundle of sticks. On the edge perched a large dark brown bird with a prominent white head and tail, leaning over the nest. Another bird with the same markings soared overhead.

"They must have chicks," David said. They heard the begging calls of young birds, barely visible in the great nest, squawking for food and wanting to fly.

"Eaglets," Lily corrected. "We learned about them in science. They're not really bald you know."

David looked at Kate, who was trying to stifle a laugh. Her seat in the boat faced west, so the early evening sunlight washed across her face and her reddish-blond hair. She seemed to glow, he thought. David got off the boat and tied it off to a small sycamore tree that had put down roots in the gravel.

"We'll stay as long as we can before the sun goes down," he said.

"Can I swim?" Lily said.

"Keep your life jacket on. There may be drop-offs," Kate said. "And stay where we can see you."

David offered his hand as Kate stepped from the boat. He didn't let go.

Lily slipped on sandals before jumping out onto the small, sharp rocks. She scoured the beach, looking for treasures to keep. Fossils, driftwood, maybe a toad.

She looked up from her search and saw her parents down the beach, sitting on a large log, facing what was left of an old bonfire left by other visitors, a few charred remnants of wood in a mound of ash. She watched them. They didn't look mad. Lily strained to hear over the waves rolling into the bay, but their voices were low. She heard only bits and pieces.

"I wanted a full house, lots of kids around the table," her mom said. "That's not going to happen, but I'm finally ready to move on."

"We could adopt," he said.

"I'm not there yet. I need to feel better."

Her mother's hands gestured, almost like sign language, but Lily couldn't understand the meaning. Her dad occasionally shook his head, sometimes nodded. At one point her mom's face looked scrunched and red. Lily thought she was starting to cry.

"Come swim with me," she yelled. Both parents looked toward her, startled, like they'd forgotten about her.

"Give us a minute," her dad said. They started talking again, but Lily couldn't hear. She decided she might as well swim alone.

"Go on, get in. They're not coming," she told herself. Sometimes she too wished for more.

She plunged in, feeling for the bottom with her toes. When she found it, she bounced and spun, pretending to be a dancer. She leapt higher and more gracefully through the water than on land.

"Nice one," she said, congratulating herself.

She stopped to check again on her parents. They were sitting close, her dad's arms encircling her mother. She was leaning against him, and she wasn't crying.

Lily turned back to the water. Below the surface schools of minnows swirled around her, and she squealed when they bumped her legs. Water striders skated across the lake's surface. A streak of silver jumped from water to sky in search of food, ignoring the boundary between water and air. For the briefest moment, the large fish seemed suspended in motion as it found a target mayfly and then flopped back where it belonged.

"Lily, let's go," her dad said. "Got to get home before dark."

She looked up to see her parents walking toward the boat, arms around each other. She got out of the water and climbed into her seat, ready to go. Dad pushed the boat from the rocky beach and hopped on last.

The sun was low. The sky—red and orange and pink—tinted the hills and was mirrored on the water. Layers of sky, land, and lake glimmered in the day's last light. To David, it seemed like there was no one else in the world, like they were the last three people alive. Kate and Lily shared the front bench, his wife holding their daughter close, facing into the wind.

"Red sky at night," Kate started.

"Sailor's delight," Lily finished. "You always say that, Mom."

"I guess I do."

"Dad said it's a good sign for tomorrow," Lily said.

Kate nodded and kissed the top of her child's head.

Hundreds of white cattle egrets flew close to the water and headed directly to a tiny island nearby. They'd taken up residence on the lake in the past few years, blown far off course from their original African homeland, first to South America and then slowly further north. Once an oddity, now acclimated. Over the hum of the engine, they heard the birds calling to each other.

"Where are they going?" Lily said.

"They roost on the island. They want to get home before dark, too," David said. He cut the engine and they moved along with the current, watching as the birds landed in willow trees at the island's edge. Egrets dotted the branches, taking their places at dusk. Black cormorants positioned themselves in a dead tree that marked the end of the island. Perched at the tip, a lone bird kept watch.

"We should keep moving," Kate said.

David looked at the deepening sky and restarted the engine. It hit on the second pull, and he backed away from the island. He took in long, deep breaths, then turned the boat and headed for the shore.

DROWNED TOWN

Standing near the churchyard's picket fence, Margaret waved good-bye as the bride and groom drove away from St. Stephen's and toward their wedding reception in the nearest town. Moments later, she watched Cam's parents ease down the same dusty road in their big white sedan that looked like an unmarked police car. Then she realized she'd been left behind. She had ridden with them.

She looked around for someone she recognized to ask for a ride. She was the outsider here, the visitor from Louisville who had come to town for the wedding. Other than the bride and her family, she didn't know these people. *Why the hell didn't I bring my own car?* The small group of wedding guests thinned quickly in the deep woods where the chapel sat. Most had already left.

Then she saw one person she recognized: Neville Burgess, the best man. She hated to ask him for another favor after the lift he had given her to the wedding rehearsal last night. Over the weekend she'd gotten the impression that he didn't like her, and the feeling was mutual. But unless she wanted to walk ten miles to the party, she had no option.

"Hey, Neville," she called out, trying to sound friendly. "Can I catch a ride to the reception?"

"I'm heading that way," he said.

"I guess Rose and Lowell forgot me," she said. He nodded and kept walking. She fell in step beside him and looked for his rusted-out pickup truck. She dreaded riding again in that filthy junker with no air conditioning. Her aquamarine silk dress would be ruined before she got to the reception. But there was only one vehicle left: a newish Jeep that sat high off the ground, black and shiny as if it had been detailed that day.

"You didn't drive your pickup?" she said.

"I brought my good truck, since it's a special occasion," he said.

Wondering why anyone needed two trucks, Margaret stepped up on the running board to hoist herself into the passenger seat, thankful for her dress's full skirt and the flat shoes Cam had insisted she wear. Neville started the engine, and soon cold air flowed from the vents. The Jeep's black interior was spotless, the opposite of the old pickup he'd driven only yesterday. Neville shifted into gear and headed down the lane toward the roads that eventually led to the main highway. As they drove off, Margaret turned for a last look at the simple frame chapel, once lost but now found and restored. Sunlight on its metal roof heightened its ethereal appearance. Despite her earlier reservations about having a wedding so deep in the woods, she now understood why Cam and Owen had wanted to marry here.

She also noticed a mountain bike mounted on the truck's rear carrier. She looked at Neville. "You planning to ride around at the reception?"

"I rode this morning. I didn't have time to unload," he said.

"The trail at Hillman Ferry or the one around Demumbers?"

"You know the bike trails around here?"

"You sound surprised," she said.

"I wouldn't have guessed you were a mountain biker, that's all," he said.

"I haven't ridden in a while. I used to ride with Robert," she said.

"Robert?"

"My late husband."

"I apologize. I didn't know his name," he said.

"No problem. Why would you?" She looked out the window as they crossed the bridge over the canal that connected Kentucky Lake to Lake Barkley. Houseboats, ski boats, and pontoons traveled in a loose flotilla. Jet Ski riders trailed the larger boats to jump their wakes.

She changed the subject. "The wedding was beautiful, wasn't it?"

"Indeed it was. They looked happy," he said. "Those two are a lot alike."

They drove along in silence, past the Dairy Dip ice cream stand, a row of antique and junk shops, and a flea market that attracted both tourists and locals. Parking lots were full of motorcycles and trucks pulling boat trailers.

"I'm still amazed we never got to know each other, you know, when we were younger," she said. "Seems like our paths would have crossed."

"If you came down to see Cam in summer, I was probably working at the marina or on a tobacco farm. I worked my way through school. Didn't have much time for loafing," he said.

His comment had a sting to it, as if he had heard of her family's wealth and judged her for it. Maybe even resented her for it. He has a real chip on his shoulder, she thought.

"And I was gone for a few years," he added.

"A construction job?"

He looked confused. "What?"

"I assumed you were a construction worker. You knew so much about the work to save St. Stephen's," she said. "And to be honest, I've never known a man who owns more than one truck."

He shook his head and laughed. "No, I volunteered my time at St. Stephen's, mostly just lifting and fetching for the ones who had skills," he said. "I left here for grad school."

"Really?"

"Now you sound surprised."

"Not really. Where'd you go?"

"A year at Oxford, then the rest of my doctoral program at Yale," he said.

Margaret's eyebrows raised. She never would have suspected this guy was an Ivy Leaguer. "Impressive. What in?"

"History. American. My dissertation was on the drowned towns of the South. TVA and the Corps of Engineers dammed a lot of rivers in this part of the country," he said.

"What's a drowned town?"

"Like our old town, where Cam and I grew up. Under water after the lake impoundment. Dead and gone," he said.

Margaret wondered why these people never got over the fact that the lakes existed.

"Do you teach?" she asked.

"Yep, at Murray State, forty miles from here. Mostly undergrad survey courses, but every few semesters I get to teach an upper-level seminar on the lost towns," he said.

"Sounds like you could have gone anywhere with your credentials," she said. As she spoke, she heard her parents' voices echoing in her own words, questioning his life decisions even though she didn't know him.

"I decided to stay here, even with all those options you implied," he said.

He seemed defensive, so she quit asking questions and looked out the window. The lake was nowhere in sight, only hills and rolling pastures with small herds of black cattle. White birds sat on the backs of a few of the cows, reminding her of some faraway land pictured in a *National Geographic* magazine. Neville turned off the main highway onto a smaller road that ran alongside a fingerlike bay.

"Are we heading back toward the lake?" she asked. He nodded, keeping his eyes on the road.

Just before a sharp curve to the left, she saw a yellow *Scenic Overlook* sign. As they drove through the curve, Lake Barkley appeared. Blue sky with wispy mare's tail clouds stretched on and on, repeated in reflections on the water. Neville pointed to the low-lying strip of tree-lined land on the opposite side.

"That's LBL, where we just came from," he said.

"Okay, now I think I have my bearings. What's this little village called?"

"Kuttawa. They claim it's a Shawnee word for beautiful, but I'm not sure about that," he said. "Old Kuttawa is another drowned town, or actually a half-drowned one. They lost everything on the south side of town next to the Cumberland River."

Along one side of Lakeshore Drive old Federal-style homes and Victorian cottages faced the lake, an arrangement that made the town look more coastal New England than inland Kentucky. White, yellow, and blue frame houses lined a single sidewalk, their front porches decorated with wicker settees and pots of geraniums and ferns. Across the road, a small park with a horseshoe-shaped beach was packed with picnickers, swimmers, and sunbathers.

"This is lovely. Very quaint," she said. They drove a few blocks to the other end of town to the Harbor Springs Inn near the marina. Neville parked and turned off the engine.

"Looks like the festivities have begun," he said, motioning his hand toward the inn. The side lawn was draped by weeping willow trees and crepe myrtles blooming pink and red. Skirted tables with wildflower centerpieces dotted the close-cropped grass. A blue-grass band played on a patio that also served as the dance floor.

Margaret scanned the crowd on the lawn. Cam's off-white dress stood out among the pastel tablecloths and rosebushes. Her head bobbed as she laughed with Owen and other guests gathered around them. Neville was right, Margaret thought. They looked happy.

She and Neville walked up the hill to the inn and entered the party through a garden trellis laden with deep purple clematis blooms.

"Thanks again for the ride," she said.

"Have a good evening," he said, as they went in different di-rections. She found herself wishing he hadn't left her and watched him as he joined a group of people she didn't recognize. She head-ed to the bar for a glass of champagne.

After the toasts, the food, and a good amount to drink, Margaret found herself alone again, sitting at a table on the far side of the lawn. The shadows grew long. Twinkle lights strung along the arbor competed with several lightning bugs floating over the grass. The smell of citronella wafted from burning candles on the round tables and from torches spiked around the edge of the patio.

She had to admit the reception had been fun so far. She had danced with Cam and Owen, separately and as a three-way after several glasses of champagne. She danced with Lowell and with Owen's father, whom she'd met for the first time at last night's re-hearsal. While on the dance floor, she noticed David, the teacher from Louisville she'd met at the brunch before the wedding. He danced with his young daughter Lily, who stood on his shoes to fol-low the moves. As Margaret left the dance floor, she saw David's wife—Kate, was it?—seated at the table closest to the band, watching her husband and daughter. They had been introduced at the Wetherfords' house, but Margaret had barely glanced up. Somehow she seemed familiar, as if Margaret had met her long before the brunch.

"I think they're enjoying themselves," Margaret said as she approached.

"Oh, hello again," Kate said. She paused before adding, "Have a seat if you'd like." The invitation sounded friendly enough, but Margaret thought she seemed a bit standoffish. Her words didn't match her expression. Still, Margaret sat down. She needed to land somewhere.

"Have we met before? You look so familiar, but I can't place you," Margaret said.

"I was wondering if you'd remember me," Kate said.

Margaret racked her brain to figure out how she knew the woman. "We couldn't have gone to school together; you're much younger than me," Margaret said. "Are you a lawyer?"

"No, but I think you represented Dr. Brian Clark at a trial. Almost five years ago. A full-term stillbirth at St. Martin Hospital."

"Yeah, I remember," Margaret said in a matter-of-fact tone. "I won that case." Margaret loved to win at trial, not because she made more money if she won, like a plaintiff's lawyer, but just because she liked winning. Defense lawyers never worried about getting their share. They got paid regardless of outcome, by the client or more likely by the client's insurance company.

"Right. You won," Kate said with a slow nod. "And we lost."

Margaret froze, and then studied Kate's face. She looked almost nothing like the plaintiff Margaret remembered, the woman who had sued the obstetrician. The woman who lost an otherwise healthy baby boy following a prolonged and difficult labor. Margaret recalled that plaintiff as someone who sat slumped on the witness stand, testifying in a lackluster and nearly incoherent manner. At the time, a confident Margaret predicted to her partners that she would win the case despite the egregious circumstances. Dr. Clark had been on the golf course during most of her labor, but Margaret's expert witnesses showed that his delay in reaching the delivery room had not caused the baby's death. The firm heralded Margaret's victory at trial, then rewarded her by naming her the new head of the litigation section.

"I'm sorry. I didn't recognize you," Margaret said, embarrassed to admit she had not once thought about this particular plaintiff since the verdict. After a trial, she only thought about the likelihood of an appeal. In Margaret's win-or-lose world, she never considered the impact on the person who lost.

"I figured you didn't," Kate said.

"How are you? How's your family?"

"It has taken awhile, but I'm okay. We have our daughter. My son would be almost six now if he hadn't died," Kate said.

Margaret didn't know what to say. In the courtroom she didn't speak to plaintiffs except to cross-examine. She rarely crossed paths with them after a case ended. As Margaret looked into Kate's pale blue eyes, now filled with tears, she felt sick to her stomach.

Kate managed a tight smile. "But we're still trying to have another baby," she said. She looked away, toward David and Lily on the dance floor. After a few moments, Kate regained her composure.

"Do you have children, Margaret?" she asked.

Margaret shook her head. What could she say that wouldn't sound cold or heartless? That she had never wanted children. That she'd done everything in her power to not become a mother. That she'd worked her ass off before the trial to defend Dr. Clark, even distinguished her legal career by coming up with a strategy that made the pompous doctor look reasonable before a jury. She said nothing. She wanted to run from the conversation. Why had Cam and the Wetherfords not given her a heads-up on who this woman was?

She watched David and Lily approaching the table. David loosened his tie as he sat down and grabbed a paper napkin to wipe his forehead. The young girl plopped into her mother's lap.

"Mom, did you see us? I was waltzing," Lily said.

"You danced beautifully, dear," Kate said as she gathered the child in her arms and kissed her.

Margaret smiled, pretending to listen as she scoured the crowd for a reason to flee. She spotted Becky, Cam's sister, sitting alone, next to the crutches she was using after her recent knee replacement surgery.

"Excuse me, but I need to check on Becky and see if she needs anything. Nice to see you again." Margaret's outright lie hung in the air between her and Kate, but she didn't care. She had to escape. She made a beeline to Becky.

"May I join you?"

"Of course," Becky said, patting the chair next to her.

"How are you feeling?"

"Old," Becky said with a laugh. She had short, thick hair of a light brown color, like her mother's before Rose went gray. She had her dad's blue eyes, even down to the smile lines etched in the corners. "I'm a month into rehab, so I'm not ready for the dance floor," she said. Becky was always an outstanding athlete, especially her tennis game, but over time she had worn out the cartilage in her right knee. Bone-on-bone osteoarthritis, the doctor had diagnosed it. She nursed her achy knee for as long as she could, until the pain became constant. Surgery was the only choice.

"How is it possible that we're old enough to need new joints?" Margaret said.

"Go figure. Seems like yesterday we were teaching you how to ski. On the hottest day of the year, I might add. And you were not a natural," Becky said. They laughed.

"I never was as good as you and Cam," Margaret said.

"Dad got us up on skis almost as soon as we could walk. That made a difference."

"You made it look so easy. It wasn't," Margaret said. She glanced back toward Kate and David's table and saw that they had pulled their chairs close together. They leaned as they spoke, their faces looking serious. Margaret regretted sitting down with Kate. She watched as Lily made her way back to their table with three servings of wedding cake. Margaret turned back to Becky.

"The other day I looked through an old scrapbook at Mom and Dad's," Becky said, "and there we were, the three of us, wearing those little bikinis. We all looked great, too, even if we didn't realize it. We were too busy nitpicking one little flaw or another, comparing ourselves to some cover girl who was thinner or taller or whatever."

"I guess we don't realize what we have until it's gone," Margaret said.

"It passes quickly, doesn't it? It doesn't take long to live a life."

"Stop, Becky, that's depressing."

"Sorry, but I look at my daughters now, one in high school and one going to college next fall, and I can't believe I'm not that age," she said. "I can't believe I'm the one with age spots on my hands, or those little wiggly lines around my lips, like Aunt Shirley used to have. Seriously, when did this happen?"

"I can't think about that right now," Margaret said, wobbling a bit as she stood up. "I need a drink."

She darted to the bar and ordered another glass of champagne, then found an empty table, collapsed into a chair, and decided she was done for the night. She had run out of things to say, and she refused to risk another depressing encounter with anyone else. She wished she could talk to Cam, but she knew better than to monopolize the bride's time. Cam needed to visit with all their guests, not just her. Margaret had arrived at the point in the evening that she'd been dreading, when the talk dried up and she was alone again. If Robert were still alive, they would have found each other about this time, rescued each other, found respite over a drink or danced without words to a slow song to refresh themselves after rounds of social talk. She finished the champagne in one long swallow. She slumped, her usual perfect posture abandoned, as she thought about how hard it was to be single at an event celebrating the concept of coupling.

"Hey, you want to take a walk?" a voice said, jarring her out of her thoughts. She straightened in her seat, turned around, and was surprised to see Neville. They hadn't spoken since arriving at the reception, just a few nods and smiles across the buffet line and the bar. Margaret had eaten dinner with Cam and Owen; she noticed Neville sitting with Owen's parents.

"Sure. I might need some walking to sober up a bit," she said.

"Come on. You need to see Silver Cliff," he said.

"I'm not sure this is the time to climb up on a cliff," she said.

"Don't worry. There's a guardrail," he said. She noticed he had shed his seersucker jacket and tie. His shirt sleeves were rolled up, exposing his tanned forearms.

As she stood, he offered his arm so she could steady herself. She appreciated the gesture, but she let go as soon as she found her balance, uncomfortable with the idea of needing his help again. A few steps in, she wobbled once more and automatically reached for his arm, where her hand remained as they navigated the uneven lawn and patio. She was glad to be wearing flats; her usual four-inch heels would have made her drunkenness more obvious. They stopped by the bar, and Neville asked for two bottles of water. "Good idea," she said, realizing she needed to drink water, lots of water, to possibly avoid a hangover.

They walked away from the inn and down the sidewalk that ran in front of the town's remaining row of houses. Along the street, homes of varying heights were backlit by the sun in the western sky. Some houses already had lights on inside. Others had candle lanterns burning on front porches where people sat in swings and rocking chairs. Several waved as Margaret and Neville passed by. Kuttawa felt like a small-town, painted-wood version of her fancier Victorian neighborhood in the Louisville Highlands.

"They aren't your typical lake houses," she said. "I don't see any A-frames or sliding glass doors or decks overlooking the water."

"These houses are much older than the lake. Most were built around 1900, maybe 1910, when this was a busy river town," Neville said.

They passed a large home with a wraparound porch and all its windows glowing. Lush potted ferns hung from hooks around the porch with welcoming wicker furniture that was painted white and stuffed with pillows. Through a bay window with a stained-glass transom, Margaret saw a group of people, maybe eight or ten, chatting, sitting around a long table set with food, flowers, and wine glasses. Through the open windows she heard laughter floating on the evening air. One couple snuggled against each other. She and Robert could have fit in there, she thought. They used to throw fabulous dinner parties.

"The houses are lovely, but it's hard to imagine a whole town here. I can't wrap my head around it," she said.

Neville pointed across the street. "See the beach and the picnic area? There used to be houses over there, too, and a business district. A bustling one. A train depot. Most of the town is underwater," he said. "Let's head this way." He motioned toward the lake.

They crossed the street to the park entrance, and he guided her toward a sidewalk that wove through the park's tall trees. Beside each tree stood a small plaque noting its Latin and common names. They stopped at an overlook, a limestone point that jutted into the lake, which surrounded the cliff on three sides. A low stone wall bordered the steep drop.

"What a view," Margaret said. The lake spread out before them in an unbroken vista that seemed to go on for miles in all directions. The sun had set, and the sky took on new color. To the east, a nearly full moon had risen.

"This is Silver Cliff. You may not realize it, but this destination is famous," Neville said.

"What in the world for?" she said. Even she heard the slight slur in her words. She tried to concentrate, determined to not sound like a drunk. She turned up the bottle and gulped water.

"There's a rite of passage for kids here. When you're about twelve or thirteen, you jump off Silver Cliff and into the lake, and hope you survive. The water's about fifty feet deep here," he said.

She peered over the rock wall and saw the water far below, maybe twenty feet down. She felt a sensation of vertigo, perhaps from the height of the cliff or the champagne, and she stepped back from the edge. She felt Neville's hand on her waist.

"No, thank you. Not for me," she said. "Add that to my list of reasons to be glad I didn't grow up here."

"What the hell's that mean?" he said in such a straightforward way she couldn't tell if he was insulted or laughing at her.

"I don't think I could jump off this cliff or live in one of these little towns," she said. "Seems like most of you don't make it out of here either." She turned from her view of the lake back to Neville. He looked irritated.

"Some of us made it out, but we chose to come back," he said.

"Why did you ever want to come back? I don't get it," she said.

"Sometimes people don't understand things when they're ignorant," he said, giving her a hard look. "You have no idea what this place is really like."

His voice sounded cold and annoyed with her, the way he had sounded yesterday when they met. She regretted this turn in the conversation. She didn't want to argue with him.

"Sorry, that came out wrong. I'm just used to city life, I guess," she said.

"Wait a minute. Where did you grow up?"

"Louisville."

"And I suspect you had other options after law school, but you came back home," he said.

Margaret shrugged. "You've got a point. But Louisville's different," she said.

"I guess it's human nature to favor your own," Neville said. She saw that he was smiling again as he shifted his view back to the lake. "You've got to admit this is beautiful." She noticed his dark blond hair highlighted by the changing sky, now an orangey pink and fully reflected on the water. The gloaming seemed to encircle them.

She tried to focus on the lake. Its swath followed the original bends and turns of the Cumberland River channel, but the lake spread wider and less restrained. The point where they stood felt like being in a crow's nest, she thought, sensing it might be the highest elevation around, a small sliver of land wedged between sky and water. In the distance, a towboat pushed barges, its engines grinding under the weight of the load. Flocks of white birds—the same kind she had seen in the cattle pastures—flew toward a small island. She breathed in, sobering a bit as she studied the water and the lights reflected from the prison further upstream.

"If you follow the river that way, you'll end up in Nashville," he said, pointing left. "Go the other direction, you'll reach the mouth of the Cumberland where it joins the Ohio River not far from Paducah. And across the lake where you see no lights, that's LBL."

"The wilderness," she said.

"It wasn't always a wilderness. It was home to a lot of people. Aunt Rose Wetherford, for one," he said, his hand indicating the direction.

Margaret squinted to see in the fading light. "Is that Mint Springs? The Wetherfords took me there by boat years ago," she said.

"There, her home was just east of that point, right across from the prison. There's less than ten feet of water over it now, depending on the time of the year. And my grandparents farmed near Sugar Bay. I guess the government decided we needed tourists more than we needed farmers," he said.

"Oh, don't tell me you're one of those guys who hates everything about the government," she said. Her head was spinning. She wondered how many glasses of champagne she had consumed, and took another drink of water.

Neville frowned and shook his head. "I don't hate the government. I pay my taxes. I appreciate my public school education and the roads I drive on. But my people were farmers. The lakes flooded their homes and took the river bottoms. Can you imagine having no say in the matter?"

"All I'm saying is that, as long as the government followed the rule of law, it was within its powers," she said.

"And all I'm saying is that sometimes the government makes mistakes, and when that happens, a lot of people suffer," he said. "If you need another example, there's a section of the Trail of Tears just a few miles up the road. Remember that story? When our government made thousands of Native Americans starve and freeze to death on a forced march to Oklahoma, all because we wanted their land." He paused for a moment, looking upriver toward his old town.

Margaret sighed. She'd heard it all before from Cam's family, and she knew how painful the history was for them. She guessed it was for Neville, too. She tried to choose her words with care, the way she spoke to the Wetherfords when they talked about the lake.

"But here the people got homes that didn't flood every year and money for their old places, right?"

"That's mostly true," he said.

Margaret made a sweeping gesture toward the lake. "And all this. It's really spectacular," she said.

"That's true, too, but some of the old folks have never been able to see the beauty. All they ever thought about was the way life used to be and what they lost," Neville said, his voice sounding melancholy. "My dad was one of them. Never got over it. He stayed mad the rest of his life."

"What a waste," she said.

"I reckon everyone chooses how they see the world, and that was his way," Neville said, watching the tugboat negotiate the dogleg turn at Silver Cliff. The remaining light dwindled as dusk moved in. "My dad mourned the loss and never saw what eventually came from it. He fished from the bank and never saw how things looked from the water."

"How could somebody have this in their backyard and never enjoy it? Cam's parents seem okay with it," she said.

"It took awhile for the Wetherfords, too. They were one of the first local families to build a house on the lake," he said.

"I guess you can tell I'm not from around here. I wouldn't have given it a second thought," she said.

"I can tell you're not from around here in lots of ways," he said, grinning. He lifted his water bottle to his lips and finished its contents. "I grew up thinking every bit of it was a bad deal. That's what I'd been told since I was a kid. My old man hollered and cussed the Corps of Engineers, but it didn't change anything," he said.

Neville paused to hear something, then motioned to his ear, indicating for her to listen. He pointed toward the shore below them where a bird squawked with a rough, harsh sound.

Margaret whispered, "What is that?"

"Night heron," he said. "And do you hear those robins in the trees? That's their twilight song."

They paused their conversation and listened for several minutes. Margaret became aware of sounds around her that she hadn't heard before, and she recognized crickets and frogs in the mix. Waves landed against the rocky beach below.

"For me, everything shifted one summer in college. I came home and worked at one of the marinas, pumping gas on the dock. Everyone who pulled in to buy gas for their boat was a stranger. Everyone out having fun on our lake wasn't from here. It just seemed wrong to me. Plus, I was hot and tired and generally pissed off like most teenagers are," Neville said. "So I took part of my paycheck and rented a fishing boat for an afternoon."

Margaret laughed. "What'd your dad say?"

"He never knew. I didn't have the courage to tell him," he said. "I went by myself and felt very disloyal to the cause, but I was hooked. I saw it with different eyes."

"That was a bold move," she said.

"Renting that boat was one of my few acts of rebellion as a kid, but I reckon it made sense. A lot of teenagers try to see the world differently from their parents," he said.

He described his first trip outside the harbor and into the main channel, back toward the old town, naturally. He had spied the few remaining houses up on Pea Ridge, looking lonesome even though still occupied, and had seen birds he didn't recognize from childhood—great blue herons, cattle egrets, bald eagles—nesting on little dots of dredged islands near the channel.

"My opinion changed that day. I gave up dwelling on what we had lost and decided I wasn't letting all this go to waste," he said.

"But you teach history," Margaret said. "Isn't that like dwelling in the past?"

"I guess so. I love history, but that doesn't make me foolish enough to think I can change the way things played out here. The towns are gone; the land is, too. The lake is here. I might as well go fishing," he said.

The moon, now high enough to scatter its light across the water, became a new source of illumination in the growing darkness. In its glimmer she could still see Neville, and she felt like she was seeing him for the first time, maybe seeing any man for the first time in a long time. Margaret could tell she had sobered up, but she felt lightheaded. She shivered in the cool night air.

"We should get back to the party," she said. He nodded.

They started walking toward Harbor Springs Inn. She felt his hand near the small of her back as he steered her through the maze of paths in the park. Darkness had transformed the park into a shadowy scene that felt far removed from the festivities. His hand transferred a small patch of heat to her skin, and although she walked ahead of him, she felt as if she were following him like a dance partner who knows all the steps. His touch was a bit firmer as they crossed the road, protective in case she hadn't sobered sufficiently, but not pushy. It lightened when they reached the sidewalk on the opposite side.

When they rejoined the reception, Margaret noticed that two of the band members had traded their bluegrass instruments for electric guitars. Cam and Owen were still dancing, looking sweaty and exhilarated, surrounded by a handful of friends. Suddenly Margaret felt tired from the long day and her intake of champagne. She wished she were climbing into bed back at the dreary state park lodge.

Neville looked at her. "You still need a ride?"

She nodded. "If you don't mind."

"I don't mind. Whenever you're ready."

As Neville spoke, Owen came over and put an arm around his shoulders. "Buddy, c'mon, let's dance. It's almost over," he shouted over the music. "You too, Margaret. We've saved the best song for last."

Margaret looked at Neville, who shrugged and said, "Sounds like it's our final act of service as wedding attendants."

"I already have a hangover, but what the hell," she said.

The lead singer stepped up to the microphone. "Get on your feet, everybody. We're going to send Cam and Owen off into happy-ever-after land, and we need your help," he shouted. The remaining guests, mostly family and close friends, made their way to the dance floor.

"Margaret, get over here!" Cam was standing near the band, her cheeks flushed, her arms gesturing to come closer. Margaret made her way through the crowd, and Neville followed. The flowers that had been pinned carefully into Cam's hair had shifted from hours of dancing.

"You look like you're having fun," Margaret said, close to Cam's ear.

"I don't want it to end, but there's some rule here about disturbing the other guests at the inn," Cam said, her face looking like she might cry. Cam never could hold her liquor, Margaret thought.

Cam embraced Margaret, who smelled the familiar herbal fragrance of Cam's shampoo mixed with the perspiration on her skin.

"Thank you for being here. I know it hasn't been easy, but I needed you here," Cam said. They stood, draped over each other, hugging tightly, reminding Margaret how she missed the touch of another person, the warmth, the scent, the confirmation that someone loved her.

She felt Cam draw away to look for her groom as the first notes of "We Are Family" began, but Cam didn't release her hand. Instead she pulled Margaret along until they reached Owen, who was singing the first lines of the song with Neville. Margaret made a slight movement toward Neville and held out her free hand, which he took. The four of them made a circle in the middle of the dance floor, singing and dancing, until Owen loosened his grip to include his parents, the Wetherfords with Becky hobbling and leaning on her kids, the neighbors from Sycamore. The circle grew until each remaining guest had been brought in and welcomed. Margaret tightened her hold on their hands—Cam on one side and Neville on the other—so that she didn't lose her place in the circle. She wanted to belong in this family. *Get up ev'rybody and sing.*

The next morning Margaret's shoulders slumped at the thought of the three-hour drive back to Louisville. Exhausted and slammed with a champagne headache, she wished she could curl up and nap for the rest of the day in the hammock on the Wetherfords' screened porch. Maybe the rest of the week. Maybe a month. Her schedule for the week ahead looked dismal, even for a person with her work ethic. She'd have days of meetings with Royer Hensen, a man who surely was in the running as the most annoying client in Kentucky. The worst part was that he was her client. The thought of him made her head pound and her stomach roll.

Royer had made a fortune blowing off mountaintops to extract coal, and when he could get away with it, he left large swaths of east Kentucky looking like a moonscape. Like a lot of entrepreneurs, after he made his money Royer set out to live the good life. Like other coal barons before him, he moved to Lexington. However, he kept his legal work in Louisville, eighty miles up the interstate, because Royer didn't want everyone in Lexington knowing his business. The partners at Marshall & Dodson treated Royer with kid gloves and tried to overlook his deplorable behavior. They made a lot of money from him. Royer Hensen was a one-man lawyer relief act.

Margaret was brought in when the lawsuits started. After his move to Lexington, Royer spent a chunk of his fortune on a series of hair plug transplants, a mouthful of veneers, and a fair bit of injectables at a glitzy med spa on Leestown Road. He transformed himself into an audacious ladies' man, at least in his own mind. Shortly thereafter, he'd been sued for sexual harassment by a group of former and current employees.

"You know and I know that's just a pack of lies," he had told Margaret at their first meeting to review the claims. "Those girls enjoyed my attention, but now they're only thinking about my money."

"Royer, please don't call them girls. I've asked you not to use that term when speaking about the women who work for your company," Margaret said.

"Really? Why would any woman not like being called a girl?" he said. "It makes them sound younger and prettier than they really are."

"Trust me on this one, Royer," Margaret said. "It's offensive, and it won't get you far with the judge assigned to your case. Her name is the Honorable Mary Sebastian." Margaret stretched out the word *her* for emphasis.

While she was away for the wedding, the associates who worked for Margaret were spending the weekend reviewing personnel files and interviewing other company executives to glean information potentially helpful to Royer. This week she would prep him for depositions. Her goal was not to disprove the allegations. Based on his behavior in her presence, she figured they were true. If she could get within firing range of a reasonable settlement, she'd consider it a win. She didn't want to take this client in front of a judge or a jury.

She got out of bed, started the coffee, and opened the drapes. Another clear summer day, the sun higher than she expected, its heat already radiating through the glass sliding doors. She must have slept later than usual. When she heard the last gurgle of hot water force through the coffeemaker, she poured a cup and stepped out onto the balcony. The lake was calm, glasslike, a light steely blue from the reflected cloudless sky. She felt like she was a thousand miles from Louisville, instead of only two hundred. Royer Hensen wasn't the only thing that troubled her about returning home. All weekend she had been surrounded by people and celebration. Despite her hesitation about coming to the wedding, now she didn't want to leave them, to return to her big, empty house. She knew she was going to miss them all.

Years ago when she and Robert first looked at the house with their real estate agent, he had worried it was too big.

"That's a lot of room for two people," he said.

"But it's everything we want," she said. The previous owners had renovated the house; it was move-in ready. The Cherokee Triangle location was a ten-minute commute to their downtown offices, and within walking distance of the Bardstown Road restaurants and coffee shops. The neighbors had inviting homes with perennial gardens along their shared fences. In fact, Margaret couldn't have imagined a better place to live. The neighbors became close friends. They had cried with her when Robert died. They brought food, took her garbage cans out to the street on trash day, and made sure her sidewalk was shoveled that first winter without him. Still, looking back, she knew he'd been right. It was a lovely home, but its unoccupied spaces accentuated her aloneness.

She was weary of solitude. She felt out of practice being with people. She had given up things she used to enjoy like book club and their monthly dinner group. With each invitation she declined and each friend she turned down, she dug herself deeper into isolation. In a city—her city—with a million other people, she had nobody.

Margaret heard her phone ringing inside the hotel room. She put her coffee cup down on the balcony table and ran to answer it.

"Are you coming for lunch?" Cam said. "I want to see you before we drive back to Nashville. Our flight leaves tonight." She and Owen had spent their wedding night at the Harbor Springs Inn in Kuttawa, but the real honeymoon would begin with their flight to Paris.

"I'm moving kind of slow this morning," Margaret said as she wandered back onto the balcony.

"Too much fun last night?"

"Yes, too much fun and maybe a smidge too much champagne," Margaret said.

"We're all feeling the champagne. Dad's pouring Bloody Marys," Cam said. "You know, the hair of the dog helps."

"Are your neighbors coming? The ones with the little girl?"

"Just my family and you and Neville today," Cam said. "Why?"

"I can't face them again. I had a very unpleasant conversation with the wife last night," Margaret said.

"What about? You don't even know them."

"Do you remember they had a stillborn baby?"

"Vaguely," Cam said.

"They sued over it. Guess who represented the doctor," Margaret said.

"Oh no. That must have been awkward," Cam said.

"You could say that. So, I ended up drinking even more than I had planned," Margaret said as she rubbed her throbbing head.

"Relax. I promise they won't be here," Cam said.

"Then I promise to come, as soon as I shower and check out." She drank the last of the coffee, which had grown cold and tasted bitter, causing her stomach to flop and her head to shudder.

The Wetherfords were only slightly less exuberant than on the wedding day.

"Everything turned out just right," Rose said as she passed the platter of country ham and scrambled eggs. Margaret decided to go easy until the Bloody Marys kicked in.

As she buttered a slice of wheat toast, she glanced across the table. Neville looked no worse for the weekend's wear. He shoveled in eggs and ham, with two biscuits covered in sausage gravy waiting on a side plate. She was staring at his plate when he looked up.

"I'll share if you didn't get enough," he said, smiling.

She shook her head. "No, I'm good. I'm not very hungry today."

"Can't imagine why," he said in a low voice.

"I'm not the only one guilty of excessive celebration," she said. Everyone around the table chuckled.

"Margaret, you need to eat a banana," Becky said. "It's the quickest cure for a hangover, or so I'm told."

"It sure is," Owen said, and looked around at his new in-laws. "Not that I need a cure on a regular basis." They laughed again. Owen had a reputation for partying.

"You're saying that you eat a banana and the hangover goes away?" Margaret said.

"Basically, yes. At least one, but more if needed," Becky said. "I think it's something to do with raising the blood sugar."

"There are plenty in the kitchen for anybody that needs one. Help yourself," Rose said.

"And the more speckled the banana, the better. Higher sugar content," Owen added.

"It's worth a shot. Otherwise, I can't imagine driving back to Louisville like this," Margaret said. She went to the kitchen, where she found a stalk of six bananas with moderate brown speckling in the fruit bowl. She hated overripe bananas, but she broke off one and had started to peel it when Neville walked in.

"How many have you eaten?"

"Whoa, I just peeled the first one," she said. She took a big bite. The sticky, sweet flavor made her shake her head, but she managed to swallow. She grimaced and took another bite, and another. She tossed the peel into the trash can.

"How do you feel?" His interest surprised her. She hadn't expected him to show any concern, but as she thought back to last night, he had shown up when she needed someone. Whatever the reason for his interest, she liked the feeling of being tended to.

"Can't tell much difference yet," she said.

"Eat another one," he said as he broke off a banana and handed it to her. She peeled it and started to eat.

"Does this really work or is it some kind of prank to embarrass me? You know, the one who drank too much," she said.

Neville laughed. "That would be an excellent joke but, on my word, the banana cure works. I can vouch for it."

She finished the second banana and pitched the peel. "I need water to get the sweetness out of my mouth," she said.

"Maybe that's how it works," he said. "You drink a lot of water to get rid of the sweet taste until you're no longer dehydrated."

She filled a glass and drank it all. Although her stomach felt full and very fluid, her general lethargy faded. She drank another glass of water. They headed back to the table.

"I think it's working. I'm almost human again," she said.

"I'm telling you, it works. Always keep bananas around the house, just in case you tie one on," Becky said. "If you end up not needing them, you can bake banana bread."

After lunch they all gathered on the driveway to send off the newlyweds. As Cam and Owen drove away, Neville walked up and stood beside Margaret.

"They're the two people I've known best my whole life. He's the right person for her," he said.

She nodded. "You knew the first husband?"

"Oh, yeah. I tried to talk her out of that one," he said.

"Me too. I never liked him. He was a real jerk and a liar," she said.

"And you're a good judge of character," Neville said.

Margaret hugged Cam's parents and wished she didn't have to leave them. Lowell handed her a small cooler. She looked inside it and found they had packed her a picnic from leftover wedding food.

"No need to stop on your way for food," Rose said. "You need to get home and rest before work tomorrow." Margaret hugged them again.

Neville carried the cooler and walked out to the car with her. "Call me if you're coming this way again," he said. He handed her his business card.

"Thank you, and thanks for getting me where I needed to be all weekend," she said. She looked at the card. *Neville Burgess, PhD, Professor of History* along with his phone number and email address, the university seal in blue and gold ink. She decided to keep it. She thought about giving him a hug, but instead she said goodbye and got in the car. As she headed out the driveway, she remembered the feel of his hand on the small of her back and the way he looked against the pink sky at Silver Cliff.

At the ramp to the interstate, Margaret kept going, back toward Kuttawa. She wasn't ready to leave yet. She drove down the main street with its single row of houses perched on the hillside overlooking the water. She passed Harbor Springs Inn where tables and chairs were stacked on the patio to be returned to the rental company. Down the road, opposite the entrance to the park, she saw the white Victorian house she had noticed last night as she walked around with Neville. She pulled over to the curb to look again.

The snow-white house sat on the slight hill with a brick retaining wall that met the sidewalk. Three large silver maples dotted the small yard enclosed by a wrought iron fence. It was a city yard, not a country one, another reminder that Kuttawa had been a real town before the lake was created. The broad porch wrapped its way around three sides of the house, and lush fern baskets hung at regular intervals around its perimeter. The porch ceiling was painted blue like the sky—haint blue, a southern tradition said to ward off ghosts, like the low-country houses she once visited in South Carolina.

Margaret studied the details of the porch and its wicker furniture, a setting that invited people in to linger over a gin and tonic and watch boats go by. She glanced higher to a third-floor window framed by fish-scale shingles and gingerbread woodwork. It was a beautiful home, but unlike last night, it now looked deserted. There were no cars in the driveway and no signs of the people she had glimpsed last night as she stared up from the sidewalk. They had been celebrating, probably nothing big like a wedding, perhaps something as simple as being together for the weekend. They looked casual in T-shirts and shorts. Maybe they were celebrating life itself. In the short time she had watched last night, she saw them eating and drinking and laughing as they sat on both sides of a long table. Votive candles had twinkled and reflected in their wine and water glasses. Even though she didn't know them, she envied what she saw. She craved what they had together.

But today the people were gone. The house had been closed up. It must be a weekend place, she decided, wondering where they lived. Perhaps Nashville, Henderson, maybe Louisville. She wished she knew them. She wanted to join them at their long, comfortable table.

Unmoored

Robert missed his annual checkup, and for six months Margaret was on him to reschedule. She wouldn't have known he had skipped it—the doctor's office always called him directly at his work or cell number—but this time, a polite woman called the house and asked Margaret to please remind him to get in touch. Margaret brought it up again as the morning coffee brewed.

"Why won't you go?" she said as she came up from behind and slipped her arms around him. "You think I like putting my feet in the stirrups? Or having the girls smashed flat for a mammogram? No, I don't, but I still go."

He laughed and turned around to face her. "That sounds almost as bad as the gloved finger reaching way up there for my prostate," he said, then kissed her and walked toward the kitchen door. "I have to get to work, but I'll think about it."

"If you won't do it for yourself, do it for me," she called out after him and headed upstairs to the master bathroom, still warm and steamy from his shower. A sweet, earthy waft of his shampoo and shaving gel hung in the humid air. She liked him to shower first. She got to breathe in his scent—the way he smelled still got her attention—plus she didn't have to wait as long for hot water to reach the second floor from the basement. The house was old and quirky, like most others in the Louisville Highlands, but Margaret loved it.

When they had first looked at the house, Robert thought it was too big and too fancy for two people. Margaret thought it was perfect, and she convinced him they needed to buy it. Typical of the neighborhood, theirs was a tall and narrow brick Victorian, a solid urban version of late nineteenth-century architecture, an era when whiskey, tobacco, and horseracing interests ruled the city. Families with names like Brown and Speed built iconic homes, racetracks, distilleries, and warehouses that still stood as monuments to the barons of vice.

Margaret Starks and Robert McKinley moved to her hometown right after law school. She had grown up in the east end, a privileged only child of doctors. He was a first-generation college grad, the youngest boy in a large family from Clintwood in southwest Virginia, a small town where his ancestors had settled before the Civil War.

Their paths had been unlikely to cross until they converged in the first week of law school at the University of Virginia. She felt the attraction when she met him at a welcome party during orientation. He wore a pale yellow oxford cloth shirt, its long sleeves rolled up in the warm September sun. She noticed that his hair and eyes were nearly the same soft brown shade, but what she remembered was his countenance. His face looked open and unassuming, maybe even vulnerable, and that made him stand out in the crowd of eager, anxious law students. They talked to each other for a long time, and by the end of the night she hardly remembered meeting anyone else. By long-distance phone call Margaret described Robert in detail to her best friend Cam, who was now in Lexington studying architecture at the University of Kentucky.

Even before Margaret learned that Robert was on a full-ride scholarship, she realized that he was smart, exceptionally smart in a class full of overachievers. He flew under the radar, though, not needing to impress anyone or prove himself worthy. When he landed at the top of their class after the first set of grades, she wondered if he was even aware of the jockeying for position going on around him.

Margaret, on the other hand, stayed aware of the competition. She tried to win in everything she did, raised by parents who expected her to come in first. She expected it of herself, too. Early on in law school she didn't excel; unlike Robert, she landed in the middle of the pack. But with the rigid habits she developed and a study schedule that few students kept, she climbed into the top 10 percent of the class and earned Order of the Coif status by graduation.

When they finished law school, they chose to live in Louisville despite multiple job offers in bigger cities. Margaret wanted to go home. She knew where she belonged. A top-notch firm, one with a long list of corporate clients that made up the backbone of old Louisville business interests, made an offer she couldn't turn down. Robert accepted a job with the public defender's office. While they studied for the Kentucky bar exam in late summer, they lived with her parents, who wouldn't permit them to share Margaret's old room. Robert moved into the recently vacated maid's room near the kitchen.

On a study break, they hung out at a small table in the box bay window at a coffee shop on treelined Longest Avenue. Margaret watched a kid on a skateboard navigate the old sidewalks that rose and fell at sharp angles where oak tree roots encroached from a narrow patch of soil beside the curb. The neighborhood was a favorite destination for people watching, especially this close to Bardstown Road.

"You're going to love living here," Margaret said.

"If I can pass the test," Robert said. He smiled and ran a hand through his hair. He rolled his head in a slow circle to relax his shoulders.

"You're kidding, right? You're the smartest person I know," she said.

"Would you put in a good word with your parents? They're still not convinced I have much to offer," he said.

"Why do you say that?"

"Margaret, come on. You must have noticed they put me in the servants' quarters, not the guest room. That's pretty consistent with the way they treat me," he said. She couldn't decide if he looked angry or just a little tired.

"Well, Thessie's room is nice, and they thought you'd like having the privacy. Have they said anything to you?"

"They've mentioned more than once that they know I could find a better job than the public defender's office. They've even offered to make a few calls on my behalf," he said.

Margaret rolled her eyes and sighed. "I'm sorry. They truly are snobs."

"They act embarrassed that their future son-in-law will be associating with poor people," he said. "Or maybe they're more appalled that their daughter's fiancé is an actual poor person from some godforsaken holler in Appalachia." He pronounced the word Appa-LAY-shuh to mimic them and their outsider mispronunciation, always a thorn in his side as a native Appalachian. For as long as they'd been together, Robert had schooled Margaret to say Appa-LATCH-uh, but she still sometimes slipped up and said it wrong. His rebuke stung her.

Yet beyond the pronunciation issue, his other words troubled her, too. She had never thought of him as, to use his words, an actual poor person. She thought of him as a kind, handsome, sexy man who ranked first in their UVA class. She knew he had needed the scholarships and that his parents hadn't dressed well for graduation, but as smart as he was and with his top-notch credentials, she knew he had potential. He would make a name for himself in

Louisville, and no one had to know he'd grown up poor. He could become better than that.

"I'll talk to them," she said.

He waved her off. "Please, don't say anything. Your folks are giving me a free place to live this summer and they're paying for the wedding," he said. "I don't want to seem ungrateful for all they're doing."

Margaret looked at him but decided not to say what she was thinking. She picked up her cappuccino and took a sip. She, too, had wondered about his job choice. He could have had his pick of any of the big law firms, the prestigious ones where he'd make a much better salary and practice with people her family knew. Instead he chose the low-paying public defender's office as if he didn't have a choice. Deep down, Margaret also thought he could do better.

The wedding date was two weeks after the bar exam. The ceremony would take place at the downtown Episcopal cathedral, with the reception a few blocks away at the Brown Hotel's Crystal Ballroom, an elegant and sought-after venue filled with gilt mirrors and chandeliers. Margaret's parents wanted their only child's wedding to be the summer's preeminent social event. Margaret hadn't paid much attention to the wedding plans while she studied for the bar, but the day after the test she shifted into high gear to catch up. Robert looked like he had run out of gas.

They sat down with her parents at their dining room table and heard from the wedding planner, a smartly dressed woman who had worked on the event for almost a year. With leopard-framed readers perched midway down her nose, she detailed the schedule from photography to hairdressers to the specific stem varieties contained in the flower arrangements.

"What do you think about the tuxes?" Margaret asked, holding out a photograph of a male model in formal wear. Robert didn't answer; he sat next to her with his eyes closed. "Robert? Are you still with us?"

He stirred, and his eyes opened. "Sorry, baby. I'm just exhausted," he said. He looked at the picture she held out to him. "Nice. I trust your judgment. Besides, I know when I'm outnumbered."

"What do you mean by that?" The atmosphere in the coral dining room grew tense. Margaret's mother, who wore an off-white knit suit with polished gold buttons that didn't clash with the décor, cleared her throat and stood up. "Maybe we should take a break. Can I get anyone a cup of tea?" As she walked through the doorway with her husband and the wedding planner, she cast a look of disappointment at Robert.

"What's wrong? Are you getting cold feet?" Margaret asked.

"Not at all. Don't make this bigger than it is," he said. "You know what you want, and these things don't matter to me."

"I don't think you appreciate how much time and money my parents have put into this wedding."

"You're right. I don't have a clue about this stuff. I don't know an orchid from a tuberose," he said. "Look, I'm just not used to things being so elaborate. In my family, we just show up at church with a handful of friends and get married."

"If the wedding doesn't suit you, maybe you should've spoken up before now," she said.

"Listen to yourself. You sound like your mother. Is that what you want?" he said. His words cut to the bone, but she knew the wedding plans were bringing out old family dynamics that she'd not bought into for a while. She had followed her parents' pretentious expectations, never considering what Robert wanted, and it was too late to change course.

"I'm sorry you don't like it," she said.

"Cut me some slack, Margaret. I'm tired and I'm feeling out of my league, but if you want this kind of wedding, it suits me fine," he said. He leaned in close and touched her face. His brown eyes had the sweetest expression, she thought. "I just want to be with you. However that happens."

The Starks family achieved their goal of hosting the season's top social event, complete with a story and wedding photograph in both the *New York Times* social pages and *Town and Country* magazine. The planner had the contacts to make that happen.

As the final surprise from Margaret's parents, the newlyweds were treated to the perfect honeymoon, a carefully curated month-long stay along the Amalfi Coast. Early in the planning stages, Robert's idea of a honeymoon in Asheville had been nixed.

"Are you sure you're okay with this?" Margaret had asked when she showed him the travel brochures.

Robert bit his lower lip as he examined the photographs. He looked at Margaret and nodded. "I've never been to Italy. Who in their right mind would turn this down to go to North Carolina?" he said. Margaret felt pleased that he liked the plan.

Her father chimed in. "Well, you've been in school for a long time and we know you can't afford the kind of honeymoon you and Margaret deserve," he said. Her parents looked at each other with a hint of self-satisfaction.

"It's very generous of you," Robert said. With a gleam in his eye, he added, "Are you two sure you don't want to come along?" He winked at Margaret. The Doctors Starks looked mortified. On their way to the airport after the wedding, Margaret assured Robert that her parents would not be calling the shots when they returned from the honeymoon.

A limousine driver met them at the airport when they landed in Naples and transported them to the harbor. They boarded a hover-craft to cross the bay to reach Capri. Despite her jet lag, Margaret marveled at the many shades of blue in the sky and water, from aquamarine to azure to deep sapphire. On Capri an open-air taxi delivered them to their hotel. During their stay, they drank limoncello and ate fresh sardines in restaurants with stone terraces overlooking the coast. They loved each other in the luxury provided by her parents.

"I'm starting to see the value in being spoiled," Robert said at dinner on the last night of the trip.

She raised her glass of prosecco and laughed. "It's always worked for me," she said.

When they returned home, they settled into a renovated carriage house in Old Louisville. They got their bar results—both passed—then started their jobs. By their third anniversary they wanted out of their rental and began looking at houses to buy.

Margaret sat in the living room of the carriage house—the ground floor space that once stabled horses—as she shuffled through a packet of real estate listings their agent had assembled for their review. "How many bedrooms do we need?" Robert had said as he sat down next to her. He handed her a glass of red wine, served in wedding gift cut crystal, and snuggled closer to her on the gray linen sofa. She shrugged and kept reading.

"If we ever have kids, we'll need room for them," he said.

"I haven't really thought about kids," she said.

"I've not been obsessing on it, but I like kids. I wouldn't mind having a few," Robert said. "Most of all, I hope we find a house and stay put forever."

Robert told her about growing up with his brother and sisters. He was one of five children, and he remained close to his siblings. Margaret, an only child, liked her small, compact family. She knew there had been another baby, a little girl named Eleanor who had died sometime before Margaret was born. Her parents never talked about what had happened. All she knew of Eleanor was the small headstone topped with a marble lamb that her parents visited every September 28. Margaret had almost forgotten there had been a sister.

"I don't dislike kids, but I don't have time right now. I can barely keep up with work as it is," she said.

"It's your body, so it's your decision," he said. "I'll go along with whatever you decide, but I hope you'll reconsider at some point. For me."

"Maybe later, but I need to concentrate on making partner," she said, wanting to put some time between their present lives and a decision to have a baby. With Robert and her busy law practice, Margaret had what mattered to her. She was doing everything right to stay on track to make partner on time, and she thought Robert would rise to the top in the public defender's office. Although she had doubted his decision to take the job, she now saw the value in his work, especially after he won a bar association award for his efforts on bail reform. He was making a name for himself. But kids? She didn't know how that fit in. Their lives were moving forward according to plan. Her plan, anyway.

As the years passed, she suspected he held out hope for a child, but he never said anything. He never pressured her. Even when they fought, he spoke his mind and seemed not to hold a grudge if he didn't get his way. Robert loved her without strings attached, which always surprised her because she'd not experienced that kind of relationship before. Most of her life she had connected love to living up to someone's expectations.

After she made partner, the subject of having kids never came up again but, like any good lawyer, she had memorized his words in case she needed to use them against him. She meant to win that argument, too. Her body, her decision.

Margaret finished her shower and dressed for the office in a starched white blouse, well-tailored blue trousers, and black pumps with high heels. Her long dark brown hair was straight and sleek from her last salon visit. Her scheduled workouts with a trainer kept her forty-three-year-old body strong and lean. She tended to her appearance as precisely as she handled her law practice. She liked the way her body looked and felt, and she knew Robert liked it, too.

She arrived at her desk an hour before the receptionist officially opened the office. With a trial starting the next morning, Margaret focused as she prepared to defend an age discrimination claim against a large health-care company, an important firm client. She expected the trial to last two days, and she expected to win.

Midafternoon, she shot an email to Robert, her message contained in the subject line: *Working late, won't be home for dinner.* In the body of the email, she added, *Love you. P.S. Want to go somewhere this weekend after I win this damn case??*

Robert sent back his response: *No problem. Playing basketball at 6 and picking up dinner on the way home. Want something? P.S. I scheduled the checkup. Love.*

During trial, the days rushed by. With Margaret's meticulous preparation, there were no surprises, including the verdict for her client. The adrenalin rush that came with winning—her career wins far exceeded losses—had subsided by the time she got home. She was exhausted.

"Congratulations, you brilliant woman," Robert said as he greeted her in the front hall. "I've booked a room in Cincinnati for the weekend. Or we could go to the lake if you want."

"I'd love to go to the lake, but I'm dead tired," Margaret said. "I vote for Cinci. It's closer."

"I thought you might say that, so I made dinner reservations at Palm Court," he said. "Grab your bag and let's go." She put her car seat back and dozed during the eighty-mile drive to Cincinnati.

When they arrived at their downtown boutique hotel, she was ready for a bourbon and a good meal. After dinner they drank port and made love on high-thread-count sheets. She slept until mid-morning. Robert had already had a few cups of coffee and read the paper by the time they headed to brunch.

"Dr. McCandless worked me in yesterday afternoon. I forgot to tell you last night," he said.

She stirred cream into her coffee, watching it transform to the proper shade. She didn't look up. "How's his finger?"

"Pleasant, as always," Robert said.

She looked at the menu, and then raised her eyes to study his face for the first time that day. Maybe for the first time in days, she'd been so busy. His eyes looked fatigued, a little puffy around the orbitals.

"Everything okay?"

"He said he felt something. A spot on the prostate felt a little stiffer than the area around it," he said.

She sat up in her chair. "What's that mean?"

"Could be a small tumor, but he said he's not worried. We'll check it again in three months, and if it's still there, he'll biopsy it."

"A tumor?" she said. Her expression changed from its usual bravado to a look of terror like a child awakening from a nightmare. It had been a tumor on her father's lung, discovered four years after she and Robert married. She'd lost her dad within a few months. Her mother died a couple of years later from a brain aneurysm. Margaret always thought her mother's death came from the stress of what they'd been through with her father. The word *tumor* triggered her most fundamental fears.

"He said maybe. Might be nothing," Robert said.

"You can't wait three months. There's no reason to wait that long," she said.

"Stop. It's no big deal. We can wait."

"You can't let this sit in there for three more months. *I* can't wait," she said.

His lips splayed into a thin, tight line. "I'm sorry if you can't wait, but I can," he said. His face reddened; his voice lowered but did not soften. "Remember what I told you years ago when we talked about having children? Do you remember what I said?"

She nodded, hearing his words echo in her memory. "It's my body and my decision," she repeated. She hadn't expected to retrieve the words for a conversation like this.

"That's right. I said I wouldn't force my will on you, and I didn't, did I?" he said. "You don't get your way about everything, Margaret." He'd never sounded so angry, like he resented everything about her and all the decisions she had made.

"I still think you're making a mistake," she said. "But it's your choice." She looked back at the menu, then tossed it aside. When the server came by to take their orders, she asked only for more coffee. "I'm not hungry," she said.

Robert ordered eggs Benedict and a Bloody Mary. After the server left, they sat in silence for a few minutes as she thought about whatever might be growing inside him. It was his body, but she loved it. Didn't she have a say in how they approached this?

"Please have the biopsy," she whispered. She felt tears overflow her eyes and spill down her cheeks, beyond her control. The waiter sped past and dropped off Robert's drink with a basket of biscuits. Robert took her clenched hand from across the table and pulled it to his warm lips, but he said nothing.

"I'm begging you," she said. "Please do everything you can to stay with me."

After his food arrived, she continued to stare at him as he took the first few bites. He looked up at her and shook his head. "You're getting all worked up for nothing, but I'll call on

Monday," he said. "I'll do it for you. Now, lighten up and have a biscuit."

The biopsy was scheduled for Wednesday. Results in a day or two, the doctor said. Soreness for a couple more days.

"Damn, I dread this," Robert said as he left for the doctor's office. He drove himself, adding that all of this would be behind them soon. She doubted that, but she didn't say it to him. She had a bad feeling.

When he called with the results, his voice sounded worn out. "It's positive. They found some cancer cells," he said.

She exhaled into the phone. "What do we do next?" she asked.

"Not sure. I see the doctor tomorrow." He agreed she could go with him.

That night they held each other, and after Robert fell asleep, she climbed out of bed to search the internet for information. She knew little about prostates, had never needed to, but now she wanted to know everything. She made notes on a legal pad as if she were preparing for a trial or a deposition. She read about radical prostatectomy, radioactive seed implants, hormone treatments, all the options. She was prepared when they met with Dr. McCandless.

"Of course, it's your decision," the doctor told them. "Every treatment has pros and cons, and some of the cons are pretty significant." He explained the possibility of impotency or incontinence or both from treatment, and the risk of metastatic bone cancer if left untreated. She glanced at Robert, who sat silently as they listened to what sounded like one bad option after another.

"Should he have a second biopsy to confirm?" she said.

Dr. McCandless shook his head. "We took ten tissue samples during the procedure. Seven showed malignancies. There's no reason to put him through that again," he said.

Margaret scoured the facts for a gap, something no one else had caught, some lapse that might alter the outcome. Had the pathologist made a mistake? Should they get another doctor to review Robert's file? Were the samples mixed up in the lab? There had to be a clue somewhere that had been overlooked. She would find a way around this mess. She'd find a way to win.

"Besides, your PSA has been inching higher for the last two years. That's why we were watching this," the doctor said.

Margaret glanced at Robert, but he didn't look her way. She wondered why he hadn't mentioned the elevated PSA, the blood test used for early detection.

"So, what's your recommendation?" Robert said.

"If I were a man your age, I'd want a durable cure, which is surgery. Remove the prostate and spare the nerves if possible," he said. "If you were seventy-five years old, we'd just wait and watch, but you're too young for that."

Margaret paid close attention as Dr. McCandless discussed nerve damage as the cause for incontinency and impotence. If there was no nerve damage from the cancer or the surgery, both functions would likely return with time. A biopsy of lymph nodes taken from the groin would determine if the cancer had spread beyond the organ. If it had spread, hormone treatment would block testosterone, which fueled the spread of prostate cancer cells. She remembered reading the word *castration* as a treatment option for advanced cases. She hoped the doctor wouldn't mention that brutal image now. Robert might refuse any treatment.

When Robert stood up, she thought he looked like he was ready to bolt. She picked up her purse in case she needed to chase him down.

"Let's get it scheduled," he said. She felt relieved. Maybe they'd caught it early. Maybe surgery would fix everything.

Before he could have surgery, Robert needed time to completely heal from the biopsy. The earliest available date was three weeks away, and as they waited, Margaret kept a schedule as rigorous as prepping for trial. She read books and studied treatises. The more she learned, the more frightened she became. She needed to talk to someone, but not Robert. She shouldn't unload all the bad details on him.

The night before, Robert brushed his teeth and finished packing a small bag for his hospital stay, predicted to be only two nights if all went well. He slid into bed beside her and began to stroke her hair.

"It's going to be all right," he said.

She nodded, slightly, and kissed him. She craved his body, thinking this might be their last time. She savored every part of him. After he drifted to sleep, she closed her eyes tightly and squeezed out silent tears. What if the physical part of their life together was over? The possibility wrecked her. She didn't know how she'd accept a bad outcome. She wanted him alive, the cancer to be cured, but the side effects of surgery could change him and immeasurably alter their life together. She didn't care that he'd be infertile. They were long past the decision whether to have children. He might have bladder or bowel incontinence. He might not be able to work again. They might never have sex again. He might die. Margaret felt disloyal thinking about the possibilities.

They had a few minutes together before Robert was wheeled into surgery. She held his hand as the hospital staff checked his temperature, blood pressure, and pulse. Dr. McCandless came through the green-curtained partition.

"I'll find you in the waiting area and give you a full report after surgery," he said, then turned and left. Margaret knew it was time for them to take Robert, who was beginning to show the effects of the sedative he'd been given. He smiled and his eyelids opened lazily when she spoke to him. She stroked his face and kissed his forehead. The nurses rolled out his gurney and headed down the hall. She stood alone for a minute.

"Please come back to me," she whispered, more of a plea than a prayer. Margaret had never prayed in her life. She wasn't sure she knew how.

When she returned to the waiting room, she found Cam sitting in a chair by the windows.

"What are you doing here?" Margaret said as they embraced, so happy to see Cam that she almost cried again. She hadn't realized until then how much she needed Cam during the surgery. The circle of people Margaret loved, and who loved her in return, was very tight—just Robert and Cam.

"I couldn't let you sit here alone all day," Cam said, explaining that she had gotten up in the middle of the night to make the drive from Nashville. For four hours Margaret and Cam sat together in the waiting room, alternating between clipped conversation and periods of silence. Margaret needed the silence, as if it allowed her to center on pulling him through surgery, as if her complete focus was as crucial as the surgeon's skill. She knew it sounded crazy, so she didn't explain her reasoning to Cam. Besides, Cam didn't ask.

During the last hour of the operation, her eyes stayed on the door where she thought Dr. McCandless would appear. He was an older man, she guessed in his sixties, known as the best urologist in Louisville. He had trained at the Johns Hopkins University Hospital which, she had learned from her research, was the hub of the prostate universe. In the 1980s Dr. McCandless had helped develop the nerve-sparing procedure, and he performed it several times a week. No chance he'd gotten rusty in his skills. Finally she saw him, and stood up so that he'd find her. He headed her way, still wearing his scrubs.

"He's doing fine," he said. Margaret wanted to hug him, thankful it was over, but the doctor kept talking. "I'm concerned the cancer wasn't confined to the organ. I had to take more tissue than I'd hoped, but I think I got a clear margin," he said. Although his words were delivered as if spoken in code, she knew what he meant. The nerves might have been damaged, increasing the odds of the bad side effects. That wasn't what she wanted to hear.

"We'll biopsy the lymph nodes. If it has spread, we'll figure out the next step," the doctor said.

We don't want a next step, Margaret thought. They wanted surgery as the only step.

"You can go back to recovery in a few minutes. He'll sleep most of the day," he said.

As Dr. McCandless walked back to the surgery suite, Margaret looked at Cam and collapsed into tears.

Robert was moved to a private room, where he slept all afternoon. Margaret needed to call his mother, and she dreaded it. Her tenuous relationship with Clara McKinley had not improved with time. Margaret remained uncomfortable with Clara's open and often fervent displays of religious belief. Except for the familial light brown eyes, she thought, Robert was unlike his family, so much so she had once asked if he'd been adopted. Robert was open and relaxed; his family members were hard to get to know and standoffish in her presence, as if they'd still not found a reason to like her. Although Robert made regular trips to visit them, Margaret was often too busy to make the long drive to Virginia.

Clara was a tiny woman, long widowed, who wore her long gray hair pinned up around her head. Since her own surgery last year to repair a broken hip, she now relied on a wheelchair most of the time. She had moved to a new assisted living facility near Wise and was too fragile to make the trip to Louisville.

"He came through surgery just fine, Clara," Margaret said. "I'm waiting for him to wake up."

Clara broke into a chant-like prayer. "Lord Jesus be with my boy. Erase all evidence of disease from his body and let him be healed," she said.

"He's doing well. I'll call a little later to give you another update," Margaret said, trying to get off the phone.

"I've had my prayer circles calling out in his name all day. We'll pull him through this, don't you know. We have to," Clara said. "And, honey, we're praying for you, too."

Margaret felt a rush of compassion for Clara. They both loved Robert; maybe they could still bridge the years of awkwardness and distance. "Thank you, Clara," Margaret said before she hung up. She didn't mention the possibility that the cancer had spread. She sent a more complete email to Robert's brother and sisters. As she typed, she stumbled over some of the words as if they were in a foreign language, one she didn't want to learn.

Cam tapped at the door, then pushed it open with one foot, her hands full with a large coffee for each of them. "How's he doing?" she said.

"Still sleeping," Margaret said.

"Go take a break and stretch your legs. I'll stay with him, and I'll call you the instant he wakes up," Cam said.

Margaret hesitated, but her back ached. "You're right. I'm stiff from sitting all day. I'll be back in a few minutes," she said.

"Take as long as you need," Cam said.

Margaret slipped out the door as quietly as she could and walked down the drab tan tile hallway toward the elevator. She worried she'd be unable to look him in the eye when she had to tell him the cancer might have spread. Maybe she'd wait another day.

Robert remained groggy, but by dinnertime he was able to eat a few bites of soft food. Margaret fed him like a baby and wiped his mouth with a soft, damp washcloth. She realized she had never taken care of anyone before. During her dad's cancer treatment, either her mother or the live-in nurse had managed the details. Margaret wasn't sure which one.

Just as the light was easing toward dusk out the square windows, the doctor appeared. She wondered how he kept these long hours every day, judging from her own level of exhaustion.

"He's doing well, so I want you to go get some rest," he said, looking at Margaret.

"I'm staying here tonight," she said.

"Oh, no. That's against my rules. You need your rest, too, because you're going to be taking care of him when he gets home," Dr. McCandless said. He gestured toward Cam. "Get your friend here to take you home. Then eat a good dinner and get some sleep."

She was too tired to argue. Robert was sleeping again, so she kissed his cheek and told him she loved him. She followed Cam to the car and was asleep before they left the parking garage.

When Robert came home from the hospital, he got stronger. The biopsy confirmed that the cancer had spread, so the goal shifted to finding a treatment that would stop fueling the cancer growth. Radiation of the lymph nodes would be the next step, followed by doses of hormones. As Robert recuperated, he kept a sense of humor, even about the catheter bag clipped to his pajama pants. His mother called daily and prayed for him over the phone line. Margaret usually left the room while they spoke.

Eventually he lost his appetite, even for the black raspberry gelato he loved. His face turned gray and puffy while his body grew thinner. They didn't talk about incontinence or impotence. After the catheter was removed, she bought disposable pads for his underwear without asking and replenished the box when it was nearly empty. They held each other in bed and talked about another trip to Amalfi.

While out running errands, Margaret stopped at the liquor store for a cold bottle of limoncello. Each year on their anniversary they shared a bottle to remember their wedding trip to Italy. The date was still months away, but she bought it, hoping that the memory of their honeymoon would help him rally. In the checkout line she noticed the young couple in front of her, ready to pay for a bottle of cheap champagne. The man's hand rested on the small of the woman's back in the gap between her T-shirt and low-riding jeans. Margaret could almost feel the touch of his fingers. When she got home, the house was silent. She grabbed two glasses and headed upstairs with the bottle, quietly, in case he was sleeping. He was sitting up in bed, propped with pillows, writing on a legal pad.

"I brought a surprise," she said, hoisting the bottle with a label decorated in lemons. "A little taste of Capri and Positano."

"Ah, limoncello in bed in the middle of the day. Am I in heaven?" he said, smiling.

She bent over and kissed him. His breath smelled metallic. "How are you feeling?"

"Not great. I may have to pass on the limoncello right now," he said.

"We'll wait until you feel better. Does anything sound good?"

He shook his head.

"Then close your eyes and rest. Maybe the nausea will pass," she said. She adjusted his pillows and slipped out of the room.

When she returned to the kitchen, she put the bottle in the refrigerator. She didn't want to drink alone.

She was tired of being alone. Robert slept so much. The smell of food often sickened him, so he no longer came to the table for meals. For a while she had taken her plate upstairs to be near him and have some conversation while she ate. When his nausea increased, she'd stopped eating her dinner in his presence. But, damn, she hated to eat in solitude. The trickle of visitors had almost stopped as he got sicker. She hadn't been to the office in weeks. Cam called regularly, but she was working around the clock to finish a big project in Birmingham.

Margaret's mood shifted from loneliness to anger, but she didn't know who to fight. She was angry about being alone, angry that he was sick. She loved him, but she was tired of taking care of him, which shamed her. Margaret knew he would take the best care of her if she were the sick one, but she wasn't good at taking care of people, even someone she loved. She missed their old life, their beautiful life before all this started. She wanted to run away, to escape the sickness and loneliness and fear of what might come next. Margaret grabbed her purse and left the silent house for a long walk past the lively shops and restaurants along Bardstown Road. She needed to peek into someone else's normal life, even a stranger's, for just a while.

At the next appointment they got bad news. A scan revealed that the cancer had spread to his bones. It was a particularly aggressive variety, the doctor said. They switched from treatment to palliative care. She shushed him when he started to talk about his funeral. To even speak of it meant he'd given up. She wasn't giving up.

On good days Robert sat at his desk and reviewed documents, the personal papers that would bring order to the chaos of losing him. He was a good lawyer. He put everything in order. His power of attorney, will, lists of bank accounts and retirement funds, a life insurance claim form, and prepaid cremation arrangements. He took care of the details of his dying. And Margaret took care of him. She lived according to his schedule. She read to him when he was awake. She sponge-bathed him and delivered his pain meds on time. She searched for foods he could stomach. She didn't go back to work. She canceled her regular hair and nail appointments, and her part grew wider and more silvery with every missed root touch-up. They still talked about going back to Italy.

"What's the most beautiful place you've ever seen?" he asked one morning, his voice sounding stronger than it had in weeks.

"That's easy. Capri. On our honeymoon," she said.

"Then put that at the top of the list," he said.

"What list?"

"Whenever you're ready, take me there or any other spot that makes you happy," he said.

Her first instinct was to shush him, but this time she didn't. She listened. For the last few days she had felt him slipping away from her. What strength remained was fading, flowing in another direction that didn't include her. Other than the little things she did for him to keep him comfortable, Margaret knew there was nothing she could do to change the course. She couldn't fix this, no matter how hard she tried. She couldn't make him get well. She couldn't win this fight, and neither could Robert.

She looked at him and nodded, grieving the finality of his words but no longer able to feign optimism. She climbed into bed beside him, raised his hand to her lips, and prayed he could still feel the warmth.

NICE PEOPLE DANCING TO GOOD COUNTRY MUSIC

The law firm's administrators billed the Nashville weekend as part celebration and part bonding experience for the lawyers and staff of Marshall & Dodson of Louisville and Boyd Hoffman of Nashville. Two law firms becoming one, the invitation read, sounding more like a wedding than a business deal. Margaret rolled her eyes, still feeling jilted by her partners who had approved the merger.

She would attend their two-day retreat; at least she got an expense-paid weekend at the Hermitage Hotel, where she could take advantage of its long list of amenities. In advance she booked services at its well-known spa—manicure, pedicure, facial, and massage—for Saturday afternoon after the meetings ended. By that point in the weekend, she would deserve some stress relief.

For Margaret, the only exciting part of the trip had nothing to do with the law firm. She'd get to see Cam. She hadn't been able to spend much time with Cam since the wedding. The newlyweds lived close to downtown in an older neighborhood off West End Avenue.

"I'm heading your way this weekend. Mandatory firm retreat," Margaret told Cam on the phone. "Please tell me you're going to be home." Margaret sat at her desk sipping a can of mineral water and watching the late afternoon barge traffic on the Ohio. She guessed Cam was looking out at the Cumberland from her office too.

"You sound thrilled," Cam said, laughing.

"Not in the least. We're merging with a big Nashville firm, the one where that asshole Marc Blevins practices. God, I can't stand him," she said.

"I met him when we designed their new offices. He seemed like a pompous know-it-all," Cam said. "Didn't you catch him once trying to get away with something in a case?"

"I should have had him disbarred," Margaret said. "He fudged some settlement agreement numbers without telling the rest of us. But you-know-who caught him and called him out for it. I should have filed a formal complaint with the bar association."

"I could have warned him that he couldn't put one over on you and your hawk eyes," Cam said.

"And now that douche bag's going to head the combined litigation sections. Technically, he'll be my boss," Margaret said. "That's a real gut punch."

"No wonder you're mad," Cam said.

"Don't get me started. I've tried to warn them about being gobbled up by a larger firm. I was the only nay vote. I've tried to make the best of it, but you know I'm not particularly good at losing. Or hiding my feelings," she said. Margaret reached into her handbag for her lipstick and compact. She had a meeting in fifteen minutes. After refreshing her red lips, she raised the small mirror to check her roots. She could use a touch-up, she thought.

"You're going along with this?"

"I don't know what to do. I've worked hard to build my practice and surround myself with the right people. I'm really picky about my team. That said, I admit there will be a lot more money in it for me. Maybe twice as much. They're bringing us up to match the Nashville salaries."

"Well, that helps, right?"

"Yeah, but money's not what I need right now," she said. "I need a life."

"I'm sorry, sweetie."

"I can't describe how lonely I am. I work all day, come home to an empty house, eat cereal or popcorn for supper, go to bed, and get up and do it all over again. It's more than five years since Robert died, and even longer for my parents. You're the closest thing I have to family, and we live three hours apart."

"I want to help," Cam said. "I really do."

"And now, with this merger, I don't know what's next. I've lived for work for so long, and now that rug's getting jerked out from under me. I'm not sure where I belong," Margaret said.

"One thing's for sure, that we're going to show you a big time this weekend. Whatever's bugging you is going to ease up with some good music and a little dancing."

"Can we go to that hot chicken joint? The kind served in a paper bag?"

"Definitely. Hot chicken always improves your outlook," Cam said. "And guess who else will be in Nashville this weekend?"

"Elvis?"

"That's Memphis, dear. Besides, I think he left the building awhile back," Cam said. "Remember Neville? He'll be in town, too."

"Of course I remember Neville. I would've never made it to the rehearsal without him. Or the reception either," Margaret said. She didn't mention that she had thought about Neville several times since the wedding. She remembered how he had provided not only rides but a timely rescue from an unfortunate conversation and a walk to help her sober up from too much champagne at the reception. She remembered the way he reflected the glowing sky and water at Silver Cliff when he talked about growing up on the river and the lake. And she remembered the feel of his hand on her back as they returned to the wedding reception, a small but memorable gesture. Indeed, she remembered Neville.

"He's coming to Nashville this weekend. We can all hang out together," Cam said.

"What's Neville's deal?"

"What do you mean?"

"I don't know. He seems private. Maybe distant. I didn't get many details about him," Margaret said.

"He's not weird, if that's what you're getting at," Cam said.

"I didn't mean it that way. I guess I wonder why he's single."

"Trust me, he's a great guy, way better than the string of losers I've reeled in over the years, at least until I woke up and saw Owen for what he is," she said. "But, just between us, if I didn't love Neville like a brother, I would've landed him years ago."

The retreat was set to begin Friday afternoon with a partnership meeting in the glitzy Music Row offices. The joint transition committee advised the Louisville partners to bring their cowboy boots and hats for the weekend get-together, a clear sign that they were all on the same team.

"I don't wear cowboy boots," Margaret had told John Watkins, her closest friend in the Louisville office. Their long relationship went back to their first days at the law firm. They had taken the bar exam the same summer, awaited the results together, made partner the same year, and otherwise marched in lockstep within the firm. At least until the vote. John had supported the merger.

"Are the heels not high enough for you?" John said. Margaret was known for her four-inch heels at the office.

"Don't tell me you have a pair," she said.

"I've never worn western boots before, but I do now. Pay me enough money, and I'll act like a team player," he said. She shook her head, trying to envision John wearing a cowboy hat and boots instead of his usual bowtie and navy blazer. "Come on, Margaret. You've got to admit it sounds like a fun weekend."

John planned to join the rest of the Louisville lawyers riding in the luxury vans hired for the Nashville weekend. Each Mercedes came with a driver, leather captain's chairs, flat-screen televisions with multiple ESPN channels, and fully stocked bars.

"I feel like I'm leaving on a college road trip," John said with a wide smile.

"No, thanks," she said. "I'll drive my own car."

"You know, you've become a stick-in-the-mud," John said.

"I have no interest in being the only woman in the locker room," she said as she stepped inside her office and closed the door. She felt her cheeks grow hot. She was still ticked off at her partners, but she was most disappointed with John.

The conference room had been rearranged for the partnership meeting, its heavy walnut table moved from the center of the room to one end to reorient the large space. From this head table the firm's new executive committee—three lawyers from Louisville, four from Nashville—faced five rows of their partners, each row ten across. Large flowcharts were hung around the room to show the modified organizational structure.

Margaret sat in the front row, thinking about how the Louisville office was outnumbered and outvoted in every decision by the executive committee. As she listened to the merger details, she learned that the newly configured firm would not be able to represent several long-term Louisville clients who presented direct conflicts with Blevins's own roster. Some of her biggest clients would be cut loose to find new representation. Her worries about the potential downside for Louisville had materialized more quickly than even she had predicted.

With a loud sigh, she turned to John in the seat beside her. "I tried to warn you," Margaret said under her breath. He squirmed uncomfortably. On Margaret's other side, a young woman partner from the Nashville office refused to make eye contact and looked down at the blank legal pad she held on her lap. At the end of the meeting, the group stood around for a few minutes, shook hands, and congratulated themselves on how smart they were.

The vans waited at the curb to whisk the partners to a party at the Country Music Hall of Fame and Museum, where they would be joined by the associates and staff to celebrate their future together. Margaret stepped aboard one of the buses and sat down beside John.

"Well, are you still happy?" she said.

"Please, not now, Margaret. I don't want to go there," John said.

"My friend, it appears you've got your boots on but your head's in the sand," she said.

"Just stop. It's done. It's going to be fine," he said.

"Whatever you say, John, but always remember I told you so." They were silent for the rest of the ride to the museum.

A throng of people stood around the lobby as drinks and food were passed by waiters in white shirts, black jeans, and boots. Someone started to applaud as the partners passed through the revolving doors. Blevins made his way to the middle of the large expanse, accompanied by Stewart Helm, the former managing partner in Louisville. He would still head the Kentucky office, but he'd answer to Blevins. Blevins took a microphone from its stand.

"Welcome to Nashville, everyone. We're here to celebrate an exciting and important day in all of our lives: the birth of Boyd, Hoffman & Marshall." The crowd cheered. Blevins smiled and passed the mic to Stewart.

"We are thrilled to have the opportunity to join you here in Nashville and get to know you. We're like one big happy family," Stewart said. Margaret shook her head.

Blevins grabbed the microphone for the last word. "Now let's have some fun," he shouted. On cue a band on the stage started playing country music that Margaret didn't recognize. She rolled her eyes and turned to the bar.

"I'd like a bourbon on the rocks. Small batch or, if you have one, single barrel," she said to the bartender.

"We don't have bourbon, but we've got plenty of Tennessee whiskey, ma'am," the man said, his enormous Adam's apple bulging over his too-tight collar.

"They're not the same. Are you sure you don't have any bourbon? It doesn't have to be top shelf."

"I'm certain of it. Mr. Blevins was particular that the whiskey served tonight be Tennessee whiskey," he said.

"Well, then, I'll take that as irrefutable proof of Mr. Blevins's bad judgment," she said. "Give me a vodka martini."

The bartender raised an eyebrow and said, "Coming right up, ma'am." His overblown southern hospitality routine irked her, but he produced an excellent martini.

Drink in hand, she headed toward John, but he made a bee-line for the men's room. She found two Louisville associates standing nearby. Both Madison Wyatt and Todd Sawyer worked almost exclusively for her, which meant she had a big say on when or if they became partners.

"Well, what do you think?" she said as she approached.

"More money, bigger firm in a growing market. What's not to like?" Todd said. He and Madison raised their glasses in a cheer. Margaret declined.

"I hope you're right. Usually if something sounds too good to be true, you can bet it is," she said. She tipped up the martini and drained it, then fished out the olive and popped it in her mouth. Madison and Todd watched and didn't say anything.

"I need another drink. Excuse me," Margaret said, and headed back to the bar, where she found herself in line behind Marc Blevins. He turned around and saw her. He had changed out of the blue plaid sports jacket he had worn for the partnership meeting into a black shirt and a sterling silver bolo tie that accentuated his graying temples.

"Well, hello. Good to see you, Margaret." He extended his hand. She didn't take it.

"You don't have to pretend," she said. "I suspect you wish I were anywhere but here."

"That's where you're wrong, Margaret. Let's let bygones be bygones."

"Uh, no, let's not. You probably know I was the only vote against the merger, and I remain unconvinced that it's in my professional best interest to answer to the likes of you," she said.

"It's a fair deal to everyone involved, especially you Louisville folks salivating for the salary bump," Blevins said. "It's a great way to build loyalty—give people enough of a raise, and they'll follow you anywhere."

God, he has a punchable face, she thought. "Don't be so cocky," she said. "I'll maintain and follow my own rules in my practice, not yours, and if I ever suspect you of anything that reflects poorly on the firm, I won't hesitate to file a bar complaint against you this time."

His smile faded. "You'll follow the firm's rules or you'll be out."

"Good riddance, I'd say." She turned away and walked toward the women's restroom, her heart racing from the encounter. She wanted to leave, but she had ridden in the vans with everyone else. She stopped outside the bathroom door and got out her phone. She typed a text to Cam.

Come get me? at Cntry Music Museum need excuse to leave

There was no response. She typed again.

Cam where r u?

She waited. "Damn it," she muttered. Then the phone chimed. It was Cam.

Just sat down to eat. Grab cab meet us Riverbirch 218 West End.

K. going out later?

Yes! R u ready to dance?

Ready to strangle someone

Yikes. U need food & drink ☺ C'mon

Heading to hotel to change. Keep me posted where to meet u

My house just around corner. U can borrow jeans & boots. C'mon

Relieved to have an exit plan, Margaret headed into the restroom. As she stepped inside, still concealed by a tiled privacy wall shielding the stalls, she heard the voices of two young women. She stopped in her tracks when she heard her name.

"Is Margaret always such a bitch? How can you stand to work for her?"

"It's not easy, that's for sure. She's a really good lawyer, but she's a mess." Margaret recognized Madison's voice. "I feel sorry for her. She has no life, and she seems angry if anyone else does."

"That's what I heard. Her husband died or something?"

"Yes, but it's been like years ago."

"She looks surprisingly good for her age. I'm surprised she's still single."

"Really, it's pretty simple. No one can stand to be around her."

Margaret was staggered. Madison with her saccharine sweetness had landed so many blows that Margaret felt punch drunk. Then she heard running water and the automatic paper dispenser rolling out fresh sheets. She ducked out of the restroom and rushed to the front doors, where she hailed a cab. She told the driver to take her back to the Hermitage.

On the short ride to the hotel, she sat silent as she watched Union Station and other landmarks flash past. She paid the four-dollar fare with a twenty and walked away before the driver could make change. Feeling dazed, she walked through the sparkling lobby with its crystal chandeliers and marble floors swirling and made her way to the elevators. Once she got to her room on the twentieth floor, she kicked off her heels, broke the seal on the honor bar, and grabbed two small bottles of bourbon. "At least somebody has bourbon in this damn town," she muttered as she sat down on the gold loveseat.

She heard a text chime in her handbag. With her drink in hand, she went to retrieve her phone and a pair of reading glasses.

R u coming? Almost done, ready to dance!

Margaret sighed so deeply her chest heaved. She wasn't in the mood for anyone, even Cam. All she wanted was to finish her drink and climb into bed. She had to face her partners again tomorrow for a half-day section meeting where Blevins would lecture on how to run a litigation section. Give me a break, she thought to herself.

Back at hotel. Too tired. Lets catch up tomorrow.

Oh no you don't. No pooping out. Neville needs a dance partner.

She had forgotten about Neville being in Nashville. She had wanted to see him, but now, in a foul mood, she didn't have the energy to talk and dance. Another text chimed.

Coming by your hotel to get you. 15 mins. Be ready

U won't take no for an answer, will u?

Nope

I'm warning u, I won't have fun

We'll see about that

Margaret headed to the bathroom to freshen her makeup and brush her teeth and hair. She changed into a pair of lean, tight jeans, a red silk shirt, and high-heeled boots. As she looked into the mirror and applied bright red lipstick, she heard her mom's voice:

Be tough. Sometimes just showing up is half the battle. Her mother's admonitions had never been easy to hear, or to live up to, but maybe she was right. Tonight Margaret would show up, even though she wanted to hunker down in the hotel by herself. Besides, Cam wouldn't let her skip out.

When Margaret stepped off the elevator, she saw Cam coming in the front door, looking carefree and contented like a newlywed should. Margaret remembered the feeling, then stifled the spark of envy that accompanied it.

"You look pretty wonderful for being too tired to go out," Cam said as they hugged. "Come on, Owen and Neville are out front. We can walk from here."

When they stepped outside, Margaret shivered in the cool night air. She thought about going back for a jacket, but then she saw Owen and Neville waiting near the Hermitage entry.

"Hey, Margaret," Owen yelled. "Get over here and give me a hug."

Sweet Owen, she thought. He was such a likeable person it was hard to feel downcast in his presence. He held his big arms open wide and they curled around her when she approached. She felt warmer in his embrace.

"You remember my best man, don't you?" he said as he released her. Margaret turned to face Neville, who stood close enough for her to smell the same spicy cologne that she remembered from the wedding weekend.

"Hey, Neville," she said. She wondered if she should offer a hug but decided against it.

"Good to see you, Margaret," he said in a calm voice with its slight western Kentucky twang. He wore faded jeans and a striped shirt, perhaps the same ones he had worn the night of the rehearsal dinner.

"I've had a long day, but I'm trying to get my second wind," she said.

"You definitely need a second wind, and maybe a third," Cam said. "We're going honky-tonking, baby." She slipped her hand into Owen's and they started down the sidewalk. Margaret and Neville fell in behind them.

"Cam said your law firm is meeting down here this weekend," he said.

"Yes, we're merging with a Nashville firm, so it seems like our world just tipped in this direction," she said.

"Is it a good thing?"

"I think it's a mistake, but I seem to be the only one."

"Being a holdout doesn't make you wrong," Neville said.

"Thank you. That's the most supportive comment I've heard in months," she said. She turned her head to look in his direction. He always looked relaxed, like he wasn't in a rush. She was accustomed to people who looked like they were counting off time in tenths of an hour.

"If that's the most support you've had in a while, you need better friends," he said.

She laughed. "You may be right."

As they crossed Broadway, Margaret noticed that the sidewalks were crowded with people wearing the same type of western hat, still clean and stark white. Tourists, she guessed. Long lines formed beneath the bright signs at Tootsie's Orchid Lounge, Layla's, and Robert's Western World. A young woman in a bright blue fringed dress and brown western boots leaned over the curb to vomit, her male companion holding her hair out of the way. Margaret held her breath as they walked past.

"You get to Nashville often?" she said.

"Every few weeks, it seems. From my house, it's only a two-hour drive, and there's more going on here than in Murray," he

166

said. "And I get to see Cam and Owen, who have renamed their guest room in my honor."

With so many trips to Nashville, he must have a girlfriend here, she thought. As if he read her mind, he added, "And, my sister lives not far away. She owns an antique shop in Franklin."

Margaret nodded. "I suppose I'll be down here more often, too, now that my firm is officially based here," she said.

"You should let me know when you're heading this way," he said.

Just then they noticed Owen was at the front of the line, waving them in.

"How'd he do that?" Margaret said as they walked past a line of twenty people or more waiting to get in.

"He knows everybody in town, especially the ones who run bars. You never stand in line when you're honky-tonking with Owen Moss," Neville said.

The walls of the bar were lined with autographed posters and instruments hung high. The music was loud and the dance floor packed. Margaret felt the energy from the crowd.

"This looks fun," she said. Neville bent closer, his ear toward her face. "What?" She repeated into his ear. He nodded and asked her if she wanted a drink. He and Owen headed to the bar. Cam squeezed in closer.

"So you've had a bad day?"

"Yeah. Not great," Margaret said. She didn't mention the conversation she had overheard in the bathroom. The words hurt too much to repeat.

"What are you going to do?"

"I don't know. I'd rather not talk about it," Margaret said. "The law firm has already ruined most of the day, but I'm not letting it spoil the night too."

"That's my girl," Cam said.

"Do they serve food here? I'm starving," Margaret said.

"They're famous for grilled boloney sandwiches and fries."

Margaret grimaced. "That's all they serve? I've never been a fan of bologna."

"Trust me, you've never tasted boloney like this. And by the way, it may be bologna in Louisville, but it's boloney here. I'll order so you don't embarrass yourself." Cam walked toward the food window. Margaret claimed a couple of open stools about the time Neville and Owen returned with four beers in frosted mugs. Cam came back with two orders of sandwiches and fries in small red-and-white-checked baskets.

"Margaret hasn't eaten yet, and we all know she can't hold her liquor on an empty stomach," Cam said.

Owen laughed and grabbed a few fries.

"Sad but true. I need to eat, even if it's boloney," Margaret said. "Did I say that right?" She reached for a sandwich triangle, heavily buttered and griddled until golden brown, and took a bite. "This is really tasty. Have you tried them, Neville?"

"Many times," he said. "I've eaten boloney sandwiches all of my life, but these are outstanding."

As she finished a sandwich, the band started a set of covers from Hank Williams and Patsy Cline to Loretta Lynn and Johnny Cash. Even Margaret recognized the songs. Cam and Owen headed to the dance floor.

"Do you want to dance?" Neville asked.

"That's why we're here, isn't it?"

The four danced to every type of country music—the rowdy songs and the crying ones—and drank until closing time at three, stopping only for bathroom breaks and more beer. They danced as couples and sometimes together in a circle. The last song of the night was a slow one, and Margaret pulled Neville close. His body felt warm and snug where they touched, one hand resting on her lower back, the other holding her hand while the singer belted out a Hank Williams standard. Neville sang along, repeating lines filled with heartbreak and longing, the high lonesome sound landing close to her ear. Margaret didn't know the song, but she recognized the feeling.

When they reached her hotel, Cam asked if Margaret just wanted to come home with them.

"I better not. I've got a meeting at nine," she said. "I need to get some sleep. I'm not used to staying out this late."

"What are you doing after your meeting?" Neville said.

A bit surprised, Margaret said, "I've got an appointment at the spa, but then I'm free until I head back to Louisville. What do you have in mind?"

Cam spoke up. "We're heading to the lake tomorrow afternoon for Daddy's birthday. The other day Mom said she wasn't feeling well, so I offered to bring a cake and fix supper. Come with us."

"Sounds good to me," Neville said, looking at Margaret. His eyes looked a little glassy. Cam and Owen also looked disheveled.

"Are you okay to drive?" Margaret said.

"Not really," Neville said. "Let's get a cab. I'll get my car tomorrow."

Cam and Owen turned to Margaret to hug her. Cam kissed her cheek and said, "Love you. See you tomorrow."

Neville stepped close, and his arms encircled her as if the dance music still played in his head. "I hope you had as much fun as I did," he said in a low voice, directly into her ear. His lips brushed hers, the contact so soft and brief, she wondered if he had intended to kiss her or if he had lost his balance for a moment and stumbled into her.

"Come on, Neville. Here's a cab," Owen called out. Neville pulled back and looked at her, smiling, then turned to leave. Margaret watched him walk toward the taxi.

"I did," she yelled. Neville spun around and cupped his hand to his ear as if he hadn't heard over the traffic. "I had fun," she said, more loudly. He gave her a thumbs-up sign and climbed in the back of the waiting car.

"I had fun," Margaret declared as the cab drove away, repeating it to herself as though she could hardly believe it. On her way up to her room, she saw herself in the mirror that covered the elevator's back wall. Her hair was a mess, her face flushed, and her lipstick worn off from eating boloney sandwiches and drinking beer. Her lips spread into a slight smile before the bell dinged to announce the twentieth floor. "I had fun," she repeated. Once inside her room, she climbed into bed, unwrapped the thin chocolate that had been left on the pillow, and let it melt in her mouth as she fell asleep.

ACROSS THE CREEK

Emmie checked the small army-green rucksack to make sure she hadn't forgotten anything. Apples. Three packs of saltines from the diner. Small mason jar of water. A Nancy Drew mystery. Some matches, a flashlight, and a towel, rolled up to fit. Everything they needed, everything she promised. Sonya Kay would be waiting where the paths crossed.

Last year, after they turned nine, Sonya Kay and Emmie were old enough to walk the woods between their houses to meet each other. Their houses weren't that close together, but there were no others in between, just trees and two paths. One path was easy to follow because it went from Emmie's house to Sonya Kay's. They'd worn it down to bare dirt and tree roots. The other was hard to locate, like nobody had a reason to be out there. They wanted to walk that other path, but they had been too scared, afraid they'd get lost and never find their way home. They thought they were ready now. They were older, ready to discover what was over there, across the creek.

They decided to start out before lunch Saturday to give themselves the entire afternoon to explore, but they had to be back in time for supper. Emmie, still as towheaded as a toddler, put on old jeans and last year's sneakers in case the path was muddy from all the rain. Her mother said it rained a lot in April to make flowers in May.

"Where you heading, honey?" Mama asked as Emmie walked toward the kitchen door. "Have you had anything to eat?"

"I had some cereal real early," Emmie said. "I'm meeting Sonya Kay. We're going for a walk and have a picnic." She didn't mention which route they were taking, afraid Mama might not let her go.

Instead, her mother smiled. "It's a pretty day for that. I wish I could go with you, but Sparky's not feeling well. I better stay with him." Emmie's little brother was sick a lot. He was treated like a baby most of the time, even though he was seven.

"His name sounds like a dog's," Sonya Kay once said, and Emmie had laughed. His real name was William Sparks Baldwin, but nobody called him that. Emmie knew that Mama worried about him. When he felt bad, Mama didn't have much time for anything but Sparky, but that was okay. Sometimes Emmie was glad he was sickly because she didn't want him tagging along. She and Sonya Kay didn't want to be bothered with little kids.

For a moment Emmie wanted to tell Mama where they were heading. Truth be told, she was half scared of their plan. She'd heard sounds coming from deep in the woods—clanging, banging sounds, like hammers hitting metal. And maybe people talking, but she couldn't tell for sure. The sounds were muffled and distant. Maybe dogs barking or maybe just the wind. She decided not to say anything. Sonya Kay would be mad if they weren't allowed to go.

Emmie picked her steps carefully across the muddy ground as she passed the chicken house and the trough near the barn. Where the mowed grass ended at their property line, the path continued through dark woods where large cedars and oaks blocked the sky. The path was drier along this stretch, and big gray rocks rose out of the ground in triangles and other pointy shapes. Some boulders were so mossy they looked as if someone had thrown a big green rug over them like the carpet on the front steps of Granny's porch. Daddy said that piece of rug had come from a putt-putt golf course that was being torn down somewhere.

Emmie saw a pink dot, way down the path. Sonya Kay was already at the meeting place, waving in her direction.

"Hurry up. You're late," she said. She looked mad. Most of the time Sonya Kay was Emmie's best friend and nice to her, but she had days when she was bossy and mean and in a bad mood. On those days Emmie would stay quiet and do what her friend told her to do. Sonya Kay got better if she had some time to boss everyone around, like she got it out of her system and felt good again. Sonya Kay was mean like that if she stayed at home too long, especially in summer when they didn't go to school. Sometimes she just got up on the wrong side of the bed, Emmie guessed.

The girls became friends when Sonya Kay's family moved to the old Wilson house, which had been vacant for years. Both went into Miss Thomas's fourth-grade class, and they sat together on the long school bus ride into town. Sonya Kay said their old house was torn down when the lake was built.

"Daddy said it's under fifteen feet of water now," she said. "He says there are fish swimming through my old room."

Sonya Kay said her father was the warden at the state prison, an old rock building that looked like a castle. He wore a gun on his belt every day, and his face always looked mad. Emmie's own daddy owned a garage and worked on cars. He could fix nearly anything, and he never wore a gun, though sometimes he got one from the closet to shoot coyotes or snakes around the chicken house. Emmie's mother stayed home to take care of their kids, mostly Sparky. Sonya Kay had two older brothers, and her mama wasn't around much anymore. Sonya Kay said she was gone but wouldn't say where.

"Did you bring everything?" she asked.

"Got it all," Emmie said, pointing to the bag slung over her shoulder. On the bus ride from school Friday, they had planned their adventure. Sonya Kay said she couldn't bring anything, and Emmie had offered to pack food for them both.

The meeting place was where their regular path made a giant T with the new trail, which led away from everything they knew. When they started, they were still in the woods. It looked familiar, like their path, with the same kind of trees and flowers. Emmie picked some bluebells near the path and put them behind her ear.

"Do you want some?" she asked Sonya Kay.

"No," she said.

Sonya Kay must be thinking about whatever made her so mad, Emmie thought. They kept walking.

A little farther, the woods gave way to a big field of grasses and flowers about as high as their heads. It was warmer without trees blocking the sun, by then high in the sky. They looked closely through the tall grass for the faint path with little flowers like red star and phlox growing along it, soaking up the hot sun.

"Can we stop yet?" Emmie asked. "I need a drink."

"No, not yet. We have to keep moving."

Emmie decided not to argue with her. They kept walking. The meadow was filled with small light blue butterflies, the ones that come in springtime. Mama always said it was warm enough to go barefoot when they saw the blue kind.

The path continued to a small creek lined with white-barked sycamore trees, its bed filled with water and smooth rust-red rocks. The trail was visible on the other side.

"We'll have to cross here," Sonya Kay said.

The water looked too wide to jump and deeper than their ankles. Emmie bent over and tested it with her fingers.

"It's ice cold. We can't walk through it."

"We have to make stepping-stones," Sonya Kay said. They looked for rocks, as big as they could carry, to make a bridge across the creek. They hauled rocks and launched them into position like steps to the other side.

"Ready?" Sonya Kay asked.

"I'm hungry. Can we stop here and eat?"

"Okay, if you really need to. You're slowing us down, but I guess we can stop for a while."

Emmie found a flat, dry spot in the creek bed to put down the rucksack. She took out the towel, unrolled it, and spread it out for their picnic. Sonya Kay plopped down and asked what they had to eat.

"We each have an apple and a package of saltines," Emmie said.

"Is that all?"

"That's all I could fit in with everything else. You said you weren't even hungry."

"I thought you'd bring something good like sandwiches or fried chicken," Sonya Kay said. Emmie overlooked the comment.

They sat in the sun and ate their rations. They shared the water, and Emmie noticed that the rim of the jar had a soured smell like it once held pickles or kraut. She saved the third package of crackers in case they got lost, even though it had been smashed in the bottom of the bag. She wanted to read some Nancy Drew, but Sonya Kay said it was time to move on. They packed up everything and crossed the creek. On one mossy rock, Emmie slipped and her foot slid into the chilly water. She wanted to turn back and head home, but she didn't say anything.

The path was hard to find until it led up a bare hill of loose, red soil. With no grass growing, the ground looked like a tractor or a bulldozer had cut into it, the way Sparky pretended when he was well enough to play outside. He built roads and towns in the backyard with his trucks and machines. Emmie's white sneaker picked up dust that mixed with the creek water to make something like red slime on her shoe. They struggled and finally topped the hill.

"Look," Sonya Kay said as she pointed. Her voice sounded excited. "Look what we've found."

They stared out toward the bottom of the hill, then back at each other like they needed to know the other one saw it, too, to confirm they weren't seeing a mirage. They saw a little town of new houses like a bigger version of Sparky's play cities, but these houses were big enough for people to live in. Real houses, not pretend.

"Let's go down there," Sonya Kay said.

"Where are we? I don't think we're supposed to be here," Emmie said.

"C'mon, big baby. There's nothing to be afraid of." Sometimes Sonya Kay sounded like her mean brothers, the ones who used to fight in the back of the school bus. They weren't allowed to ride the bus anymore. They got kicked off, and the warden had to take them to school each morning on his way to the prison. Mama said they might have to go to reformatory school if they didn't straighten up soon.

Emmie hesitated. She wanted to turn around and run home. She didn't know where she was. Daddy and Mama had never mentioned that another town was so close. She wondered if they knew it existed.

Sonya Kay scowled. "We came all this way to explore and discover something, and now we have. Don't tell me you're going to chicken out now that we're here," she said.

The town was quiet and empty. It didn't look right. Emmie didn't see any people or cars along the bright black streets. She'd have to go, though. Sonya Kay didn't take no for an answer when she made up her mind.

"All right, but we can't stay long. And we must stay together," she said. At church camp she had learned about the buddy system, the rule for swimming in the camp lake. She wanted to follow the rule in this strange place.

"Come on, I'll beat you there," Sonya Kay said, taking off down the steep red clay hill. Emmie followed her footprints down. Sonya Kay always liked to be first, and Emmie didn't mind if she won.

They reached a glistening deep black road that smelled like the tar used on the school roof in second grade. A few streaks of red mud from the scalped hill oozed onto the pavement like blood seeping from a scraped knee. Emmie turned to read a big wooden sign—ROAD CLOSED—planted in the mud and painted bright school-bus yellow. As they walked into the town, Emmie reached for Sonya Kay's hand as she thought about the buddy system. She wanted to like the pretty new houses because she could tell Sonya Kay did.

The houses were close to each other, much closer than Sonya Kay's house to hers. Some looked ready for people to move in, while others were missing a roof or had holes where doors and windows might fit. Boards stood like matchsticks to show the outline of what might become another house. The girls walked past stacks of wood that smelled like the lumberyard where Emmie sometimes went with her dad.

"Let's look inside." Sonya Kay pointed to one that had green shutters. "This one."

She shook free of Emmie and ran toward the nearly finished house. Its yard was cleared of bricks and wood, but there was no grass. Boards lined up to make a bridge for crossing the mud, like the rock one they had built at the creek. The windows and the front door were closed.

"We can't. We don't know who lives here," Emmie said.

"Nobody lives here," Sonya Kay said. "It's empty, so it won't hurt if we go in and look around. Plus, there's nobody to see us."

She walked up on the front porch and looked in the windows.

"See, I told you it's empty. There's no furniture," Sonya Kay said. "I'm telling you, nobody knows about this place. We're the first ones to find it." She reached for the doorknob, opened the door, and headed inside. Emmie didn't want to lose sight of her, so she went up the steps and into the house. Sonya Kay was walking through the rooms.

"Here's the living room, and there's the dining room and the kitchen," she said.

"How do you know? There's no furniture or stoves or refrigerator to tell which is which," Emmie said.

"I figured it out," she said as she opened a door under the stairs. "And here's the cutest little bathroom. Look, it's got a pink toilet!" Emmie stuck her head into the room to see it. She wished she had a pink toilet and sink.

"I wish I lived here," Sonya Kay said.

"Why? You'd live too far from me." Emmie couldn't imagine her family living anywhere but home.

"We could still see each other," Sonya Kay said. "We could walk to the creek and meet each other there."

"Maybe your parents will buy one of these new houses," Emmie said, hoping that it couldn't be true, even as she said the words. She wanted Sonya Kay to always be at the other end of their path.

"Nah, they won't. They don't have enough money for something like this. Besides, I don't think my mama's coming back. She's been gone three weeks now," she said.

"Where's she gone?"

"Daddy says she's shacked up with some old man over in Livingston County. He says he's going to get a divorce and she'll not ever get to come back home," Sonya Kay said.

"Your mama's not coming back?"

"No, she's not. She might as well stay over there in Livingston County. We all hate her anyway."

Emmie felt sadness rise up in her. Why would their mama leave and not take them with her? She felt sorry for Sonya Kay and even her mean old brothers. But then she thought about Sonya Kay's daddy who acted mad all the time and wore that gun. Sonya Kay had said he sometimes got real mean and whipped them all with a belt, sometimes with his fists, even if they hadn't done anything wrong. When Emmie played at their house, she had noticed him staring at her like he'd like to whip her too.

Not long ago, Emmie walked the path to Sonya Kay's house and saw her friend running toward her, running away from home. Her face looked flushed, and on her cheek there was a mark in a deeper red the size and shape of a grown-up's handprint.

"Let's go to the meeting place. I don't want to be around here," she said, out of breath from running. Emmie heard crashes from inside the house. A man's voice sounded loud and angry; a woman's was crying. "Stop, you sonofabitch," the woman had screamed. Sonya Kay grabbed her hand and they ran. When they reached the middle ground between their houses, they sat down so Sonya Kay could catch her breath.

"He got mad at breakfast," she explained, "because my mama fixed oatmeal. He doesn't like oatmeal. He grabbed her by the hair and punched her right in the face. I tried to stop him," she said, touching her own face. "That's when I ran out."

"We need to tell on him. My parents will know what to do," Emmie said.

"Don't you dare. He'll kill us for sure," Sonya Kay said. She made Emmie promise she wouldn't tell.

Most of the time Sonya Kay said nothing about her parents, even when she had blue spots on her arms. Emmie wondered if her friend wanted to run away and live like she didn't even know them. Any of them. Maybe that was why she said she'd like to live in one of the empty houses in a town that no one knew about. They wouldn't be able to find her.

They walked inside two or three more houses, running up staircases, some without handrails or anything to hold on to. Emmie couldn't look down or she got dizzy. She started to like the new houses and imagined living here and what it would be like if they lived together. They could be sisters, since she didn't have one and Sonya Kay didn't either. Maybe then Sonya Kay would be happy. They had come across a town that somebody built, just waiting to be found.

"I want this bedroom," she said. It had a big window that looked out to the street and the fresh concrete sidewalk.

"Okay, that one's yours," Sonya Kay said. "I want the room across the hall."

"What color is your room?"

"Pink, like my coat."

Emmie felt a rush of disappointment, because pink was her favorite color and Sonya Kay knew that, but Emmie didn't want it to ruin their life together as sisters. She'd let Sonya Kay have pink. They were just pretending anyway. "All right. I'll take blue," she said. Sonya Kay smiled.

In the late afternoon light, the house grew shadowy fast. Emmie realized it must be getting late. "We need to go. We have to get home before dark," she said.

"I wish I could stay," Sonya Kay said, looking around the town. "Well, come on, let's go," she said. Her face looked mad again as she started walking toward the red hill.

They didn't talk as they walked back. They crossed the creek and the field, and then found their way through the darkening woods. When they reached their meeting place, they said goodbye and ran on, Emmie to the left and Sonya Kay to the right. Emmie could barely see her way home, and she ran as fast as she could when she saw its lights. Mama looked happy to see her as she came in the back door, and the house smelled like meatloaf and mashed potatoes. Emmie looked out the window and didn't see any lights on at Sonya Kay's house. She wondered what they were having for supper that night.

After church on Sunday, Emmie's family went to Granny's for dinner and didn't get back until suppertime. Sonya Kay got on the bus Monday morning once again looking mad. She had on the same dress she had worn to school Friday. A tiny dot of ketchup on the collar reminded Emmie of the fish sticks and tater tots they had in the cafeteria Friday, and in her mind she saw a replay of Sonya Kay eating her lunch and dribbling that little spot of ketchup. Emmie could tell that her friend wasn't feeling right, so she said nothing. Maybe Sonya Kay would get over it when they got to school.

"When are we going back across the creek?" Sonya Kay said.

"Maybe Saturday? It takes too long to get there, and we'd never make it back before dark if we leave after school," Emmie said.

"Saturday's so far off. I love that place."

"How come? There's nobody there."

"Exactly. There's nobody yelling and fighting. I'm tired of hearing it," Sonya Kay said.

"Has your mama come home yet?"

She shook her head. "I don't think she's coming back. He said he'd kill her if she ever stepped foot on his property again."

The thought of her daddy killing her mama made Emmie's stomach hurt. Sonya Kay's daddy had a gun, and he was probably a good shot. He might have already shot some of those convicts at the pen because they're bad people. Sonya Kay's mama wasn't bad, though.

"We have to wait for Saturday," Emmie said.

Sonya Kay gave her a mean look like she didn't want to hear it. She didn't mention crossing the creek again the next day, but then on Wednesday she got on the bus smiling. She said she had gone to the town again after school, all by herself.

"Why did you do that?" Emmie said. "We're supposed to use the buddy system."

"Well, buddy, I needed to go and you wouldn't, so I went by myself," Sonya Kay said. "He was asleep when I got home from school. I don't know why, maybe he was sick. The boys were fighting over the television, so I slipped back out and headed on over to New Town. That's what I named it."

Emmie liked the name Sonya Kay had picked but thought she shouldn't have gone alone or been in the woods after dark by herself. Emmie wondered if she should tell Mama about New Town and what was going on at Sonya Kay's house, but she had promised not to tell. She couldn't break her promise.

"He didn't even know I was gone. He didn't wake up until sometime this morning. He was frying eggs and bacon before he went to work," she said. Her trip to New Town made her happy, so Emmie tried to feel happy too.

On Thursday morning the bus driver stopped in front of Sonya Kay's house, honked the horn, and waited a long time, but she never got on. Emmie saw the warden come out on the front porch, looking like he just got out of bed and motioning for the bus to go on. She must've gotten sick, too, Emmie thought. She won't like spending the day at home with her daddy even if she's bad sick.

Sonya Kay didn't come to school the next day either. Emmie noticed Miss Thomas cleaning out her desk.

"Where's Sonya Kay?" she asked.

"She's moving to a new school. She and her mother are moving to be with her mama's people down in Fulton," Miss Thomas said, her voice like the silk ribbon on a blanket. Emmie had never heard Miss Thomas raise her voice, not once, even when the boys acted up and shot spit wads into the girls' hair. "Seems they've had some family trouble lately, and her daddy says that Sonya Kay needs to be with her mother. We're going to miss her, aren't we?"

Emmie nodded and felt her throat tighten. She had thought Sonya Kay—her best friend, her buddy—would always be just down the path. She would feel lost without her.

After school she walked to the meeting place and sat down, hoping there had been a mistake and Sonya Kay wasn't really gone. She sat for a few minutes, watching the house. It looked empty and lonely, too, without her. If she was with her mother, they couldn't ever come back. She'd get shot if she came back.

The woods were almost dark, so Emmie started for home. Maybe she's really gone, she thought. Before she reached the edge of her yard where the trees opened to reveal the lingering light, she heard sounds on the path, the one that led across the creek. Maybe Sonya Kay was coming to find her, returning from her New Town. Perhaps Miss Thomas misunderstood the message about Sonya Kay and her mama leaving here.

But Emmie knew this couldn't be Sonya Kay, who moved along as quiet as a deer. Whoever was coming along the path from New Town was making a lot of noise. Emmie hid behind one of the large mossy boulders and peeped around its edge. She saw Sonya Kay's daddy, his warden's uniform splotched with red mud, the hem of his pants wet, the gun on his belt. He reached the T in the path and turned right toward his house, and Emmie watched him until he was just a shadow moving. She heard the screen door slam, then got up and ran for home. She didn't tell anybody what she had seen, just like she had promised, but she never returned to New Town. He knew what was across the creek.

A few days later Emmie heard a commotion in the direction of Sonya Kay's house. Like before, she hid and watched. Sonya Kay's father and her two mean brothers loaded a truck and trailer with everything from inside. They hauled out the drab velour couch and the kitchen table, the beds and mattresses, even Sonya Kay's little white dresser with its tilting mirror in the middle section. When one of the brothers let down his end too early and a piece of furniture hit the ground, the warden cursed and smacked the boy hard on the ear. Emmie was glad they were leaving. She hoped she never saw them again. Maybe a new family would move in. Maybe they'd have a girl her same age.

For some time Emmie stayed close to home, so lonesome that she even played trucks and cars with Sparky in his little dirt towns. She came in to get a drink of water and heard her mother talking on the telephone. Mama's voice was low, but Emmie heard her mention the warden and decided to listen. Without making a sound, she crouched in the hall near the kitchen door, unnoticed, with a good view of her mother standing at the sink. Mama looked out the window as she spoke to the person on the other end of the line, the long phone cord stretched way out behind her.

"That's right. His wife and the little girl are missing. They never showed up in Fulton, don't you know," Mama said. "I think her people are from there." She paused to listen.

"They say the mother's not shown up for work in some time, and now that little girl's gone, too." She paused again. "Lord, bless their hearts." As Mama was saying that she appreciated the call and telling the other person goodbye, she turned around and saw Emmie. Their eyes met, and Mama gave her a hard look. She took a few steps and hung up the phone.

"How long have you been there?" she said. Emmie didn't answer. "I asked you a question, sis."

184

Surprised by Mama's displeased tone, Emmie jumped up and ran out the front door. "You come back in this house right now," Mama called after her. Emmie ran toward the edge of the woods, where she scrambled into another hideaway behind the trunk of a large winged elm tree. "Emmie!" her mother kept calling in the distance, but she didn't answer. She was thinking about her missing friend. She wondered if Sonya Kay's mama had taken off with that old man from Livingston County and made Sonya Kay go with them. Or maybe Sonya Kay finally ran away from all of them, like Emmie had thought she would. Maybe she had gone to New Town where no one could find her, and she was living in one of those pretty houses, all by herself.

SIGNS

Rose Wetherford watched her selections ride the checkout belt toward the Wonder Market cash register. A box of soda crackers. Six cans of white beans. A pink kitchen sponge. Frozen cheese pizza and a plastic bucket of vanilla ice cream. Hand lotion in a bottle decorated with oranges. She believed she had everything she needed for supper. She hadn't brought a list.

"That'll be $23.76," the young clerk said without looking up. Rose continued watching the items head to the bagging area, studying the back of the red pizza box that pictured an oven door, its dial set to 425 degrees, and a photo of a golden-brown baked pizza. Her stomach rumbled. She glanced at her wristwatch, which said it was already four-thirty, but Rose doubted it could be so late. She hadn't eaten lunch yet. The watch must need a new battery, she guessed. It wasn't keeping time.

"Mrs. Wetherford, can I help you find something?" a man had asked as he approached her in the baking aisle. His face looked young, but his head was slick, and Rose couldn't tell if he was bald or shaved or terribly ill. The name tag on his blue shirt read *Rodney, Assistant Manager*. She thought she knew him from somewhere.

186

"No, I've got everything I need," she had replied, then pushed her cart to the checkout lanes at the front of the store. Perhaps she had taken too long to shop. Did the assistant manager think she was shoplifting? Maybe she'd start making a list.

"That's $23.76," the clerk repeated more loudly. The raised voice got Rose's attention, and she gazed into the young woman's small hazel eyes, but Rose didn't recognize the eyes or the face that contorted as the clerk pursed her lips. Her name badge said *Tammy*, but Rose didn't know anyone by that name. She looked around and saw nothing familiar. She didn't know the people in line around her or the towheaded teenage boy holding the two bags, waiting. They all seemed to be waiting.

"What did you say, honey?"

"I said $23.76," the clerk said, louder still. She raised her right hand to inspect and then bite at her nails.

Unsure of what to do next, Rose leaned against the black bumper guard that padded the metal lane. Something wasn't right, but she didn't know what. She felt like she was putting together a jigsaw puzzle, but some of the pieces were scattered or lost. Nothing fit together in that moment.

"What shall I do?" she said in a low voice to the clerk. She didn't want anyone else to hear, but she needed an answer.

"You're going to pay me for these groceries," Tammy said with a smart tone.

Rose heard the words and wanted to follow the clerk's instructions, but she seemed to be moving in slow motion. People waited on her to move, to correct her lapse, to figure it out. She stroked her handbag strap.

Something bumped into Rose from the rear, so she turned around. The woman behind her, groceries already piled on the conveyor belt waiting to be scanned, had tapped her with the edge of her cart. "Sorry," the woman said, but to Rose her face appeared impatient and unapologetic. The woman's fingers strummed the cart's blue handle. A little boy in a dinosaur shirt stood beside her, biting into a doughy sugar cookie as he stared. Rose heard a baby start to cry nearby.

"How much did you say?" Rose said as she opened her purse and found her wallet. The clerk said the amount. Rose pulled out several bills and studied them, knowing she needed to pay but unable to put together the right amount. She had already forgotten the number the clerk had said and was too embarrassed to ask again.

"Is this enough?" she said as she handed over a couple of twenty-dollar bills.

The clerk nodded, entered the amount into the register, and quickly made change. Mechanically she ripped off the paper receipt and turned to hand over the change to Rose, who had already walked away, moving toward the automatic door, the bag boy following her.

"Ma'am, you forgot your change," the clerk yelled after her, but Rose kept walking past newspaper racks and vending machines toward the parking lot. The bagger went back for the change and caught up with Rose outside, searching for her car.

"Wait, Mrs. Wetherford, here are your groceries," the boy called out. He braced the bags against his chest with one arm and with the other handed her the change and receipt. Rose stared at his face. His distinctive hair color, a blondness rarely seen after preschool, helped her remember him, and a small wave of relief swept over her.

"Why, thank you, Bradley. I didn't know you were working here," she said. She had taught his class during vacation Bible school not long ago, and she had known his mother, Emmie, since she was a towheaded little girl, a classmate of Rose's own daughter Camilla. The girls had gone to the new elementary school in Sycamore, a town built from scratch right before the Corps of Engineers finished the dam that caused the Cumberland to rise out of its banks and swallow the places Rose had known all her life. Forty years ago, the water overtook the old river town where she had lived as a newlywed and young mother. Sometimes the flooding seemed so fresh it could have happened yesterday.

"I can't seem to find my car," she said. "I don't know what's wrong with me today. Must be tired or something." She attempted to laugh it off, but inside she felt scared.

Bradley scanned the lot and spotted the silver minivan parked next to the ice machines.

"Is that it, over there?" he said as he tipped his head in the direction of the vehicle.

"I believe you're right, Bradley," she said as they walked toward the van. After she clicked to open the back cargo door, she studied his face as he put the bags inside. "You sure favor your mama when she was a little girl," Rose said.

The boy smiled and headed back inside.

Rose sat down in the driver's seat but didn't move for a while. She pulled down the visor and flipped up the cover to check herself in the mirror. She should have taken time to put on lipstick before heading to the grocery. Cam had reminded her years ago when she was just a little girl. "Mom, you look happy when you wear lipstick," little Cam had said on the way home from a Brownie Scout meeting.

Rose dug in her purse to find a tube of pink lipstick. She applied the color to her lips and fluffed her hair with her hands, then started the car. She drove out of the parking lot, wondering what she would fix for supper. Maybe she should take a nap before she started cooking.

A few miles down the road, she missed the turn that led home. She drove on, making a series of turns on a narrow winding road that felt familiar. As she passed a sign that read *Kentucky State Penitentiary 2 Miles,* she rolled down her window to smell the mossy dampness of the river she knew was close by. An old unpainted barn stood near the shoulder of the road, clearly listing from its foundation. She had stopped there with Lowell awhile back to buy a bushel of ripe tomatoes from Mr. Taylor, the farmer who sold vegetables from a small stand beside the barn. She had canned twenty quart jars of tomatoes that summer.

She drove on, the light shifting as she headed west. The prison water tower came into view, along with its guard turrets and limestone walls topped with razor wire glinting in the sunshine. The road curved, and she saw the familiar small scattering of buildings outside the prison fences, including the shop where inmate crafts were sold like souvenirs to townspeople and visitors. Leather goods made by the prisoners were especially fine and sold as soon as they were displayed in the windows. The wallets and purses were so well made everyone wanted one. They never wore out.

Beside the large beech tree, she made a hard left turn onto Water Street to head home, but she noticed something looked different. The river was high. It must have come up fast, she thought, after she left for the store. Squinting in the bright sun, she noticed that the old stone wall along the steep street had turned to rubble. When she realized that the road ahead was covered by water, she pushed hard on the brakes, finally coming to a stop before the pavement ended at the lake's edge.

Her heart hammered in her chest as she saw the swirling waters and recognized where she was. Years ago, before the lake, this street had paralleled the river and led to her house. After the lake's impoundment, the same stretch of pavement had been converted into a ramp with direct access for launching boats. She knew that. What she didn't know was why she was there. She hadn't lived in the drowned old town for more than forty years and rarely visited, especially by herself.

She glanced at the dashboard clock. Lowell would be home and surely wondering where she was. He'd give her that look, the one she had seen on his face lately, one that conveyed a mix of worry, impatience, maybe even pity. He never said anything, just gave her that look. She had known Lowell Wetherford for most of her life, been married to him for more than fifty years, but she had never seen that expression on his face before. It frightened her. The first time she had noticed it, she had accidentally left a pan on the stove with eggs boiling for breakfast. She wasn't gone long—just a trip to the bathroom down the hall—but he had acted like that little mistake was a big deal.

"You could've caught the house on fire," he said. The kitchen was smoky, filled with a stench of burned eggs and hot aluminum. With a magazine he fanned around the smoke detector to make it stop beeping. She watched him move the pan to the sink and fill it with water that hissed when it made contact. When it cooled a bit, he scrubbed hard to remove any sign of the scorch. He glanced up at her, and she saw that look.

"I can clean up my own messes," she said as she snatched the scouring pad from his hand. She wanted him to say something, to reassure her that everything would be okay. When he didn't, she wanted to hit him. She had never laid a hand on her husband or her children or grandchildren, but she had a strong new desire to smack him. When Lowell walked out of the room without saying a thing, she grew angrier. Her hands trembled when she put the pan in the rack to dry. Something wasn't right.

Rose heard a voice asking, "Ma'am, you need some help?" then saw a fellow walking toward her van carrying a fishing pole and a tackle box. She didn't recognize him and, from a lifetime lived near the state penitentiary, she knew better than to ask this stranger for help. She shook her head, shifted the car into reverse, and hit the gas pedal while easing off the brake. The rear tires spun in a soft layer of silt deposited on the boat ramp. She punched the gas, slinging mud, forcing the van up the hill to a flat spot where she could turn around and get back on the road. She wanted to go home. She needed to get the ice cream to the freezer before it melted. As she drove, she realized she could no longer deny that something was wrong. As much as she dreaded having the conversation with Lowell, saying the words out loud and seeing that look on his face, she knew it was time to talk. She could ask Lowell for help.

REFRESHER COURSE

Margaret hadn't thought about sex in a long time, at least not in the context of herself having sex again. Since Robert died, she had tamped down those thoughts. The gap between fantasy and reality hurt too much to think about. His face, his touch, his taste and smell lingered deep inside, and the memories left her feeling sad and broken. She willed herself to stop.

But lately, in the bedroom left unchanged since his passing, she often awoke from dreams that left her wanting love. And sex. Her thoughts weren't random, anonymous visions of men's bodies or their parts, but about one man in particular, Neville Burgess. And they could be traced to the night a few weeks ago in Nashville when they held each other on the dance floor and when, as they said goodnight, his lips swept across hers with the barest touch that Margaret now believed was a kiss. That night, she traded her early indifference to him for a lusty attraction.

Early on she had dismissed him as a good old boy from western Kentucky, certain they had little in common. Bit by bit, as she learned more, she had to admit he intrigued her, and although they hadn't spoken since that night, she thought about Neville often and in every way. When she imagined them together, she didn't see herself in her nearly fifty-year-old body. She envisioned her younger self, back when sex was a normal and regular part of her life. She looked and felt the way she had when she and Robert became lovers at age twenty-two, with a slender body that moved with grace and strength as called upon. She wasn't sure she still had it in her.

Before getting out of bed, she looked across the room to the chest of drawers and the box that held Robert's ashes. He remained a ghost in the room. The sight of the box reminded her of her failure to decide where to distribute his ashes, her failure to get on with life. She also felt ashamed of her recurring thoughts of Neville. She got up, put on her robe, and headed downstairs.

With coffee made and NPR playing in the kitchen, she opened her laptop to check emails. It was Saturday. She wasn't in her normal rush to get to her office. As long as she got there by midmorning, she could finish up some work she wanted to have off her desk before Monday. Among the inbox stack of Amazon offers and *New York Times* headlines, she spotted Neville's name. She clicked on his email first.

> *Hello Margaret,*
>
> *I'll be in Louisville the weekend of November 15–17 to present a paper at a conference. Staying at the Seelbach Hotel. Any chance you'll be in town? I'd like to see you again.*
>
> *Neville*

She smiled and nervously tapped her fingers on the keys without typing. He would be in Louisville in two weeks. She looked at her calendar, then hit Reply.

> *Hi Neville,*
>
> *Great to hear from you. I'll be in town that weekend. Let me know when you're free and we'll work around your schedule.*
>
> *Best,*
>
> *Margaret*

She reread her words and thought her tone sounded terse and businesslike. Did she want it to sound businesslike? She reconsidered, then inserted another sentence. *I look forward to seeing you again, too.* She hit Send and headed upstairs to get dressed.

Daylight streamed through the shutter louvres in the marble bathroom. Margaret rarely saw the room in this much light. She rarely saw herself in this much light. On weekdays she was up and dressed before the sun, when the room was darker and more forgiving of flaws. Stepping out of the shower, she studied herself in the mirror that covered the wall above the double vanity. She was still slim, but her waist looked thicker and undefined. She turned around and saw her ass looking long and flat. Later, when she put on her bra, she noticed a slight ridge along its back strap.

She hadn't kept up her usual exercise regimen for a while, but she hadn't realized how much it showed. Late in the summer she had twisted an ankle when her stiletto heel caught in a sidewalk crack in front of her office building. As she recovered from the injury, she'd been unable to work out and had not gotten back into the routine. The stress of the law firm's merger had drained her energy and motivation for weeks if not months. She couldn't recall the last time she'd had a hard workout. Parts of her body that she had never worried about looked slack and soft. She wondered if the looseness she saw in the mirror extended to parts she couldn't see. She wrapped herself in a towel while she dried her hair, currently a tad longer than her usual shoulder-length style and quite a bit darker than her natural rich brown. Her grays were growing resistant to the dye, her colorist said, getting harder to cover, a situation that, without proper care, created results that were too dark, too harsh for an aging face. The explanation stung. At her last color appointment, a miscalculation of formula made her hair turn midnight brown, almost ebony, but she didn't have time to sit any longer at the salon for the mistake to be fixed. Margaret wasn't thrilled with the shade but going gray wasn't an option. She'd ask for a color correction or additional highlights at her next appointment. She dressed in jeans and a sweater, then headed downstairs to think about what she needed to do to prepare for Neville.

Except for Cam, Margaret hadn't had a guest inside her home for a long time. She walked through the house to assess what it needed to welcome a visitor again. Although the house was impeccably designed (and spotlessly clean, since there was no one to dirty it), last year Margaret concluded that the interiors looked tired and in need of a refresh. She hired her friend Natalie to update every room, except the bedroom. Robert wouldn't recognize the house now, but their bedroom was the same. Margaret hadn't changed anything in the room since he died, except for cleaning out his closet. Maybe it was time.

She reached for her phone and called Natalie, who ran a small interior design shop on Baxter Avenue. Margaret rushed through the pleasantries and got to the reason for her call.

"How much time do you need to redo my bedroom?"

"So, you're finally ready," Natalie said. "What's his name?"

"What do you mean?"

"Most single people redo their bedroom when someone comes into their life," Natalie said. "Am I right?"

"Maybe," Margaret said, dragging out the word in a songlike way. "Well, yes. Someone I met at a friend's wedding. We've spent some time together and flirted a bit, nothing more, but he's going to be in Louisville in a few weeks. I'm not saying anything's going to happen, but I'm ready to redo the room."

"Good for you, Margaret. I'm happy for you," Natalie said.

"So, how much could you do in two weeks?"

"Depends on what you want. If it's just bed linens and painting the walls, we could do that quickly, depending on the painter's schedule," Natalie said. "I've actually got a bit of time this coming week because another project has slowed down. The cabinets aren't finished yet."

"What about a new bed and mattress?" Margaret said. Maybe it was time to get rid of the ones she had, she thought. Robert had died at home, in their bed. She'd kept the pillows and mattress because his scent remained in the fabric.

"Depends on whether the item is in stock or if it needs to be special ordered or fabricated," Natalie said.

Margaret had no time or energy for furniture shopping or looking through catalogs. "You know what I like. I love every room you've done for me, so just make it all work together," she said.

"I have a couple of pieces in mind, so let me see if they're still available," Natalie said. "And I'll check with my painter. If she's available, we could start by midweek."

"Perfect. You make all the decisions, and I'm sure I'll love it," Margaret said.

After she hung up, she ran upstairs and looked around the bedroom. Everything in the room could go except for the chest of drawers that had belonged to her parents and a desk that Robert had used when he was too sick to go to his office. She took photographs of each and emailed them to Natalie, who assured her that she had everything under control.

Before she left the room, she glanced again at the wooden box on top of the chest. It had sat there for five years, seen daily but nearly invisible to her. She walked toward it and studied the walnut inlay against the curly maple lid, tracing the design with her fingernail. He still waited for her to keep her promise to take his ashes to a place she loved, a place that made her happy, but she didn't know where that might be. They had talked about Capri where they honeymooned, but the thought of being there alone did not make her happy. Instead it paralyzed her with anxiety. She opened the top drawer of the chest and restacked items to make room. She stroked the top of the box, then picked it up, lowered it into the space, and slid the drawer closed. Maybe it was time.

If there was a chance of intimacy with Neville or anyone else, she wanted to be ready. Margaret was always well dressed on the outside, but she'd not thought about being seen in lingerie in years. She'd go shopping for a few things for herself. Nothing she owned qualified as sexy. She wasn't even sure what that meant these days.

She felt like every part of her needed refreshing. Her membership at the gym had lapsed, but she would rejoin. She searched for the local Y's class schedule and found a spin class starting in two hours. And maybe she'd hire a trainer to help her tone the thickening midriff and saggy ass. She needed longer than two weeks to fix it all, but she had to start somewhere. She rarely missed a Saturday morning at the office, but she felt certain Todd and Madison could handle the work without her. She typed a text to them: *Something's come up won't be in today. Continue school case. Call me if Qs.*

Knowing that Natalie would take care of anything related to the house, Margaret made her own list of everything she needed to do, head to toe, to prepare for Neville's visit. She checked her calendar again, confirming her regular appointments for hair and nails the day before his arrival. She'd request the color correction for her hair, and maybe she'd get a facial and a Botox touch-up, too. She called the skin spa and scheduled the appointments for next week, which would give the treatments a few days to settle. Remembering the dull wintery skin she had seen in the mirror that morning, she scheduled a body polish, too.

She thought back to a magazine article she had read, probably in *Cosmopolitan* or *Glamour* or one of the others she read only at the hair salon. The story was about a type of exercise—the name escaped her—that toned and strengthened *those* muscles. She typed in *muscle exercises for women,* hoping that vague search would bring up the topic she wanted. She got videos for triceps and thighs, as though those were the only muscles women cared about. She re-typed *exercises for women and sex* and scanned the search results.

"Kegel, that's it," she said. Her search also delivered ads for vaginal rejuvenation, waxing, bleaching, tightening, and other cosmetic enhancements. She winced as she read the details. She had no idea there was so much public discourse about women's privates. She shook her head and muttered, "Hell, no," feeling out of date and out of practice in every way.

Her friends who had been through childbirth used to talk openly about doing Kegels as they prepared for delivery and post-partum recovery, but Margaret hadn't heard the word in years. No one talked much about sex anymore, at least not around her. May-be it was a younger woman's conversation, or maybe she spent too much time alone. She read the detailed instructions on how to do Kegels and watched a couple of medical videos about the benefits. As she practiced, she caught herself thinking of Neville.

His last email said he would arrive in Louisville late Thursday af-ternoon. The conference at the Filson Historical Society began Friday morning, with Neville's keynote address scheduled right af-ter lunch.

"I've made dinner reservations at the hotel for Thursday night," he told her over the phone. "And if you don't have anything better to do, come to the conference, for as much or as little as you can stand. I know a history conference may not sound enthralling, but I'd like for you to come."

Margaret smiled, flattered that he wanted her company. "I'll check my calendar," she said.

"Is your office close to the Seelbach?"

"Just down the street. Do you want me to meet you there?"

"If you don't mind. I can't leave Murray until my last class gets out at one o'clock. That's Central time. I might be cutting it close for dinner at seven-thirty," he said.

"No problem. Text me if you're running late," she said.

Her bedroom remodel was almost finished. The room had been painted in restful shades of ivory and gray. Natalie had found a spectacular handmade silver leaf headboard. The new carpet was soft on Margaret's feet, and she liked the way the small crystal chandelier sparkled in the morning light. No one would suspect the makeover had been accomplished in less than two weeks. Whether or not anything happened this weekend, the room was ready. Even if he never saw her bedroom, she liked the transformation.

Margaret wasn't as sure about herself. Her personal makeover was taking longer. Working out with the trainer exhausted her and made her muscles ache, but she couldn't see much change. Her body didn't respond to diet and exercise as quickly as it used to or as rapidly as she wanted. She wished she'd started months ago. New lingerie was neatly folded in the second drawer of the chest, which had been returned to its spot after the painter finished. She repeated the Kegel exercises at least three times daily as recommended, maybe more when she spent an entire day seated at a conference table.

For Thursday, she planned a light work schedule to give her time to get ready for Neville. She needed to proof a brief for the third time so it could be filed before 5 p.m., but her team would handle the filing details. Despite what she had told Neville, she would not be meeting him straight from the office. She would head home to dress for dinner, maybe have a glass of wine to calm her nerves, before heading to the Seelbach.

Her anticipation built through the day. As she reread the brief for what she hoped was the last time, she realized something was missing. A section that had been in the previous drafts was now deleted. The error left a huge gap in their argument.

"Tell Madison to get in here. Something's wrong with this," she called out to Veronica, her assistant. In a few moments, Veronica stepped into Margaret's office, her face looking colorless.

"Madison went home with the flu," she said.

"Then get Todd," Margaret said, irritated.

"I've already checked. He's in court with Mr. Helm," Veronica said.

Margaret looked up, managing a scowl between her brows despite the recent Botox treatment. "I guess I'll have to fix it myself," she said. With a red pen, Margaret marked a part of the text and held it out for Veronica.

"Please look back through last night's revisions. Something's disappeared, and we must retrieve those sections," she said. "We can't file it like this."

Margaret looked at her watch. It was almost four, the time she had planned to leave. She wanted everything to be right for tonight, but she had to stay and shepherd the document. She couldn't remember the last time she'd handled the details of filing a brief. Her heart pounded. The armpits of her blouse were wet. At four-thirty she received confirmation of the filing. She had to get home, shower, do hair and makeup, dress, and get back downtown to meet Neville. She didn't want to be late.

Margaret pulled her silver BMW onto the cobblestone drive and surrendered it to the valet. She steadied herself in her four-inch heels and straightened her black Chanel jacket, then climbed the short flight of steps to the marble-floored lobby. Light from faceted chandeliers, wall sconces, and table lamps warmed the formal, high-ceilinged space.

She found a seat in a gilt armchair near the fountain and sat down to text Neville: *I'm here.* Margaret realized that her breathing was fast and shallow. She closed her eyes and took in several deep, sustained breaths, and started to feel better. She flinched when she felt a light touch on her shoulder.

"Are you napping?" Neville said in a low voice. He stood beside her chair and smiled down at her. He extended his hand and when she took it, she felt him pulling her up to stand in front of him. Still holding her hand, he bent to kiss her, another light touch on the lips. This time she knew he intended to kiss her. Her breathing sped up again.

"No, just resting my eyes. It's good to see you," she said. He looked handsome, she thought, with his dark blond hair slicked back in a style more city than country for a change. She liked it. She'd only spent time with him at the lake or honky-tonking in Nashville. He usually had on jeans and boots or beat-up athletic shoes, but tonight he wore a blue blazer and gray trousers, a white shirt without a tie. Even dressed for dinner, he looked like he spent a lot of time outdoors. His deep blue eyes, with a few crinkles around the corners when he smiled, seemed brighter than she remembered.

"You look beautiful, as always. A little taller than usual. Must be those heels," he said.

"Right. These aren't lake shoes," she said.

"We've got a few minutes before our reservation. Would you like a drink?" he said. She nodded, and they walked down a short flight of stairs to the bar. Margaret looked around, thinking the space looked different, more modern than the last time she was here. She noticed small glass tiles as iridescent as seashells applied to the bar wall. Sheer linen drapes floated across the windows along the sidewalk on Muhammed Ali Boulevard. Small candle lamps sat on each bistro table.

They headed to a table with an upholstered corner banquette. She slid into the seat, not too far from the edge. Her leather pants made the slide nearly impossible. Neville went to the other side of the crescent-shaped bench, moving further toward the middle to close the gap.

"Welcome to the Seelbach," the server said as she approached the table. "What can I get for you folks?" The young, fresh-faced woman wore her shiny chestnut-colored hair pulled back in a ponytail. Margaret wondered if she was old enough to legally handle alcohol.

"I'll have a glass of prosecco," Margaret said.

"I'll take a beer," Neville said. The server started naming brands, but he stopped her. "Surprise me. Pick something local and interesting. Thanks." The server walked back toward the bar.

"So, how's the merger coming along?" Neville asked. "Last time I saw you, you weren't too happy about it."

"I'm trying to make the best of it. I'm still the only one who's not jumping up and down about it," she said.

The server returned with the drinks. She set a tall stem of prosecco in front of Margaret, along with a tiny bowl filled with fresh raspberries. "The berries are wonderful in the prosecco, but I didn't want to make assumptions," she said.

"Lovely idea," Margaret said. She lifted a raspberry from the top of the heaping bowl and plopped it into the sparkling wine. She watched bubbles form around the fruit as it sank to the bottom.

"And for you, a local amber called An Oldham But a Good One," the young woman said. "It's made at a small brewery in the next county." As she set the frosty mug on the table, Margaret glimpsed a delicate garland of daisies tattooed around the server's small wrist.

"Sounds like a great choice. Thanks," Neville said.

Margaret noticed that he smiled at the server and had thanked her multiple times since they sat down. His gratitude was a bit over the top, she thought. The service was good, but why wouldn't it be? They were at a nice place; the server was getting paid for doing her job. Maybe he was hitting on the young woman right before her eyes, a thought that both infuriated and saddened Margaret. She took a sip and said nothing. She watched as he brought the mug to his lips and took a long swallow.

"This is tasty. Want to try it?" He slid the mug toward her.

"Sure, but I'm not much of a beer drinker." She took a taste, then another.

"I think she likes it," Neville said, laughing. "You might be a beer drinker, after all."

She pushed the mug by the handle back toward him. "I didn't know anything made out in Oldham County would taste so good, but I'll stick with my prosecco."

They drank and nibbled a few olives and roasted nuts from a white divided dish the server had also delivered to the table.

"So, you're going to stay with the firm?"

"I don't really know what else to do. I thought about leaving, going to another firm or even starting my own, but they've offered such sweet deals to the people who work for me, they won't come with me. I'd be leaving on my own. I've spent years training them, and I don't want to start from scratch with untrained lawyers and paralegals." She paused for a moment. "To be honest, I'm sort of tired of what I'm doing, anyway. I never thought I'd ever say that."

"What's changed?"

"I don't know. With the merger, I've seen us reduced only to numbers. How much money we generate is all that matters, not the quality of the work. Maybe the bloom is off the rose," she said.

"You still like the actual work?"

"Yes and no. I love practicing law and I'm an exceptionally good lawyer, but most of my clients are big companies fighting over money. Or assholes who happen to be rich enough to pay me four hundred dollars an hour to represent them." She thought of Royer Hensen, the wealthy businessman and serial workplace harasser. He generated a mountain of legal fees and had helped her rise to the top of the firm, but she could hardly stand to be in his presence.

Neville reached over and laid his hand on hers. "If money didn't matter, what would you do? What's your dream job?" He looked directly at her, his expression open, waiting to hear her answer. His interest felt genuine, something more than just being polite or having good manners. No one had asked her a personal question in a long time or seemed interested in listening to her answers.

"I'd still practice law. I'd just find different clients," she said.

"Then you should find a way. You're too smart to not love what you're doing," he said.

She hadn't thought about work in that way for a while. Truth be told, money wasn't an issue. She had made a lot of money, and she'd inherited more than she'd ever need in a lifetime as the sole heir of her parents' estate and sole beneficiary of a life insurance policy through Robert's job. Still, she didn't see a way out. She'd be lost without work.

A little before eight they made their way to the restaurant on the second floor. Each time his hands touched her, even the slight brush against her shoulder as he held her chair, her pulse quickened. She hadn't looked at the menu when the waiter came for their order; she asked for the salmon without worrying how it was prepared. "I'll have the same, please," Neville said. After dinner, lingering over coffee, she began to wonder what would happen after he paid the bill. She didn't want to leave him and sleep alone in her remodeled bedroom.

Without a spoken plan, they left the dining room holding hands and headed down the wide flight of marble steps that led to the center of the lobby. At the foot of the stairs, Margaret hesitated for a moment. A left turn would take her to the valet stand to retrieve her car and head home. To the right was the bank of elevators that might transport them upstairs to his room. As the thoughts rushed through her mind, he let go of her hand. Maybe he was calling it a night. She looked at him, searching his face for a hint of disinterest or a signal that she should leave. Instead, she saw the same beautiful expression that she'd seen all night, and she realized he was waiting for her to decide how the night would go. It was her call.

She reached for his hand and, while holding his gaze, slowly kissed each fingertip. Together they turned toward the elevators. When they reached his door, he fumbled with the keycard until the lock's tiny light turned green, and they stumbled into the room. They had begun to undress each other when her self-consciousness resurfaced. She wondered if she should let him see her this way, bare and without cover. Then she cast aside that moment of doubt like a cumbersome article of clothing she no longer needed or wanted. Her reclaimed body felt beautiful and strong as she pressed close to him.

THANKSGIVING

As Neville rotated the sixteen-pound turkey in a plastic tub filled with brining solution, he looked at the kitchen clock and wondered where she could be. Margaret tended to underestimate the drive from Louisville, but she'd had sufficient time to reach his house. He hoped she hadn't gotten lost. He had sent his full address with GPS coordinates as well as written directions. She called earlier from a gas station in Princeton as she made her way down the West Kentucky Parkway.

"I'm at Dublin's. Want me to pick up some barbecue for the weekend?"

"Absolutely. How'd you know it's my favorite?"

"Either I'm very smart or I've heard you mention it about a hundred times," she said. "It smells so good I'm not sure I won't eat it all before I get to your house."

"Keep your eyes on the road and your hands off the barbecue. And be safe coming across the bridge. It's still not finished," he said.

Two weeks had passed since their first night together. That unrushed, slow-simmering dinner at the Seelbach had led to an entire weekend together. Neville took every free moment he could manage away from the conference and still qualify for reimbursements. Margaret came to the history conference to hear his speech on the drowned towns. With her long dark hair, red dress, and intent expression, she stood out in the audience of historians dressed in tweed and corduroy. When she smiled at him, he lost his place for a moment. He realized he couldn't make eye contact with her if he hoped to make it through the talk. She paid close attention and asked astute questions during the Q&A session. Margaret's queries were as precisely framed as those asked by experts on the topic.

"Nice job, professor," she said afterward. Then she invited him home, where he awoke the following morning in an elegant bedroom with a crystal chandelier, smooth white sheets, and Margaret with her hair draped over a monogrammed pillow. He returned to the Seelbach later that day to pick up the rest of his things and extended his stay with Margaret for another night.

To Neville, it seemed only natural to invite her for Thanksgiving. They'd have five days together, including the holiday meal with the Wetherfords. When he asked, she quickly agreed to come. "I'd love to. I hate holidays alone," she said.

He sometimes had difficulty connecting this woman with the one he had met in passing years ago through Cam, or even the one he'd met again at Cam's wedding a few months back. Before, Margaret seemed pretentious and spoiled, a snob who had dismissed him based on initial impressions. She wasn't the first person to judge him for his accent or what he wore or where he came from, but he had wondered then how Cam could be friends with someone as entitled and condescending as Margaret. Lately his opinion of Margaret had changed. Maybe his first impression had been wrong, too.

Neville lived on Kentucky Lake, as close as he could find to the college campus in Murray where he taught and still be on the water. His timber frame home of wood and glass—"rustic minimalism" he called it—had views of the southern portion of the lake. Further to-ward the horizon he could see LBL's western shore. He loved the riv-ers, and the lakes that sprang from them. To him, they were one and the same.

After Margaret accepted his invitation, he spent a few days cleaning and putting away the clutter, mostly books, that had accu-mulated on tabletops. With the fresh memory of her tasteful home in Louisville, he worked to make his own more welcoming. It would never be elegant, but he wanted it to feel hospitable. He collected his guitars and banjo from around the house and took them to his study. He bought new sheets and a bedspread for his room, and replaced the cushions on the porch swing. The bird feeders were filled and Scout's bed washed. A bottle of prosecco chilled in the refrigerator. He searched three groceries for fresh raspberries and bought flowers at the Piggly Wiggly floral shop.

He was getting worried about her. He paced until he heard the dog barking and caught sight of headlights coming up the long gravel driveway. He went out the front door and waved. The west-ern sky was orange and pink, and trees that had already lost their leaves were black in silhouette. Geese honked as they flew toward the safety of the water for the night. It was Wednesday evening, the day before Thanksgiving, and they had all weekend together. He strolled to the car to welcome her.

The next morning he slipped out of bed early to fix coffee and get the turkey in the oven. He had offered to help with the meal at the Weth-erfords. Lately it seemed like they could use a hand. His own parents had been gone for years; his sister Nan lived in Tennessee. He often spent Thanksgiving with the Wetherfords. He had known them since childhood, and he loved them, even though there was no blood rela-tion. They never complained when he showed up empty-handed, but this holiday Neville wanted to help out. He also wanted to check on Aunt Rose. Cam mentioned that her mother wasn't doing well. The family had scheduled a consult with a neurologist.

"Something's not right," Cam said. "She's walking funny like she's lost her balance, and Dad said she couldn't find her way home from the grocery the other day. Can you imagine how many trips she's made to and from that grocery?"

"That doesn't sound good," Neville said.

"Her doctor couldn't find anything, though. They've referred us to a doctor in Lexington, so we're going right before Thanksgiving," she said.

"Let me help with the meal for a change," he said.

Cam thought for a moment. "Can you do turkey? Since it needs to thaw for a couple of days and then be brined, I'm not sure we'll be able to juggle it all."

So Neville volunteered, not mentioning that he'd never roasted a turkey in his life. He approached the task like he did everything, including his job as a college history professor: calm, confident, and ready to research everything written on the subject. He assumed he could figure it out. On food websites, he found multiple versions of so-called fail-safe recipes for Thanksgiving turkey. He also wrote down the 800 number for a turkey emergency hotline. He had not realized that there was a world, maybe even an underworld, filled with cheats and hacks, dedicated to putting a cooked bird on the table.

After he started the coffee, he retrieved the turkey from the tub of brining solution and patted it dry. He reread the instructions for prepping it to roast. With the temperature and the timer set, he slid the aluminum foil roasting pan into the oven and washed his hands. From the materials he had read, he learned the details on reducing the risk of salmonella poisoning.

He organized a tray with cups, creamer, sweetener, sugar, and blueberry muffins he'd picked up at the organic bakery near campus. He clipped one red rose from the bigger bouquet and put it into a juice glass, the only thing he had that worked as a bud vase. He headed back to the bedroom, where he found Margaret awake and standing at the window that faced the lake, wearing the white terry robe he had bought the same day he shopped for sheets and towels at JCPenney.

"Good morning," he said. She turned and smiled. She looked radiant, enveloped in morning light reflected from the water. The sun had just cleared the trees near the shore at Fenton Landing.

"Would you like some coffee?" he said as he set the tray down on a table near her. He turned to her and they embraced, their bodies comfortably fitting together. His hand untied the robe and slipped inside, feeling her nipples harden as he lightly swept over her body, bare under the terrycloth. His arms surrounded her inside the robe, and he pulled her closer. He felt her tug at his jeans. Her skin was warm and soft, her touch gentle at first. Without releasing each other, they eased sideways to find the bed. They made love without hurry.

"I think the coffee's gone cold," he said as they lay together. "I'll go make a fresh pot."

"Don't leave," she said.

"I'll be right back. I have to check the turkey, too," he said. He got up, slipped on his boxers, and headed to the kitchen. The room smelled like roasting turkey. When he opened the oven door, he saw that the bird's skin had taken a golden glow in the heat. He guessed he was doing something right.

At two in the afternoon, they arrived at the Wetherfords with a turkey that looked like a photograph in a cookbook.

"Whoa, that's beautiful. And it smells delicious," Cam said when Neville removed the foil tent and displayed his accomplishment on the kitchen counter. He strutted around the room, high-fiving Margaret and Cam, who was still cooking. The kitchen was stacked with pots and pans.

"How's your mom?" Margaret asked.

"Not well. She's very confused from the trip to Lexington," Cam said.

"By what the doctors said?"

"No, by just being in a different situation. She seems disoriented today, like she's not the same person. It's really starting to scare me," Cam said. "And when I went to set the table, I found a stack of unpaid bills under the placemat at her seat, like she's been hiding them. Some were months overdue."

Margaret and Neville looked at each other. They both loved Rose, who had been like a second mother to each of them over the years.

"Where is she?" Neville asked.

"Dad's helping her dress."

"Tell me what I can do to help," Margaret said.

"Can one of you finish setting the table? I quit when I found those bills. And I need someone to mash the potatoes and someone to put more wood on the fire," Cam said.

Neville looked at Margaret. "I'll carry the wood in. Do you want to set the table?" She nodded.

"Owen should be back soon. Can you believe there was no toilet paper in the house, anywhere?" Cam said. "He drove into Sycamore to get some. I hope he finds a store open on Thanksgiving Day."

"You should have called. We could've brought some," Neville said.

"We didn't realize it until someone needed it." She laughed. "Mom must have forgotten to buy it. She's always been the shopper, not Dad."

They heard voices coming from the other end of the house as the Wetherfords navigated their way to the kitchen door. Rose held to her husband's arm. Her physical deterioration caught Neville off guard. For an instant he remembered how she had looked when he was a boy, the smiling, dark-haired, busy woman she used to be, always quick to pull him close or offer an oatmeal cookie when he came to play. He had difficulty reconciling his flashes of memory with what he saw. She was noticeably feebler, though she was smiling. He walked over and gave her a careful hug.

"Happy Thanksgiving, Aunt Rose. How are you?"

"Doing fine," she said softly, and she studied him for a time. He started to identify himself, to save her the embarrassment of not recognizing him, but she interrupted. "Why, Neville, I'm so happy to see you," she said.

He felt relieved. He shook hands and locked eyes with Cam's father, who looked tired and drained of color. "How are you, Uncle Lowell?"

The older man nodded. "Doin' fine," he repeated.

"And here's Margaret Starks from Louisville, Mama," Cam said. Margaret approached to hug her, as she always had as a guest in their home.

"Yes, I know Margaret. She's a pretty thing, isn't she? Just keeps getting prettier," Rose said.

"You're right about that," Lowell said. Margaret kissed them both.

"How's the meal coming along, Cam? I've been no help at all today," Rose said. She looked at Margaret and in a low voice said, "I just don't feel like myself."

"We've got it all under control, Mama. Go sit down and we'll have it on the table in no time," Cam said.

The Wetherfords headed to the family room, where the muted television played a college football game. Neville helped them get situated and then tended the fire. He came back into the kitchen. "What did the doctor say, Cam?"

"Can we talk about it later? I just can't right now," she said. He noticed her eyes had filled with tears. He went to her and put his arms around her, which prompted her to collapse into his chest. He held her as she cried silently.

"Close the kitchen door," she whispered to Margaret. "I don't want her to hear me."

The doctor in Lexington thought she had a rapid-onset form of dementia, possibly Alzheimer's. "She was so uncooperative during the cognitive testing that they couldn't get a clear picture of her level of function," Cam said, and grabbed a piece of paper towel to dab her cheeks. "She was very agitated from the moment we got to the clinic. She didn't know where she was, and the mood kept spiraling downward. She cussed when they asked her to do simple games. You know Mama. Have you ever heard her cuss?"

Margaret put her hand on Cam's shoulder and kicked into lawyer mode, trying to find any other causes for the behavioral changes. "Has she had an MRI? A PET scan? There might be something else going on. Have they checked her meds? It might be as simple as the wrong dosage or a drug interaction," she said.

Cam nodded. "They've done every scan and EEG and X-ray possible. We'll get the results next week. There's no sign of a stroke or tumor, no thyroid imbalance, UTI, nothing," she said. "And they don't have a specific test for Alzheimer's. The diagnosis itself seems fuzzy, mostly based on symptoms and function."

The kitchen door swung open a crack, and Owen stuck his head in. "May I come in?"

"Of course, silly," Cam said. "We're talking about Mama."

Owen entered the room carrying an economy-size package of toilet paper. "No chance of running out again this weekend," he said. They laughed together, and Owen hugged Neville and Margaret.

"Glad you're here. We need a shot of happiness," he said.

The Wetherford family gathered around the trestle table in the dining room that overlooked the lake. Lowell and Rose sat at each end of the table. Cam's sister Becky, her husband Blake, and their two teenage daughters were on one side, with Cam, Owen, Neville, and Margaret on the other. Lowell sliced the turkey, which was unanimously proclaimed a success. Becky had made the dressing and gravy with a recipe that didn't require pan drippings, and Cam fixed green beans, mashed potatoes, and corn pudding. The teenagers had made pies that tasted like pumpkin but not exactly. Everyone asked for extra dollops of whipped cream.

"Let's go around the table and tell what we're thankful for," Lowell said. "This year we'll start with the newest member of the family, Owen." Cam and Owen had now been married for five months.

"That's easy. I'm thankful Cam finally said yes," Owen said. Everyone chuckled. Cam leaned over to kiss him.

"And I'm thankful you kept asking," she said.

They continued around the table. When it was Margaret's turn, she said, "I'm thankful to be here, with all of you. You're my family."

"I'm thankful you're here, too," Neville said, smiling at Margaret and taking her hand.

"Okay, you two, we've got children present," Owen said.

Rose was next in the rotation. She paused, looking uncertain what she should say. Lowell cleared his throat and spoke up. "I'm thankful for each one of you at this table, and for Rose, and what we've made together." His eyes were wet and full, his voice quavered. Cam stifled a sob, and Owen put his arm around her shoulders.

Becky's family went next. The rotation came back to Rose. She stared into the distance, out toward the lake. Then she began to look at each person seated around the table, slowly moving around the circle, lingering on their faces as if to collect information she knew she needed. About the time they decided to give up and clear the table, she spoke. "I'm thankful for love. That's what I was trying to think of. Love," Rose said.

Neville swallowed hard, then looked at Margaret, who sat with her head down, eyes closed. He couldn't look at Cam. No one said a word. At last Becky stood up from the table.

"Mama, why don't you lie down for a while and rest," she said, her voice thin and unsteady.

"I'm not tired. I'll help clean up," Rose said.

"We've got enough help. At least go sit down in the den and watch TV," Becky said.

Rose complied, led by her husband to the next room. Within minutes she was asleep in the brown leather recliner. She slept while they cleaned the kitchen.

"Want to take a walk?" Neville whispered to Margaret.

"I think I'll stay and talk to Cam. You go," she said.

Neville grabbed his jacket and walked down to the lake's edge with its mix of small white rocks, brownish red gravel, and occasional mussel shells. The shore was wide this time of year when the water level was at its lowest after the drawdown at the dam. Winter pool, they called it. He picked up a handful of flat rocks and sent them skipping across the lake's cold and glassy surface. The landscape was beautiful, but for Neville and most people from the old river towns, its beauty was always intertwined with loss and sorrow. For many, like the tourists and the construction workers who had built it, the dam and lake projects had brought unexpected opportunities; for his people, it stood for destruction of home and history. Some were able to move on and build new lives. Others, especially the old people, never recovered, never figured out where they belonged. For some, including his own father, the beauty of the transformed landscape never compensated for what was taken. The missing parts haunted them.

As a boy on another dreary winter day, Neville had stood with his father on a hillside in Eddyville where their old town used to be, not far downstream from where he now stood. The demolition had been completed, and a scenic overlook with a marker on a grassy knoll had opened to the public. From a young age, Neville had known the old town like the back of his hand. He had explored every inch when he got his first bicycle, but when they returned, he didn't recognize the altered setting. Landmarks were gone, except for the old prison and some of its outbuildings. Convicts and their guards were the few people left behind. Neville guessed that they wished they could leave, too.

That day, he saw firsthand the damage that had been done. The wounds. The land was scarred from an accelerated demolition as the lake level rose faster than expected with heavy spring rains. Chunks of concrete and bricks littered the uneven ground where basements and cisterns had been filled. Crudely cut pipes jutted out of the ground.

"Over there was the crossing," his father said, pointing to what used to be the western edge of the Cumberland River. A section of road on the other side that once led to the ferry landing ended with no warning at the lake's muddy bank.

"That's how we went to see your granny between the rivers," his father said. "Do you remember going?"

Neville nodded even though his memories were vague and patchy, broken up with time and distance. He couldn't admit to his father that he didn't remember.

"Those sons of bitches," his father muttered, and threw down his cigarette as he turned to leave. Neville had followed his dad back to their truck without a word.

As an adult, Neville tried to live in the present, grateful for what existed instead of dwelling on what had been lost. He thought about the deep happiness he had only recently found with Margaret. Neville had loved before, but not like this. Being with her conjured the beauty of connecting to another human being, the pleasures of exploring another human body. He felt it to his core. He knew about Margaret's deep sorrow when her husband died. Cam had told him her worries as her friend's grieving dragged on. He didn't begrudge her loyalty to her dead husband. Knowing that she'd loved another person so completely made him love her more. Maybe she was moving beyond her staggering grief.

But his own feelings of joy were tempered by what he'd witnessed that day, as the Wetherfords, his second family, faced an uncertain future. He hoped the doctors were wrong, but he feared the worst after seeing Aunt Rose's decline. He zipped his jacket and kept walking, rubbing the rocks between his fingers and palm, occasionally stopping to launch one across the surface. He reached down for another handful and noticed a long piece of asphalt, half buried in rocks and mud but still clinging to the earth. Only during winter's low water were remnants like it visible. It was an old road, abandoned or rerouted when the lake was built, eroded by the water that covered it most of the year, but somehow outlasting his elders who once drove their big Chevys and Plymouths along this stretch of highway. Neville wished he could remember where the road went, and the missing places and people along the way.

REMODEL

Elmer sped up when he reached the interstate, trying not to be late for his one-o'clock showing. As a general rule, he didn't show property on Sundays, but Neville had called the night before, saying he had a friend from Louisville who was interested in an old house that had just been listed. Elmer scheduled the showing as a favor to his nephew and because, with fifty-some years in the business, he hated to miss a sale.

"Uncle Elmer, you know anything about the old Greer house over in Kuttawa?" Neville had asked.

"Let me think." After a short pause, Elmer said, "Is it that big frame house with the wraparound porch? Just across from the park entrance."

"You never forget a piece of property, do you?"

"Try not, but it's getting harder to keep it straight, especially with all those new subdivisions," Elmer said.

They planned to meet at the house, which was unoccupied, with a key box entry on the door. The listing agent couldn't make it—the Baptist church didn't let out until 12:30, and her family ate Sunday dinner after that—but she gave him the code to get in. Neville's friend needed to get back on the road to Louisville by the middle of the afternoon.

He took the Kuttawa exit, then eased down the ramp and turned toward what was left of the old river town. Only old folks like Elmer remembered that there used to be a thriving downtown with a bank, multiple churches, car dealerships, hardware stores, a dress shop, grocery, and filling stations. Places to eat and drink, places to loaf. Now there was just one main drag that was primarily residential with a few side streets no longer than a block or two. A lakeside park. A boat dock that floated above where the train station once sat. He tried to picture the town when it had been whole.

As Elmer rounded a sharp curve, he slowed down and pulled onto the shoulder, then slipped the car into park. The view at this spot still captivated him, even after all these years. A broad and open vista, a layering of water and sky against Land Between the Lakes. He'd been all over that strip of land, often on foot, walking properties as part of his appraisal business. Memories of the exile of thousands of people still saddened Elmer, but he was a practical man. There was a price to be paid for progress. He put the car in gear and drove on to the house at 3714 Lakeshore Drive.

He spotted the realtor's sign and turned onto Second Avenue, a steep short street that led to Iron Mountain. Only in country as flat as western Kentucky would a little hill like this one be called a mountain. The house was the one he remembered, built on a corner lot on what used to be Oak Street, a former tree-lined boulevard where the town's finer homes had been built. As the highest point in town, this area was out of reach from act-of-God river floods or later man-made lake levels. High ground always sold at a premium; poor people were the ones stuck in flood zones. That was just a fact of life.

Elmer pulled into the driveway and parked under the carport at the back. He surveyed the structure—he knew where to look for problems—and saw that this one needed a paint job and soon. But the house was pretty, with gingerbread carved into the eaves and around the windows, if a person liked that sort of thing. Old frame houses needed a touch-up every few years, especially on the western exposure where weather and strong afternoon sunlight took their toll.

He crossed the wraparound porch to the front door, noting several rotten boards that would need to be replaced. At the door, he fished out a piece of paper with the code that, when the correct numbers were entered, would spring a key hidden inside the lockbox compartment. His hands trembled slightly as he pushed the numbers. "Oh, hell," he muttered. After two more tries, he got the key and unlocked the door. Elmer felt a chill in the house and searched for the most likely location for the thermostat. He wanted to get the place warmed up before Neville and his friend arrived.

Elmer walked through the house, turning on lights and assessing its features. Refinished hardwood floors and what looked to be original oak woodwork, a big kitchen, two full baths, and nice closets for an old house. He guessed it was built during Kuttawa's early days when tourists flocked to a big hotel at the nearby mineral springs to "take the waters" as a cure for whatever ailed. He found an information sheet on the kitchen counter. Built in 1905, he read, long before the dam's dedication in 1966.

"Uncle Elmer?" a voice called from the front door.

"I'm back in the kitchen," Elmer said. He headed toward the entry hall and saw Neville, a nephew from his wife's side, standing with a tall, attractive woman with long dark hair. He noticed that she wore boots with tall heels, which confirmed for Elmer that she wasn't from around here.

He and Neville shook hands and then embraced. Neville motioned toward the woman.

"Uncle Elmer, this is my friend Margaret Starks. She's also a good friend of the Wetherfords. She's a lawyer in Louisville," he said. Margaret extended her hand to the older man.

"Oh, sure. I know the Wetherfords," Elmer said. "You must be about Cam's age, I'd say."

"You're right. We were college roommates and friends ever since," she said.

"Then I'll bet Lowell Wetherford taught you how to water-ski. He always got a big kick out of teaching kids to ski," he said.

"Oh yes, it was a memorable experience. I might have been the least talented student he ever worked with," she said.

He noticed Margaret starting to look around the room. Over the years Elmer had learned how to read buyers. This one was not a tire kicker. "So, you're looking for something on the lake?"

"Well, sort of. I fell in love with this house a few months ago when I was here for Cam's wedding," she said. "When I learned it was on the market, I wanted to come take a look."

"That's the spirit. I like a buyer who is patient enough to wait until the time is right," Elmer said.

"Well, I don't know how patient I am, but I may be spending more time at the lake. And more reason to be here," Margaret said, smiling at Neville. Elmer caught a glimpse of Neville's face as he looked at Margaret. Why, he's sweet on her, Elmer thought. His own face broadened into a smile. Neville had always been one of his favorite nephews from when the boy spent time with Elmer's own kids. Cousin time, they called it. They all loved their cousin time. They rode bikes or swam all day, wallered together on the sofas and floor watching television at night. His four kids had been close to both Neville and his sister, Nan. After college, Neville was the only one who came home, another reason Elmer loved him. The rest of the kids were scattered from Tennessee to Colorado to Hilton Head Island.

"Y'all go look around and see what you think. If you're still interested, you'll want to get it inspected, but I think it's in fairly good shape for its age," Elmer said. He watched as Margaret walked into the living room and studied the bay window with its stained-glass transom.

"I like the high ceilings," she said. She walked toward the dining room, which faced west and featured an identical window. The afternoon sun glistened through its colored glass. "Isn't that beautiful?" she said, turning to Neville. He came to her side and put his arm around her. Elmer noticed that they held hands as they walked into the kitchen.

"It needs updating, but it's big enough to do a nice kitchen," she said.

"You like to cook?" Elmer said. If Neville was interested in her, Elmer wanted to know what kind of person she was.

"I'm not much of a cook, but I like nice kitchens. For the caterers." Her eyes, nearly the same green color as in the window's stained glass, twinkled when she laughed and when she looked at Neville.

"I'll head down to the basement and check out the furnace and the hot water heater while you look at the second floor. Take your time," Elmer said. As a real estate man, he'd learned that he didn't need to hover over the more independent-minded buyers. They needed privacy to imagine themselves living in a place. He thought Margaret might be in that category.

Elmer went down the steep basement stairs, lighted with a single bare bulb hanging from a white ceramic fixture. Although the main part of the house had been remodeled at some point, the partial basement was more of a cellar than usable square footage. A dank smell rose from the earthen floor of the adjoining crawl space. Something would need to be done about that, he decided. He used his flashlight to check out an ancient gray furnace that was working but probably needed to be replaced in the next four or five years. He stomped a spider, then observed a fairly new hot water heater. Natural gas. A bright green plumbing inspection sticker showed it had been installed three years before.

When he returned to the main floor, he heard their footsteps and laughter coming from upstairs. He went out to the front porch and sat down to wait in a white wicker rocking chair. The house was perched on a small rise, and its wraparound porch provided a view of the park across the street, the marina, and a public beach. Over at the park, boys and herons fished at water's edge. The ribbonlike branches of great willow trees tickled the surface.

As a younger man he'd driven through Kuttawa many times before the old road was rerouted to its present location on higher ground. What had been a neighborhood street become the main thoroughfare for the homes still standing. Every house and business on the other side of the road had been purchased by the government and then demolished because they sat at or below the 367 mark, the elevation above sea level. Permanent iron markers indicated the Corps boundary line on every tract along miles and miles of shoreline, allowing the U.S. Army Corps of Engineers to raise and lower the lake's water levels as needed for flood control. Strictly enforced rules against building within the Corps boundary meant the town could never be rebuilt.

The clearing and moving went on for years, not only the people and buildings but every tree and grave, too. A lasting image for Elmer was the sight of long rows of emptied graves for a cemetery relocation. By the time the dignitaries cut the ribbons and the floodgates closed to seal this area's destiny, the land itself looked like a bomb had ripped it apart. People had moved on to brand-new towns, where they were joined by folks from other lost places. At the time, Elmer didn't think much about the scale of what was happening, but looking back, the projects were monumental.

The glass storm door swung open, and Neville and Margaret came out on the porch. They sat together in the wicker swing that faced the lake.

"What do you think?" Elmer said.

"It needs a lot of work, but—I know this sounds crazy—I love it," Margaret said. "Somehow it feels right to me."

Elmer nodded. "The mechanicals are in fairly good shape. Basement looks dry. Furnace will need to be replaced sometime. Roof may have a few more years on it. The disclosure says it was redone after a hailstorm about twelve years ago," he said.

"What do you think about the price, Uncle Elmer?" Neville said. "Can you talk 'em down some?"

"We'll sure try." Elmer laughed. "I've never been one to pay list price on anything."

"I like the way you think," Margaret said.

Elmer studied her for a minute. Her eyes moved around the porch, the yard, the surroundings, like she was memorizing every detail about the house.

"So, you're moving here? You're going to live in Kuttawa?" he asked.

"I'm considering. I'm not ready to leave Louisville completely, so that gives me some time for renovations. Do you know any good contractors?"

"There's one that lives right down the street and up the hill a ways. I expect you want things done right, and you won't find a better carpenter, if you don't mind his, uh, what do they call it now, lifestyle," Elmer said.

"What's that supposed to mean, Uncle Elmer?" Neville sounded annoyed.

There was a pause in the conversation as Elmer struggled for words. "I'm talking about Tom Wallace. I thought you boys went to school together," he said.

"Of course I know Tom. He's a great guy, and he's the one who figured out how to save St. Stephen's," Neville said, turning to Margaret. "I think what he's trying to tell you is that Tom is gay. Is that right, Uncle Elmer?"

Elmer's face flushed. He didn't want to have the conversation. "Now, you know it doesn't matter one bit to me, but it does to some folks, especially some of the church people around here," he said. "Some say they like him, that he does good work, but they won't hire him. Won't support the lifestyle, they say. I don't know what the hell that even means."

Neville shrugged. "Just another way of judging people," he said. There was silence, and Elmer wished he'd never brought up the subject.

"If you tell me Tom's the right person for the job, that's all I need to know," Margaret said.

"I thought you might say that, but I don't want to assume anything about anybody these days," Elmer said. "Seems like everybody's picked a side to be on."

"And as for those church people you mentioned, they need to know right off the bat that I won't share that pew with them," she added.

She's tough as nails, Elmer thought.

"Well, now, all right," he said. "I've known Tom since he was a boy, and you won't find a finer feller. Or a better contractor. Maybe he could come over and give you an estimate before you make an offer."

"I have to head back to Louisville this afternoon. Could you ask him to come look it over?" She opened her small shoulder bag, pulled out a business card, and handed it to Elmer. "Have him call me, and I'll explain what I want."

"Do you need time to sell your house in Louisville before you can buy this one? We can write in a sale-of-home contingency," Elmer said. There might be a problem with financing if her house didn't sell fast enough, or she'd have to get into a bridge loan.

"I don't plan to sell my place. I won't need financing. It will be a cash transaction," she said.

"We don't see many all-cash buyers around here, especially in this price range," he said. "If you want my advice, I'd for sure lowball them if you won't have any contingencies. We might get a good bargain."

"Let's see what Tom thinks and go from there." Margaret stood up and looked around. "I get a good feeling here. I have ever since the first time I saw it."

After Neville and Margaret left, Elmer called Tom, who said he'd be right over. As Elmer waited on the porch, he heard the honking of Canada geese and spotted them flying in V formation across the bay. Elmer liked to watch birds. He was fascinated by the great distances they flew in migration, even tiny ones like the hummingbirds that summered around the lakes and spent winters in Mexico. Somehow birds used the stars or instinct or some kind of radar for finding their way, returning year after year, recalling where they'd found sufficient food and habitat. He'd read about geese and how flying together made for much easier migration than going it alone. As a group, they felt less wind resistance and could fly farther, faster. Humans could learn a lot from birds if they'd take the time to notice, he thought.

Elmer caught sight of Tom coming up the sidewalk, wearing a ratty blue sweatshirt and baggy, paint-stained jeans, which was pretty much his constant uniform. Elmer noticed how much Tom resembled his late father, with the same stout frame and quick stride, as if he had a job to do. Tom wore a St. Louis ball cap, too, making him fit in with nearly every other baseball fan around here.

"That was fast," Elmer said.

"I'm motivated," Tom said as he climbed the brick steps up to the porch. "I'd love to get my hands on this place."

They shook hands, and Elmer handed Margaret's business card to Tom. "Here she is. A real go-getter, this one. I liked her," he said.

"Let me take a look around," Tom said, and headed inside. Elmer could hear him moving around the house from the basement to the attic. He hoped there weren't surprises. There would be a lot of disappointed people if the deal didn't work out, himself included.

Elmer had known Tom and his family since the day he appraised their house between the rivers. Tom was just a kid when his family fought to keep their homeplace. Several generations of Wallaces had lived on the land for more than eighty years, but those kinds of histories or hardships or protests didn't matter. Sure didn't stop the buyouts, either. Back in the day, Elmer had lain awake at night, thinking about the ones being forced to give up their homes. Some were cheated by appraisers who were too cozy with the Corps or TVA. Elmer had tried to be fair and do right by everyone, but sometimes he wished he could go back and recalculate some of his final numbers.

In the end, Tom's parents had moved their frame bungalow by barge across the Cumberland to a piece of ground above the Corps boundary, high enough not to flood. After relocating, the Wallace family could stand on their front porch and look across the lake to the hillside where the house had once sat. Part of its original foundation and several majestic sycamore trees were still over there, and the family returned to the land each July to pick blackberries where fence rows were once strung. Jonquils planted nearly a hundred years ago bloomed in spring, untended, surviving long after the kinfolk who set out the bulbs.

After his parents died, Tom renovated the house, taking it down to the joists and studs and rebuilding it. Elmer had admired the boy's determination, and others did, too. The project launched his remodeling business. His preservation work was well known throughout western Kentucky. Elmer thought back to his earlier conversation with Neville and Margaret, and he regretted what he'd said about Tom. For a man who prided himself on treating people fairly, his words couldn't pass muster. He knew he had spoken out of turn when he saw the flash of disappointment on Neville's face. He worried that his nephew would think less of him for carrying tales like an old busybody instead of simply sticking with the truth of Tom's skills and integrity. He couldn't defend his own words, and he never wanted to alienate Neville. He wouldn't make that mistake again.

Thirty minutes later Tom joined him on the porch. "What do you think?" Elmer said.

"It needs some updating and cosmetics, but this old house is as solid as a rock," Tom said.

"You'd take the job if she offers it?"

"Oh, hell, yes. I'd love to bring it back," Tom said. "And I'm about to finish that job over in Cedar Bluff. The old house they're turning into a bed-and-breakfast. You should come see it."

"Best call Neville's lady friend tomorrow and tell her what you think. We don't want somebody to jump in here and steal it out from under us," Elmer said.

The men shook hands. "Thanks for recommending me, Elmer. I need the work," Tom said. The older man nodded. Tom headed down the sidewalk toward his house.

Elmer went back inside and made his way around the house turning off lights. He lowered the thermostat back to sixty degrees and locked up. As he stepped off the porch, he heard the honking sounds of more geese, flying in formation, using stars or magnetic fields or the lake itself to find their way home.

WATERSHED

Margaret pulled into the driveway and spotted Tom Wallace sanding gingerbread woodwork by hand, high on an aluminum ladder propped against the second floor of the house. He had promised to wait for her so he could show her the progress since her last visit to Kuttawa.

As she stepped up onto the porch and Tom climbed down from above, she saw that his light brown hair and clothes were sprinkled with flecks of white paint and wood shavings. A few had adhered to his brows and lashes, making him look like a shaggy old man. Since the remodeling work had begun on the house, she believed Tom put in as many hours on the job as she did in her law practice, and she admired him for that. She had gotten the place at a good price, but she counted Tom Wallace as the best bargain in the deal. He knew how to get the job done. She also enjoyed his company.

"Hey, how's it coming?" she said.

Tom ran his hands through his hair to shake out paint chips and then dusted off his T-shirt. "I'd say pretty well. The inside should be done in a week," he said.

They walked around and through the house as Tom pointed out changes. New custom fish-scale siding had replaced rotted sections. The original Ionic porch columns had been scraped down to bare wood. A dark gray roof had been installed. Tom showed her where he had woven a patchwork of new wood sections to salvage original exterior moldings where possible.

"That looks like a jigsaw puzzle," she said. "I can't imagine how you made the wood fit together like that." Tom never bragged on himself, but he seemed to appreciate when she noticed the finer points of his work.

"We'll start the exterior painting as soon as nighttime temperatures stay above forty degrees," he said. "That's if you decide on the colors." He smiled. The paint colors were an ongoing conversation. She had promised to make the decision three weeks ago.

Margaret made a face like an exaggerated wince. "Sorry it's taking me so long," she said. "I just want to get them right."

From an old photograph displayed at the Lyon County Museum she had learned that the house—locals called it the Greer House—had been a fashionable Victorian Painted Lady in its heyday. Multiple paint colors had been used to accentuate its ornate gingerbread woodwork, but at some point in its long history the color scheme had been simplified to an all-white version, probably during the Great Depression when money was tight. Margaret wanted to return it to its more colorful past. She picked five different shades of blue for the moldings and alternating rows of fish scale, but she still needed a sharp accent color for the balusters and the fan-shaped carvings around the upstairs windows. Yellow or purple or orange, she couldn't decide. She needed to be certain.

"It'd be a lot easier to choose if you saw the colors on the house instead of those sample cards," Tom said. "Get Emmie to mix you those little cans, and I'll slap some paint on for you to see."

"That's a great idea," Margaret said. She promised to head to the paint store first thing in the morning. Emmie, a tall quiet woman who owned the store in Sycamore, was another childhood friend of Neville's and Cam's.

Margaret wandered through the house, noticing additional details she had missed before, like fan shapes carved into the newel post and egg-and-dart plaster moldings around the dining room chandelier. Sunlight sparked the stained-glass windows in the living and dining rooms.

"It's prettier than I ever dreamed," Margaret said. "I don't know how to thank you."

Tom nodded. "It's a beauty, and built like a fortress," he said. "I've heard that the man who built it ran the lumberyard, so he used the finest materials he could get his hands on. It'll be standing long after we're gone, I expect."

The remodeled kitchen stretched across the back of the house, with reclaimed wood floors, marble countertops, and floor-to-ceiling cabinets painted a soft gray. The effect wasn't dissimilar to her Louisville home—her decorator Natalie had advised along the way—but this house had a view of Lake Barkley from its front porch and many of the rooms.

"When can the furniture be delivered?" she said.

"Give me a week on the inside," Tom said. "Another month for the outside."

"And I'll be ready for the summer. I still can't believe it," Margaret said. She noticed Tom checking doors and windows as they walked through the house. "Don't worry, I'll lock up. Neville's coming by a little later." She had spoken to Neville on her drive from Louisville, and he sounded upset. When she asked what was wrong, he said he didn't have time to explain. He had a class to teach. They'd talk about it that night.

"You want me to shut off the water? I'd hate to have another leak on these floors," Tom said. During the remodeling, there had been a few glitches, including a frozen pipe in an upstairs bathroom that burst and ruined the hardwood floor in the adjoining hallway and the ceiling in the study directly below.

"If you'll show me where the shutoff is, I'll do it. I need to know, anyway," she said.

He led the way down the basement stairs and pointed out a valve with a red wheel handle on a copper pipe about an arm's length above. "Turn it clockwise until it stops," he said. "I'll be back tomorrow morning if you get the paint samples, or Monday if you don't, but call me if you need anything. I'm just down the street."

"If you're not in a rush, I've got cold beer in the cooler," she said. "I can't offer a chair but we can sit on the front steps."

"Sure, but I need to run home and take a shower. I feel pretty gritty from sanding wood all day," he said.

"Okay. Maybe Neville will be here by then," she said.

While Margaret waited for Tom to return, she walked through the house again, trying to imagine how it would feel to actually live in these rooms. Louisville had always been home, except for her years away in college and law school. She could have chosen to live anywhere, but throughout her life Louisville had been her ideal place. Now the city felt less idyllic, less like she belonged there. Nothing and nobody in Louisville—not family, dog or cat, even a potted plant—needed or depended on her. Her home was quiet and empty. Over the years she had turned down so many invitations that her friends quit asking.

Work had always felt right, but since her law firm was gobbled up in the merger, that too had changed. Maybe she didn't belong there either. As she had told Neville a few months back, she still liked practicing law but wished she had different clients. She had grown weary of defending unsympathetic and unlikeable jerks like the serial workplace harassers and doctors who took time to complete their golf games instead of rushing to the delivery room. Perhaps she still possessed the basic materials for rebuilding a life in

Louisville, but here she was, in a half-finished old house far from home, both in miles and history, feeling more optimistic than she had in years.

She still couldn't explain the emotional connection she felt, but it had only grown since the first time she saw the house, the night of Cam's wedding reception. The scene she had glimpsed through its front windows from the sidewalk, a small gathering of people eating and drinking and laughing as they sat at a long table in twinkling candlelight, had beckoned to her. Even though she didn't know the people, she wanted to join them at their comfortable table or re-create that scene for herself. When she learned the house was on the market, Margaret felt like a gift had been delivered, just for her.

She walked out to the car to retrieve a small cooler, then carried it back to the porch and sat on the top brick step. The wicker swing had been moved to the shed while Tom was working on the porch. She checked her phone; Neville had texted, saying not to worry, he was running late. She opened a beer, an ale from a small craft brewery just outside Louisville that Neville liked. She had never been a beer drinker, but the flavor had grown on her. She saw Tom climbing the steep driveway.

"Feel better?" she called.

"Almost human," he said.

"Here's a cold one to kick off the weekend," she said. She opened another beer and passed it to him. They clinked the bottles together, and Tom sat down on the step below her. His hair was still wet and brushed back from his face. The ends were starting to dry.

"So, you've been here since you were a kid?" she asked.

"Yep. I have memories of living between the rivers, but we left when I was about six. Before the dam was finished. I've lived my whole life in the same house, though," he said, and nodded toward his place down the street. He described watching his child-hood home as it was lifted from its foundation, then hoisted up and onto a barge for the trip across the Cumberland. He met Neville not long after, when he enrolled at the new school in Sycamore.

"Both of us played every sport we could, and we were in Scouts together. Neville always told the scariest damn stories around the campfire," he said, laughing.

"What kind of stories?" Margaret asked. She wanted to hear more about Neville as a boy.

"He'd tell tales about digging up graveyards and ghosts that haunted old homeplaces. You know, things we heard about when the lakes were built," he said. "He told us one about a little girl and her mother who disappeared and were never found. The story got even scarier when we found out it was true."

"That happened around here?"

"Yeah, the little girl's daddy was the prison warden for a while before he got fired. He was legendary for his mean streak," he said. "When you think about it, it's funny that Neville used to scare us by telling us true stories. Wouldn't you know he'd become a history teacher?" They both chuckled. Tom took a drink and motioned out toward the lake. "Look at that."

Following his gaze, Margaret saw hundreds of white pelicans filling the bay inside the riprap jetty. The sky beyond looked like a magenta curtain that backdropped the scene. "Wow, that's breath-taking," she said, lingering on the view for several moments. "I'm still shocked to see pelicans here. They just seem out of place, like they're too exotic to survive in this climate. Maybe it's my own ig-norance. I don't really know anything about pelicans."

"They actually do very well here. We're on their migration path, and they seem to be staying around longer each year, like they like it here," he said. "I heard it's because the winters don't get as cold anymore. They can hang out longer and still catch an easy fish dinner whenever they like." Tom's words reminded her of Neville, both the sound of their slight western Kentucky accents and the way they spoke with knowledge, maybe even reverence, about the birds and the other creatures that lived around the lakes. They shared a deep love for it all.

"Did you ever think about living anywhere else?" she asked.

"I took off for New Orleans when I was younger to learn carpentry and restoration work. It was fun for a while, but I didn't feel like I belonged there," he said.

"I've felt like that here, like I'm an outsider and will never quite fit in," she said. "But sometimes I feel the same way in Louisville. Since my husband died, that doesn't feel right either." She paused and glanced at Tom; he was still looking out toward the lake.

"I guess no place is perfect," he said. "New Orleans was an easier place to live as a gay man, you know, more accepting, less judgment, but it wasn't home. Here, I put up with inhospitable comments now and then, but I'm living where I want to be. Mostly people are all right."

"Really? I'd think they'd be pretty opinionated."

"They are, but I understand how to get along here. I know where I shouldn't take a date for dinner, if you know what I mean," he said, meeting her eyes with a matter-of-fact expression. "I wish things were different, and I suspect change will come. Eventually."

She nodded. "What about your family?"

"My parents died awhile back. I have two sisters over in Paducah and a brother in St. Louis. We get together a few times a year. I have them over to the house at the holidays. They like seeing the old place and showing it to their kids."

"So you're still close?"

"I'm close to my little sister. She's great. The others, I wouldn't say we're close, but we're okay," he said. "It's like there's a code of silence, a line we don't cross if we want to get along. A lot of families have their own don't-ask-don't-tell policy when it comes to their gay kinfolks, or for that matter, anything else they don't want to talk about."

"Must be hard to have that wall between you, though. I know my family had its own share of barriers and rules that had to be followed," she said.

Tom nodded, his mouth forming a slight frown. "Still, it would be nice to have someone, family or friend, ask about what's going on in my life, not just a conversation about my business or which house I'm remodeling," he said. "I'd appreciate being asked if I've fallen in love or found a good man. You know, normal questions."

"I hear you. I've not had anyone ask after me, either, other than Cam and her family," she said. "If I didn't have the Wetherfords, and now Neville, I'm afraid I'd be without anyone who gives a damn about me. That's why I've decided to adopt them, and I think they've adopted me."

"I guess some of us have to create a family for ourselves," he said.

She nodded and paused for a minute. "Hey, by the way, are you seeing anyone?"

"No, but I've met someone with potential," he said, and smiled at her. "I think I'm going to like having you down the street."

She smiled back. "You want another beer?"

He shook his head and stood up. "I appreciate it, but I better go. I'm meeting some friends for a barbecue sandwich before Dublin's closes," he said. "And next time, you come sit on my front porch for happy hour."

"I will," she said. "I'll let you know when I have those paint samples tomorrow morning."

She watched him as he headed home, and then she saw Neville's Jeep pull into the driveway.

"There you are," he said as he got out and walked toward her. He looked tired, tense, she thought, maybe even angry. He wrapped his arms around her and held her close. "From what I can see, the house looks amazing."

"It does. Tom is first-rate. Want a beer?"

"I'd love one. I've had a hell of a day."

"What's happened?" She handed him his drink, and they sat down on the same porch step.

"Remember, I'm part of a group of former landowners and descendants from between the rivers?" he said. She nodded. "Our work is mostly tending the cemeteries and St. Stephen's Church, but we got word today that somebody's pushing to redevelop Land Between the Lakes," he said, his dark blue eyes changing to a steely squint. "I can't believe they're about to get this done before we even heard about it."

"Are you kidding? They can't do that," she said.

"There's a group of developers lobbying Congress to modify the laws that protect LBL. They want to build hotels, marinas, condos, whatever, on property we were forced to give up."

"That's just not right," she said.

"Well, the history goes like this. When they bought out everyone, they took the land by eminent domain for the express purpose of creating a public recreation area," Neville said. "They gave their word that the land would never be developed commercially, and now they're reneging on that promise."

"Depending on how far they've gotten with this plan, it sounds like you'll have to contest it. Might have to sue and get an injunction to stop the development," she said.

"That's what we're thinking," he said.

"But you keep calling it a promise not to develop the land. Wasn't there a written agreement or something to that effect put in the law?"

She watched his face transform from looking ready to take on a fight to one filled with uncertainty. "We're looking into that," he said. "We're meeting tomorrow morning at St. Stephen's. We don't have a lawyer yet, but do you think you could come and listen, maybe steer us in the right direction?"

"I'm happy to help, but I have to warn you it's a lot harder to prove a promise that wasn't written down, especially when it involves land," she said.

"I know," he said with a long sigh. "There's not been anything easy about this situation for the last forty-some years."

She snuggled closer to him in the night air and stroked her hand along his cheek.

"We'll figure it out," she offered.

Through phone trees and email alerts, word traveled quickly about the development plan. The onetime residents were ready to fight. By late Saturday morning the normally quiet lane leading to St. Stephen's Church was packed with cars and trucks. Someone brought a portable microphone for the standing-room-only meeting and turned it over to Neville as soon as he and Margaret entered the building.

"We all know the promises that were made when they forced us out," Neville said. "The land was supposed to remain a natural area in perpetuity for free public use like hiking, fishing, camping. It was never intended to be redeveloped at all, let alone as a for-profit resort with hotels and restaurants and condominiums."

Many in the crowd nodded in agreement and clapped their hands.

"Get it, son," one man hollered.

"That's right," a gray-haired woman called out as she held high her original contract, yellowed and dog-eared. Middle-aged people in the crowd had been children when they were forced out with their families. Others were grandchildren and great-grandchildren who had been brought up with stories of the removal.

Margaret listened and took notes. She got Neville's attention, indicating she'd like to speak.

"I want to introduce Margaret Starks. She's a lawyer from Louisville," he said. "I know a lot of you don't trust strangers, but don't think of Margaret as a stranger. She's been friends with Cam Wetherford since college and she's been coming here for years. She knows this place and loves it and, well, I'm just saying you can trust her. I trust her."

A few people in the crowd chuckled. Several had heard that Neville had a new girlfriend from Louisville. He motioned for Margaret to come to the front, near the altar, and he handed her the microphone.

As Margaret stood before the packed church, her eyes scanned the crowd. She saw familiar faces like Lowell Wetherford, Mr. Moss and Owen, Uncle Elmer, Tom Wallace. She saw Emmie who had mixed her paint samples that very morning. She recognized Russ who worked at the marina and others who looked familiar that she didn't know by name. She knew these people, liked them, felt an unexpected yet undeniable bond with them, and from the looks on their faces she could tell they were worried. She knew how to help them. She had the skills that they needed, and in that moment, in their presence, she admitted to herself that she might need them as much as they needed her.

She started to speak, explaining that they needed more information before deciding how to attack the proposed redevelopment. They needed to know the plan's current status and who was guiding it through the legislative process. Perhaps they could stop it in its tracks by working with local elected officials and congressional delegations. If that didn't work, they might have to seek an injunction to halt further action by the government until a lawsuit determined their claim on the old promise against development. "The details will dictate our course of action," she said, pausing to take a deep breath. "And if you want me to represent you, I will take this case pro bono, at no charge to you or your organization of former residents."

Someone in the audience started clapping; another whistled. Soon all of them were on their feet, applauding. She had surprised herself with her offer to work for free, but she couldn't walk away from them. She looked at Neville, who also seemed shocked by her offer. "Are you sure?" he said in her ear as he covered the microphone.

She nodded. "I'm sure." She didn't need their money. She had found the clients she had been hoping for.

After the long meeting at St. Stephen's and a late lunch with Neville at Belew's Dairy Bar, she headed back to Kuttawa. When she arrived at the house, she saw that Tom had already painted the test colors on several sections of woodwork, and as soon as she saw the samples, she knew the bright yellow was exactly what she wanted. She texted Tom with her choice so he could start on the exterior painting next week. The Kuttawa house was nearly finished, and she might be needing it soon as both residence and law office.

She moved a comfortable chair from the shed out to the porch and found a box about desk height that had once held cans of drywall mud. With her laptop and notes from the meeting, she started outlining a plan of action. If the plan couldn't be stopped early, litigation would be complex and time-consuming. There was a good chance the firm would say no to her taking it. Boyd, Hoffman & Marshall rarely represented plaintiffs, especially pro bono plaintiffs in a case that could drag on for years before a decision was rendered. She wouldn't be surprised if the Nashville partners, especially the repulsive new head of the litigation section, would prefer to represent the rich developers. That would set up an ethical conflict within the firm and deny her the opportunity to represent the displaced families. She decided she was taking the case no matter what the executive committee said, even if that meant she had to resign from the firm.

"I'm not giving up," she muttered to herself as she snapped the laptop closed. She looked out at the park. The lake level was approaching summer pool, but few swimmers were brave enough for the early-spring water temperature. All afternoon the sound of laughter had wafted to the porch from the playground and the basketball court, but the crowd had thinned. She decided to go for a walk, and she grabbed a sweater.

At the edge of the empty swimming area she noticed a couple, probably in their late twenties, sitting on a blanket on the small sandy beach, unaware of her approach as they cuddled and kissed. Margaret tried not to stare, but the woman's bikini caught her eye. The suit's vital triangles, three small patches of red-and-blue fabric, looked as if tiny Confederate flags had been folded ceremoniously to cover the woman's private parts. Margaret watched as the man slid his hands over the woman's skin, laughing as he teased, alternately pretending to warm her or to undo the strings tied at her neck and back. Margaret looked away and kept walking through the parking lot. Something growled from inside the cab of a shiny red pickup truck, and she turned to see a large brindle dog drawing a bead on her from the other side of the half-open passenger window. She quickened her pace.

At times like this Margaret still wondered if she would ever fit in here. She knew this end of Kentucky had strong ties to the South, but the open display of Confederate flags still startled her, whether on swimsuits or flying on flagpoles or mounted from the beds of pickup trucks. She hadn't grown up with such displays, but as much as she loved Louisville, she recognized that her hometown had its own share of division. The symbolism was more subtle, perhaps nearly invisible, but it was there, usually in the form of a prominently positioned hero statue dedicated to a revisionist history, or in the proliferation of white-flight bedroom communities from the days of court-ordered school desegregation. Maybe no place was perfect.

She detoured to walk the shoreline rocks. She discovered mussel shells, opened but still joined like wings, plain, almost homely compared to the fancy shells she had collected as a child. Back then she only wanted the prettiest ones. On beach trips with her parents, she always picked up shells. "Keep only the best ones," her mother had told her. If a shell had the slightest flaw—the tiniest chip along its edge or a faint discoloration in its finish—it was discarded. For varieties she was unable to find on her own, her parents purchased pristine examples from a shell shop. It had been a beautiful collection, but so fragile that, with time, most of her prized shells had crumbled to sand. Margaret bent to pick up a lake mussel and studied its sturdy, common beauty. She tucked it in her pocket and walked on.

When she reached Silver Cliff, she left behind her thoughts of flags and broken angel wings as she watched a tugboat in the distance push its barges through the bend in the channel. She speculated on where it was headed. From the west, the low sun sent pink streaks across the water. The swath of land across the lake took on a brilliant green cast, its trees budding in the warm and humid spring air. Egrets and cormorants flew toward a small island to roost in scrubby willow trees. They squawked and called to each other as they made their way home in the gathering darkness.

Margaret breathed deeply as she took in the panorama brimming with motion and life. Its flow had become part of her. As she studied the view, she wondered if this might be the right spot for Robert, too. He had asked her to scatter his ashes in a setting where she found beauty and happiness, and for years she had put off a decision as she pondered an ideal location. She now saw the place for what it was, one transformed by immeasurable loss but where something beautiful rose from all that was missing. Like a bird using stars or instinct in migration to locate favorable conditions, she had returned year after year to find people here who welcomed and loved her. In their company, she felt stronger, the journey easier than going it alone.

MINT SPRINGS

Cam studied her mother's face, searching the familiar wide-set brown eyes for something recognizable like a spark of warmth or curiosity or recognition. Instead she saw a countenance interwoven with worry, disconnect, sometimes alarm. The new normal. Cam wasn't sure her mother still knew her, not all the time anyway.

"What must I do?" Rose Wetherford asked, again. No matter how many times she asked the question, the answer never satisfied her.

"Mom, I've come to visit you. What would you like to do today?"

"I want to go home."

"We are home, Mom."

"What are you talking about? I don't live here." Her voice rose a notch in pitch. By late afternoon, she'd need medication to ease the agitation that grew during the day.

Cam looked at her dad in his recliner, his expression tired and helpless, as though he'd heard the question a million times in the past few months. Rose had declined quickly—"rapid onset," they called it—as if her life's memories flowed through a spillway

245

and floated downstream to a distant and hard-to-reach place. Once that gate had opened, nothing seemed to stem the flood, with the most recent memories plunging first, leaving only the oldest ones remaining. Sandbagging with medicine, therapy, even daily prayers did little to slow its swiftness.

"Which home are you talking about? The one in Eddyville before the lake?"

"I never lived there. I live across the river," her mother said.

"Or the house that you and Daddy built in Sycamore?"

"I'm talking about the house where I've always lived. At Mint Springs, between the rivers. All of my people live there."

The words startled Cam. Mint Springs was where her mother had grown up, her family homeplace. For more than a hundred years, the big brick house with double porches was a landmark near the banks of the Cumberland River. Visited by the Marquis de Lafayette on his American tour after the Revolutionary War. Spared by both Confederate and Union soldiers making their way south along the waterway. Toppled by bulldozers forty years ago when they built a monumental concrete dam a few miles away. It was torn down, its venerable trees uprooted, the Clarkson family graveyard moved up the hill about a half mile from its original location. The cemetery was the last visible connection to what had existed before Mint Springs drowned in the rising waters and disappeared beneath the lake's surface.

"I want to go home," her mother said.

Cam exchanged looks with her father, who looked as if he could use a respite. A drive and a change of scenery might be good for her mother and probably easier than staying here listening to repetitive questions all afternoon.

"Then let's go," Cam said. "We'll pack a lunch and head out."

Cam walked into the kitchen to gather a few items for a simple picnic. She made a couple of pimento cheese sandwiches, for which her mother still had an appetite, and wrapped them in aluminum foil. She added bananas, some napkins, and water bottles from the refrigerator.

Her dad came into the room. "Are you sure you want to do this?"

"Absolutely. It might be good for her, and you need a break. Why don't you take a nap while we're gone?"

He nodded but looked worried.

"You know she could get angry if things over there don't suit her. She's not going to like it when you tell her the house is gone," her father said.

"Don't worry, Daddy. I can handle it," she said. As she looked at him, she realized how thin he had become. His body felt shrunken when she embraced him.

They helped Rose navigate the walker to the bathroom. She could still use the toilet with assistance and frequent reminders, but her diaper was wet this time.

"We need to change your underpants," Cam said. She gently tore the cloth sides of the adult-size diaper and put it in the trash can, then untied her mother's shoes and helped her out of her pants. At first, after the initial diagnosis, Rose resisted wearing a diaper—"I don't need that thing"—but it had become an accepted part of the new routine. In her mother's presence, Cam always called the diaper underpants. She packed a spare for the outing.

She and her father accompanied her mother down the ramp, built of yellowish lumber a few weeks ago, from the kitchen door into the garage. Rose shuffled along, unsteadily, her gait altered as if she had sustained some unknown physical injury. The doctors had explained the usual progression of the disease, and Rose Wetherford seemed to be a textbook case. Loss of short-term memory, loss of mobility, loss of names, faces, locations. Loss and more loss, Cam thought. It was heartbreaking to watch. Somehow her mother seemed able to hold on to her oldest memories—her parents, her original home, the words to old hymns she had sung as a girl at Mint Springs Methodist Church—all while losing her grip on the present.

When they reached the silver van, Cam and her dad worked together to hoist Rose into the front passenger seat. Lowell had begun parking his sedan outside so they'd have more room in the garage to accommodate the walker, or a wheelchair when that day arrived. It couldn't be long, Cam thought, as she watched her dad stretch the seat belt out as long as it would go and then reach around her mother to secure the latch. He patted her thigh and kissed her cheek. "You girls have fun," he said, and closed the van door. "Call me if you need me, Cam."

She nodded and backed out of the garage. As she headed down the driveway, she looked at the overcast skies and hoped the predicted rain would hold off. She caught a glimpse of her dad in the rearview mirror, standing stoop-shouldered next to the house, watching them leave. Even from a distance, he looked broken and sad. She hated to see him like that, but she didn't know how to fix things. She was having a hard time dealing with the diagnosis, too. It was uncharted territory for all of them.

Nearly every weekend Cam came from Nashville to help care for her mother, giving her dad and her sister a break. With each trip she found that more of her mother had slipped away. Cam grieved the missing pieces, like her mother's sense of humor and adventure, even her mobility. Her mother's essence seemed to be leaking from her, cell by cell, from a brain under attack. The playful light in Rose's eyes was extinguishing from within, leaving a person who was still physically present but missing vital parts.

Despite being forty-eight years old, Cam felt like a child as she faced her mother's illness. She dealt with the details like an adult— the doctor visits, the medications, the provisions in the long-term care policy—while deep inside she wanted to lie down and kick and cry. Her mother was leaving her, and she wasn't ready. She didn't think she would ever be ready. She needed her mother to hold her and stroke her hair, tell her everything was going to be okay. Cam knew it wasn't going to be okay, but she wanted to pretend. A world without her mother was unimaginable.

"Nothing looks right," her mother said. "Are you sure you're on the right road?"

"I'm sure, Mom. The roads have changed."

"I don't see the ferry. We always ride the ferry to get home."

"It's okay. I know where we're going." Cam glanced over reassuringly and saw her mother studying her.

"Tell me who your mother is. Do I know her?"

The question was formal and distant, as if spoken to a stranger, and the realization that her own mother didn't recognize her stung. She tried not to make a big deal over it, but tears welled in her eyes. It had happened before, and it hurt, but her mother eventually circled around and reclaimed the knowledge of her. Cam knew it was just a matter of time before that bit of information washed away with all the rest. She too would be swept from her mother's memory. Cam wondered if she should tape a picture of herself to her mother's walker as a reminder, a way of deferring the inevitable, the way she had tried as a child to keep Francis LaClede's memory alive. She hadn't known the dead boy, but after she scavenged his photograph from the old town's ruins, she had secretly kept it all these years, tucked away like a bookmark in sheet music from Miss LaClede's lessons, a memorial not only to that long-lost boy but also to her piano teacher, dead herself for so many years now. On occasion Cam would retrieve the worn shoebox shrine and open it to study the gathered items, her personal ritual for remembering.

She was unable to speak for a moment. She swallowed several times, took in deep breaths, and finally answered.

"Yes, ma'am. You know my mama. You've known her for a long time." The answer seemed to satisfy Rose Wetherford.

From the main road through LBL, Cam made several turns and headed east down a long brown gravel road that led to the Clarkson cemetery in what used to be the farming community of Mint Springs. A handful of homes and businesses had once sat almost exactly across the Cumberland from the state penitentiary. Most everything had been torn down in preparation for the lake. The few houses that survived the impoundment were later cleared to make way for the national recreation area to be called Land Between the Lakes. Residents, including many of Cam's relatives, had fought the federal projects. Old photos showed protestors holding signs telling TVA to go away, to leave them alone, but the government's power of eminent domain marched on, claiming it all for the public good.

Cam was still young when her grandparents were forced out. She had only vague memories of visiting the old family farm. These days when the water was at winter pool, its lowest level, remnants of Mint Springs reappeared. The stone foundation of the old Methodist church came into view, as well as some scattered bricks. Most of the town names between the rivers were forgotten. Cemeteries became directional landmarks and the setting for annual summer homecomings for displaced former residents and their descendants. To tourists and newcomers who didn't know the history, the recreation area looked like unspoiled, unsettled meadows and woodlands.

As Cam drove the gravel tracks, the green median of tall grass brushed against the van's undercarriage. Long mud puddles lingered from rain earlier in the week. Dragonflies hovered over the water and scattered as the car approached. Cam parked in shade that ringed the small collection of tombstones where her ancestors had been relocated as the lake encroached.

Cam went around the car and opened her mother's door. "Mom, take my arm. I'm afraid the ground is too uneven for your walker," she said.

Once her mother got her feet under her, they slowly commenced making their way toward a rough wooden bench built as an Eagle Scout project by a distant cousin a decade or so before. They walked past the graves of Rose Wetherford's parents, her brother Pete, her grandparents, great-grandparents, aunts, uncles, and in-laws. She didn't seem to notice them. She was looking toward the lake in the distance, a sliver of bluish green.

"Isn't this beautiful, Cam," she said. Cam hadn't heard her mother say her name for several weeks. She had begun to wonder if her name was lost, never to be uttered again by the woman who had given it. Cam took comfort that she wasn't nameless yet, or motherless.

"Let's have a seat," Cam said. They settled on the bench, then Cam remembered the picnic lunch in the car.

"Are you hungry, Mom? I've got lunch in the picnic basket."

"I believe I could eat a bite," Rose said.

Cam headed back to the van, thinking how their family order had shifted. The woman who had taken care of her all her life needed to be reminded it was time to eat. Time to go to the bathroom. Time for bathing. For Cam, the youngest in her family, taking care of others didn't come naturally. She was never responsible for a younger sibling. As an adult, she'd remained childless. She felt inept and uneasy at caregiving, yet ashamed of herself for her impatience in the role. But this was her mother, she thought. She'd have to figure it out.

As she walked toward the bench with the picnic basket, she saw Rose looking around as if taking in everything in sight. Cam worried that her mother didn't recognize where she was, which might upset her and trigger the onset of agitation. Sometimes she looked afraid, as if the world seemed strange and unknowable. Other times she turned combative and paranoid. On bad days she would curse, spit, and scratch. The neurologist had prescribed an antianxiety medication for those times. In her pocket Cam carried an extra dose in case the anxiety skyrocketed.

"You all right?"

"I'm fine. I always sit here and wait for Papa as he works the river bottoms. I carry his lunch to him every day," she said, blurring the boundaries between present and past. She looked content. Her generous smile had returned.

"What does he grow down there?" Cam decided to ask questions and truly listen to the answers. She didn't know how much longer her mother would be able to tell stories.

"Corn, hay, mostly, in those big fields. And smaller patches for tobacco and potatoes, and then we have our garden closer to the house. Right down there on that little rise that never floods. That's why my great-grandfather built there. Never floods around the house, not even in bad years like 1937."

Cam surveyed the landscape toward the water. The shoreline was completely different than it would have been before the lake. The water stayed high because of the dam, a level similar to a natural flood. The actual home site was invisible, as if it had only existed in dreams or never at all.

"Does the prison look the same as always?" Cam asked.

"Yes. Like a castle. On summer nights we have the windows open, and we can hear their voices. The prisoners and the guards."

Cam laid out the food and drinks, then unwrapped a pimento cheese sandwich and handed half of it to her mother.

"See that grove of trees yonder," her mother said, pointing to a stand of old beech and ash close to the water's edge. "That has always been the prettiest spot. Cool no matter what the temperature is. My grandpa tied the mules out there to cool off after a long day of plowing. Papa switched over to tractors, but he kept a few horses for us to ride around the farm. They grazed out there under the shade of those trees."

After taking a couple of tiny bites from the sandwich, Rose pointed out the calls of a bobwhite and the loud thumping of a woodpecker, and then closed her eyes and breathed in deeply. "Smells like clover and honeysuckle."

As Cam finished her lunch, she marveled at the change in her mother, who continued to look directly toward the former site of her home. She knows the setting despite its altered appearance, and despite her illness, Cam thought. Her conversation, which seemed lost many days, came easily as she spoke. A gentle breeze, westerly, blew against their backs.

"A place needs water to feel like home," Rose said calmly. Her mouth lifted into a faint smile as though something peaceful washed over her. "When we moved to higher ground, we knew we'd never get flooded again, but I missed seeing the river every day. So did Papa."

She started to hum, then sang in a clear, steady voice. "O they tell me of a home far beyond the skies, they tell me of a home far away, they tell me of a home where no storm-clouds rise, O they tell me of an unclouded day." She paused for a moment, lips pursed, a look of worry developing in her eyes.

"What's wrong, Mom?"

"I'm remembering the next verse."

"What's that song?"

"I don't know the name, but we sing it in church every Sunday," she said. Her face relaxed as the words returned to her. She started singing again.

"O they tell me of a home where my friends have gone, they tell me of that land far away, where the tree of life in eternal bloom, sheds its fragrance through the unclouded day."

Cam was unfamiliar with the song. She had never heard her mother sing it before. The music flowed from somewhere deep inside, unheard during their life together as mother and daughter, but newly resurfaced in Rose Wetherford. When she stopped singing, she studied the landscape as though she had found a thin place that more closely connected heaven to earth, water to land, past to present. Her face looked pleased with everything around them.

"I'd like to live here, wouldn't you?" her mother said, turning to look at Cam, her expression warm and true as if for an instant she had found those missing pieces.

Cam nodded and followed her mother's gaze back toward the lake. Beneath its shimmering waters lay a forgotten world, yet in that moment and through her mother's eyes, Cam sensed its loveliness, not only for what it once was but for what still existed. Despite profound loss—those unstoppable and devastating changes that had forever altered the landscape, sometimes beyond recognition—it remained a place of beauty, seen and unseen, transformed but still lovely.

"Yes, Mama," Cam said, reaching for her mother's hand. "This feels like home."

ACKNOWLEDGMENTS

About ten years ago I walked along the shoreline in Old Kuttawa, Kentucky, in winter when the lake level is at its lowest. For the first time I witnessed the foundations of houses, scattered bricks, even railroad spikes near where the train station used to be. The images haunted me. The drowned towns and the many lost places felt close, their histories not so distant. I began to research the dismantling of the river towns prior to the impoundments, as well as the deconstruction of communities in the place now known as Land Between the Lakes. Although I grew up in nearby Paducah, I had not considered the profound personal losses of the few for the benefit of the many when the lakes and LBL were created. I want to express my gratitude to those who lost their homes and communities to the Kentucky Lake, Lake Barkley, and Land Between the Lakes projects. Thank you for the sacrifices made on our behalf and in the public interest.

Through review of archival collections and conversations, I read and heard accounts that reflected a deep sense of grieving for these places. The grief and longing have continued through several generations, reminding me of my own parents' move from Appalachia to Paducah in the early 1950s. While my family's move was not a forced relocation like those in the lakes region of western Kentucky, I witnessed my parents mourn the fact that home as they remembered it no longer existed.

Drowned Town is fiction based on historical events. The history is documented in nonfiction, memoir, and poetry in books like *Between the Rivers: History of the Land Between the Lakes* by Betty Joe Wallace, *A Country Boy from Owl Hollow* by Clyde Lyon, and *New Covenant Bound* by Tony Crunk. Constance Alexander's excellent oral history series, *Connecting People and Place*, gave former residents the opportunity to tell in their own words about life Between the Rivers.

I want to thank my literary dream team—University Press of Kentucky, Hindman Settlement School, and Silas House—for believing in these stories and making this book possible. I couldn't ask for better care and skill in bringing my work into the world. Silas, I'm grateful that you're the kind of writer who understands rural people and places, and the kind of editor who nurtures the potential of a story and the storyteller. Thank you for your big, openhearted view of everything.

I'm grateful for my teachers and friends at the Appalachian Writers' Workshop and in the Murray State University MFA Program, who have given advice and encouragement in equal measure; the writing group members and friends who have suffered through the early versions, including Rebekah, Chris, Alex, Nan, Lynn, Nancy, Wilma, and the Glory Group; the journal editors who published several of these stories along the way and provided welcome sustenance to a new fiction writer; and the valuable lifeline of family, those essential connections based on blood, marriage, love, friendship, instinct, or other favorable conditions.

And to my loves—Alex, Alexander, John, and Allysan—thank you for sticking with me through all the rough drafts, as well as our time spent walking shorelines together.

CREDITS

"Across the Creek" was published by *New Madrid Journal* in 2014.

"Drift" was published by *Limestone: Art. Prose. Poetry* (now *New Limestone Review*) in 2015.

"Dry Ground" was published by *Appalachian Heritage* (now *Appalachian Review*) in 2016.

"Mint Springs" was published by *Still: The Journal* in 2016.

"View from Within" was published by *Sequestrum Literature and Art* in 2018.

"Signs" was published in *Anthology of Appalachian Writers* XI in 2019.

"For What It's Worth" was published by *Appalachian Review* in 2020.